The Southern Comfort Christmas

by

Barbara Lohr

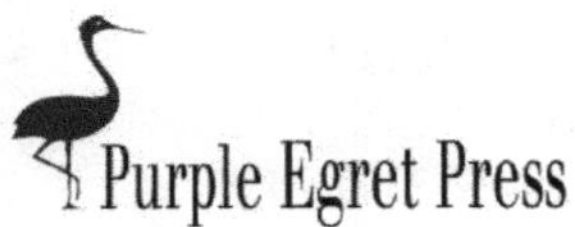

Purple Egret Press

Purple Egret Press
Savannah, Georgia 31411

Cover Art: The Killion Group
Editing: The Editing Hall

Print ISBN: 978-1945523-01-4
Digital ISBN: 978-1-945523-00-7

*For Ted and the city that
has become our love song.*

Chapter 1

Georgina Darlington's brow wrinkled. Harper Kirkpatrick figured fighting all that Botox wasn't easy. "Oh dear, I'm afraid this just won't do. No, no. This just won't do at all." Her client dismissed Harper's hard work like yesterday's grits.

"But we talked about this for some time, Mrs. Darlington." They'd never made it to a first name basis. Maybe they never would. A muscle twitched in Harper's right eye. She was running out of time. The decorations were slated to go up in about a week. And Harper was going to be married in a month. Perspiration prickled along her hairline. No matter what, she had to sell this idea.

Maybe Georgina had forgotten their earlier emails. "You wanted something different, new and fresh. And you were open to lime green and aqua, as you wrote in your emails. A really unique holiday color scheme, or so we thought then."

It damn well rocked. *Georgina, snap out of it!*

Harper's stomach growled and she sucked it in. No lunch today. Might help her fit into her mother's wedding dress, which was about a size 0. "I attached some sample photos to the emails, remember?" Georgina's expression was set in stone, and Harper clamped her lips shut. No way was she going to plead.

"Oh, sugga. I do not recall that. I certainly do not." The hand that had never touched dishwater or wielded a Swiffer waved away hours of Harper's work. The bitch had just plain changed her mind. "You know I cannot abide emails."

Seeing red by this time and not the holiday kind, Harper struggled to remain composed. But she never knew when to stop. That was just a sad fact of her life. "Actually, I didn't realize that or I wouldn't have sent one. Your email address was on the card you gave me." Harper pressed one hand gently to the twitching eye.

Who didn't email? But okay, this was the South. Things moved at a different pace down here. Like molasses in January. Curbing her Chicago practicality—and tongue—could be so hard. "You didn't want the red and green you had last year. They were so, well, standard." *Boring. Dusty. Handed down from your parents.*

Taking a ladylike sip of her sweet tea, Georgina winced. This morning even the tea wasn't measuring up. One more tablespoon of sugar was slowly stirred into the tall glass with a long-necked silver spoon. "Unique but *tasteful.* I mean, sugga, you may be from the North but down here we have to stay within some, well, boundaries."

The words hit Harper like a blowtorch. Georgina had just about called Harper Chicago white trash right to her face. Beneath her hot pink and green striped sweater, Harper's heart galloped while her face flamed and her eye twitched. She could hardly catch her breath, she was that mad. Slowly reaching inside her bag, she fingered her purple inhaler.

Another sip. Another teaspoon of sugar. Finally, a smile. Now

Georgina Darlington, president of the Savannah Women's Society, was pleased with her drink. But Harper was far from pleased. Infuriated was more like it.

Feeling under siege, Harper gave it one last try. "But I ran the lime green and aqua past you. Dropped off the samples. Didn't Leotia give them to you?" Too late, the arch of Georgina's brows told Harper she'd thrown the housekeeper under the bus, and she didn't mean to. But cripes, Harper had already ordered the garlands, wreaths and holiday ornaments she'd agonized over in the vendor catalogues. Leotia had assured her the samples would reach the lady of the house.

And maybe they had.

Hadn't Cameron warned Harper? "If you're going to work with southern belles darlin', be ready to pay the toll."

According to Cameron, the men also could dig in their heels about a stained glass transom or an ugly family heirloom they insisted on incorporating. Her interior design business had started with Cameron when she was the nanny for Bella, Cameron's little girl. What started out to be fun and exciting, often a collaborative venture, sometimes turned into trial by fire.

The sun drilled through the leaded glass windows. She didn't need a mirror to know her neck was turning pink. In stressful situations like this, her Irish Kirkpatrick skin didn't do her any favors.

Spread out on the Darlington dining room table that gleamed under the crystal chandelier, the garland samples were a lighter, fresher green than the usual Christmas choices. Sure, the lowcountry look Harper had pulled together was a departure from the usual apple red and spruce green. Instead, her uniquely colorful samples lay like a wanton northern trollop who'd sadly misjudged her client—not that she was taking this personally. Glittery lime green and aqua ornaments. Oyster shells and palmetto leaves. Sand dollars and starfish. How excited she'd been when the plan came together in all its splendor on her drawing board.

Was this just one more thing she'd gotten wrong? The Darlingtons had a huge party scheduled for the first Saturday in December, so they had to move this project along. Had those nods and appreciative sighs merely indicated that Georgina's mind was elsewhere?

Harper's mind felt fried and now both eyes burned. Last night she'd worked hours finishing the sketches of the main rooms in the mansion, along with the hallways, doors, and pillars. Glory be, she'd even taken time with the four powder rooms. This project would shine, showcasing the distinctive holiday theme that would provide additional flare to her portfolio.

But if Harper blew it, she wouldn't get the referrals Georgina had broadly hinted at when they began working together in September. Stomach plummeting, she glanced outside. Barely moving, gray moss hung listlessly from the live oak trees that arched over the driveway and portico. She'd been hung out to dry.

"We talked about all of this in a follow-up call." Why hadn't she sent notes after that phone meeting? For a sickening second she was right back in SCAD, the Savannah College of Art and Design, letting key points slide and procrastinating. Too busy to tie up loose ends that inevitably caught her in their snares.

Bella Bennett and her feeding disorder might be the only endeavor Harper had seen through successfully to the end. Her heart warmed at the thought of her achievement. Glancing back at her client quickly iced her spine.

Georgina threw her a brittle smile. "That last time we talked? Frankly, my mind's a blank." *No kidding.*

"I was rushing off to an appointment that day, as usual." Her martyred words suggested the committees of Savannah could not function without her. The hysterical laugh building inside Harper felt alarming. But Georgina was off, running through an exhaustive list of her community duties. As the grandfather clock in the hallway ticked the morning away, Harper sat at the table that would seat twelve and kept smiling. The words flowed around her, sticky with insincerity, sucking her into the Christmas from hell.

And this was just one of her difficult clients. Brittany Bedford was next.

"You do understand, don't you, dear?" Batting her eyes, Georgina paused.

"Yes, of course." It was useless to argue. "I'll get back to you with some revisions." Sometimes she marveled that the South hadn't won the War of Aggression, as they called it. They might have done better if they'd left it all up to the women.

"When will I see those revisions, dear? Oh, I do hope that will be soon with Thanksgiving next week and all." Lips pursed, Georgina waited.

"Within a week." Schedules and plans tumbled in her brain.

Georgina's mouth wrenched harder, smaller. How did the woman's husband ever kiss her? Cameron knew Montgomery Darlington, who apparently was just as persnickety as his wife.

"Early next week. I'll email you. Or call." Harper had just sealed her doom. The coming weekend would be hellacious. Georgina's satisfied smile in place, they wrapped up. After sweeping together her samples and sketches, Harper fit them into the portfolio marked Darlington. Somehow, she made it to the door without bonking Georgina over the head with the weighty package.

Once outside, she sucked in a deep breath. End of November and fifty degrees. This was why she hadn't moved back to Chicago after graduation. Rotten luck that the warmer weather kept the pollen and mold active. Her chest felt tight as she hurried to the SUV, stowing her portfolio in the back next to the two others.

One down and two to go. Things couldn't get much worse, could they?

Needing a serious attitude adjustment, she punched on the radio. "Jingle Bell Rock" sheared her nerves. There should be a law that Christmas music could not be played before Thanksgiving. Her pulse raced, and she dug out her inhaler to take a couple of deep breaths.

Hello, air. Do your job.

But as she backed out of the driveway, she white-knuckled the steering wheel, endless lists scrolling through her head. She couldn't even think about everything that had to be done in the next week.

Planning a wedding in Chicago when she lived in Savannah had not been easy. Thank goodness, her mother had insisted on handling the entire affair. Organization had never been Harper's forte. She was glad to leave important decisions to her mother, like whether they should have beans or asparagus.

Had Mom picked up her wedding gown, in storage for the past thirty-five years? Alterations might be necessary—like letting it out four inches and spanning the distance with white lace. That had been her mother's suggestion.

"I'll be Home for Christmas" came on the radio. As she drove, tears leaked from Harper's eyes, and she dashed them away. Wheels squealing, she took a corner too fast and the portfolios rustled against each other. Yes, she wanted to be home, but Chicago wasn't home anymore. Not really. Cameron's mansion just off Victory Parkway had become her home.

Catching the sparkle of the diamond on her left hand, she smiled. The tension in her neck eased. Anywhere Cameron was, that was home.

His arms? Home.

His lips? Home.

His—whatever. Definitely home.

She had to pull it together. Cripes, she'd been so emotional lately. When had she ever felt this stressed out? Like, never.

What was she thinking when she took on these Christmas gigs? It's not as if the wedding was a surprise. They'd been engaged since Valentine's Day, for pity's sake. Then the other weddings had come up—McKenna's and then Selena's. Why had they ever thought the holidays would be a great time to have the ceremony? Thank God

McKenna, Harper's older sister, was up in Chicago and could help their mother. "We'll take care of everything. Don't you worry about a thing," her sister had assured her.

Exactly. Because Mom had been waiting for the marriage of her youngest daughter forever. "You know, I can't be running up there to check," she'd told McKenna during one of their Sunday night calls. "Not with Bella and everything. And Cameron is busy with his own work. Are you sure you can handle this? Otherwise we can dial it down."

"Not to worry. I've got this. Don't you see? Your wedding is the make-up for mine. Mom finally gets to plan a wedding in Chicago. You should see the lists taped to their refrigerator. She's in her glory. My own destination wedding in Santa Fe was a huge disappointment."

"Are you kidding me? We loved it!" For Harper and Cameron, the five days in Santa Fe had been a perfect romantic getaway.

"So did we. A wedding is a very personal thing, and we wanted to escape all the hoopla, the endless line of Oak Park firemen and policemen, the neighbors where we trick or treated for years." Then McKenna seemed to remember that she was describing the wedding that awaited Harper and Cameron. "Not that all of that isn't wonderful."

McKenna's tone had switched from nostalgic to practical. A midwife at a Chicago hospital, she was like that. "We had a party later for our old friends and neighbors when we got back from Santa Fe. But now Mom gets to do it right, as she says. Your Oak Park wedding has become my redemption in her eyes. Thank you very much."

The call ended. Harper loved her older sister like crazy, but those final comments had been a downer. McKenna had mentioned all the elements that Harper felt ambivalent about. After all, at twenty-six, she hadn't lived in the Oak Park house for eight years. Time and distance had caused a divide. Her friends were here now. Her heart was here. How she wished she felt better about this.

Her stomach growled, reminding her she needed food. A quick glance at her phone told her she had forty minutes before meeting with Brittany Bedford. The last thing she wanted was to pass out on the Bedford's sun porch. A quick lunch grabbed at Goose Feathers would give her time to regroup before the next meeting.

Finding a place to park was never easy in downtown Savannah. Finally, she wedged the SUV into a tight spot near Ellis Square. It was easy to pick out the students by their tats, piercings and hip clothing. Being a student at SCAD gave you carte blanche. You could be as bizarre as you liked, and Harper had developed her own unique style. Smiling at the people rushing past in their lightweight jackets and sandals, she adjusted her hot pink head scarf.

Within fifteen minutes, she was seated with her unsweetened tea and a warm panini breakfast sandwich that smelled like heaven. Sinking her teeth through the fresh crust, she savored the spicy slice of salami under the scrambled eggs. Chewing slowly, she glanced through the window of the French Bistro-themed cafe and tried to relax. She tried imagining Georgina in a warm circle of light. No good. Somehow that warm circle turned into a fiery pit. For a second, she was tempted to call Cameron for comfort. He was always able to get her back on track.

But hey, she was a big girl. Sometimes she thought she leaned on him too much, as if she were riding on his coattails. Building her own identity was important to her, but if her first call this morning was any indication, she was doing a crummy job with it. Keeping up with her deep breathing, Harper finished the panini, took her last sip of the tea and cleared her table. With a quick trip to the ladies room, she reapplied her coral lipstick and adjusted her scarf. She didn't have time to do anything about that messy braid. Ten minutes later, she was on to the next client, humming along to "All I Want for Christmas is You" as she headed south on Abercorn.

When she pulled up to the Bedford mansion on the posh street in Ardsley Park, the sun bounced off the ornate ironwork. Savannah architecture could spin Harper right back in time. Looking at the Doric arches and long windows, she could almost hear the rustle of hoop skirts. Thank goodness Cameron was part of the Preservation Society that had taken on the mission of saving historical Savannah for future generations. Together with some business partners, he was developing the Broughton Street Corridor, bringing in upscale shops and landscaping the street while preserving its historical character. She was so proud of him. The last thing the city needed was another parking garage—at least that was her take on it.

Scooping portfolio number two from the back, she sprang up

the steps. Hazel answered on the first ring, hair pulled back in a neat bun.

"Good morning, Hazel."

"Miss Harper." Hazel nodded. "Mrs. Bedford is expecting you. This way, please."

The heels of Harper's black boots clicked on the marble floor. This would be where the day would turn around. Brittany would be the client who reinstated Harper's faith in herself. This meeting would remind her why she'd turned from fashion design to interior decor. Desperation had nothing to do with it, although every other career attempt had gone bust following her graduation.

Well, every career but being a nanny. Although scary at first, being Bella's nanny had fit her like one of the snug tops she managed to shrink in the dryer with frightening regularity. Snug but making her look oh, so good.

Brittany Bedford was waiting in the side sunroom, reading the paper as she lounged in a wicker chaise. The blue and aqua drapes and cushions looked very Vera Bradley. Standing, she waved Harper over to a glass-topped table. In her distinctive British accent, she said, "I just know you've thought of something that's positively brilliant." Anticipation sparked in her eyes and Harper's spirits lifted. Now, this was more like it.

"Oh, I think you're going to like this, Mrs. Bedford." How long did it take to be on a first name basis with one of these matrons? Why was she Miss Harper and Brittany got to be Mrs. Bedford?

But soon Harper would be called Mrs. Bennett. Testing the name in her mind, she almost fell smack onto a coffee table.

"Oops, sorry about that." Usually her bruises only lasted a week. The boots helped.

Dressed in a sleeveless sheath that made it clear she never took second helpings, Brittany Bedford was always "well turned out," as Harper's mother would say. Every bit of crepe skin was probably coaxed from her middle-aged arms during weekly massages, followed by a mani-pedi. Her silvery blonde hair fell to her shoulders in beautifully coiffed waves that made Harper uncomfortably aware of the unkempt braid she'd slung over her shoulder that morning. No time for anything else.

Scraping her confidence together, Harper slid the portfolio onto the table. Mrs. Bedford had specifically asked for a historical British theme, very much in keeping for her. Brittany hailed from London and had met her husband Beau at a polo match. He kept horses at some Georgia farm. They had two children in college and both were studying overseas.

"I want guests to feel they are entering a Charles Dickens novel," Mrs. Bedford had said when they first met. What fun. Who could resist that challenge? Opening the large portfolio, Harper began laying out the palette, color swatches and product samples while she chattered about her research into the Christmas traditions of Merry Olde England. "As you can see, we would use velvets, suedes and brass to echo the rich traditions..."

"The colors are so dark." Mrs. Bedford frowned at the burgundy that two weeks ago had felt "like home, the streets and parlors of London" when Harper had brought over samples. How her client liked to remind everyone of her British heritage. She'd even hinted at an ancestral duke or two. "And so much gold."

"B-brass." Harper could hardly get the word out. "You asked for brass."

"Good heavens, are those bugles?" She pointed to a sketch where three French horns were embedded in a lush garland framing one of the arched doorways.

"I believe they're hunting horns." Well, that was a stretch. Actually, they were French horns but she figured Mrs. B. wouldn't know the difference. "You wanted a hunt theme to be incorporated and specifically mentioned bugles. I mean, horns."

Cripes. What had Brittany Bedford said that day? Bugles, horns or French horns? Harper's mind froze and apparently so did her thought process. Her lips felt as if she'd just come from the dentist, shot full of novocaine. Her confidence melting in the sun streaming into the enclosed sun porch, she fingered her sketches with miniature horse figures, riders in costumes and dogs, lots of dogs gone-a-hunting. Pipsqueak, Bella's darling mutt, had been her model. She'd been so proud of her work.

But a lot of head shaking and tsking was going on. The disapproval fanned out like high tide on the Georgia marsh, from the drawings of their fabulous front door and pillars, through garlanded doorways, to the gigantic tree and festive serving tables Harper had sketched out for Mrs. B. By the time her client set the drawings aside, Harper felt they'd been violated. "Harper, you might simply adore this but for us? I'm sorry, dear. But I just don't think so." The three-carat diamond on her left hand winked when Mrs. B. fanned her fingers over her chest as if to slow her shocked heart.

I'm out of time. Out of time. The words echoed in Harper's head like a pealing bell.

Studying Harper with a pensive gaze, Mrs. Bedford tapped her tiny gold pen on the pad in front of her. "You know, I was counting on you. You were highly recommended because of your engagement to Cameron."

When would she stand on her own merit?

Then she remembered the book Connie, their housekeeper, had given her the Christmas before. The *Martha Stewart Housekeeping* book that Harper sometimes used as a doorstop. What would Martha say? Harper listened for her muse. Martha would probably not say, *Take a flying leap.*

Nothing came. Her shoulders slumped. "No problem. Seems that we had a little miscommunication. You'd like something brighter? More contemporary?" With no time to waste, Harper had to pin this down.

Picking up a magazine from the coffee table, Mrs. Bedford rifled aimlessly through the pages. "What about plaids? They're so cheery." Holding some article away from her, she smiled wistfully. "My father used to take me to Scotland for Christmas. Such wonderful times."

Harper thought her head might spin right off her shoulders. Maybe she'd watched the *Wizard of Oz* one too many times with Bella. "One week?" she asked brightly, sweeping up hours of work that had suddenly been relegated to the trash.

"Four days?" The magazine hit the glass table like the crack of a whip.

"Yes, of course." Packing up her samples, Harper fought the panic blazing across her chest. Somehow, she would do this. If she were going to work here in Savannah, she had to meet the expectations of her clients. And they were high. Cameron had warned her.

"Aren't you getting married soon?" Mrs. B. asked brightly when they reached the front door.

"Yes. Christmas."

Was she clapping with delight? "Oh, how lovely. What could be more beautiful than a Christmas wedding in Savannah?"

A Christmas murder. In this case, yours.

"We're getting married in Chicago." Harper's smile slipped.

"Oh. I'm sure that will be acceptable too." Mrs. Bedford looked positively blissed out. Some women got everything they wanted without lifting a finger, or so it seemed. Did Harper ever want to be one of them? Not really.

"Now, just to be clear." Black boots wide, Harper made one last stand. A lot was riding on her getting this right. This was probably how the mayor of Savannah had felt when he rode out to meet Sherman, surrendering in exchange for not torching the beautiful city. Pleased, Sherman presented Savannah to President Lincoln as a Christmas gift. Mrs. Bedford would no doubt claim any of Harper's success for herself—that is, if she were successful.

"What type of decor do you expect to see when you think about your Christmas, Mrs. Bedford? What do you imagine?"

Eyes distant, the taskmaster fingered her pearls. "Plaids, Harper.

Beautiful, cheerful plaids. Just surprise me!"

"Fine, you've got it."

She stepped out into the sunshine, and the door closed behind her. Tripping on the way down the steps, Harper caught herself just in time. But the portfolio slipped from under her arm, hitting the steps. Because she hadn't snapped the elastic around it, her drawings and samples spun into the dirt surrounding the pink flowering kale, so popular here this time of year. By the time she'd scooped her work up and crammed it back into the portfolio, some pages were streaked with dirt and others were torn. What did it matter? She threw the mess into the back seat and climbed into the SUV.

This day had DISASTER stamped on it in capital letters.

Chapter 2

How could this be happening? Snapping off "Silent Night," she asked that question all the way out to Tybee Island. At first she'd been so excited, so flattered to be asked to handle these projects at the finest homes in the city. But she hadn't planned on the attitude. And she sure hadn't figured in the time crunch. When they'd booked her during the summer, her own wedding seemed so far away. Now? Her clients and her family were chasing her down like hounds, as Cameron would say.

Her phone went off. Maybe it was Cameron. She wanted to hear his sweet voice assuring her that everything would be fine. Wanted to feel the warmth that would cascade through her body, as comforting as hot chocolate on a cold Chicago day.

But it was her mother. "Hi, Mom. How's the weather in Chicago?"

"Oh, you know. It's snowing again."

Every conversation seemed to begin with a weather report. And Chicago didn't come out on top. Driving east to Tybee Island on Hwy 80, Harper passed between rows of age-old palm trees. With the sunroof open, the light filtered in and out of the long fronds. Savannah might get chilly in December but the blizzard conditions with occasional ice storms? That didn't happen here, and Harper didn't miss it a bit. The thought that they might end up traipsing around in wedding gear during miserable weather slung an anchor around her neck.

"Sweetheart, how's it going? Aren't you excited about your big day?" Maureen Kirkpatrick, or Reenie as she was called, was unfailingly cheerful.

"Oh, fine." No way was she going to unload on her mother, who had been a housewife all her life. Not that it was easy to raise seven children, but she'd stayed with what she knew, which was Chicago.

Harper had her pride. Since she'd chosen Savannah, she didn't want her mother to think she'd made a wrong choice—about Savannah or about Cameron.

"Your guest list, dear. You seem to be missing a few people. Those *must haves*, you know."

Must haves? What was her mother talking about? "Where are you?" Harper asked. "Sounds like a tornado is howling behind you."

"Oh, just the storm," her mother said crisply. "You know how it is."

Her stomach sank. "Oh, Mom. That's why Cameron's family won't come to the wedding. They can't handle the snow."

"That's ridiculous, Harper. They're the very names who are missing from this list. What family doesn't want to see their child married? How could they refuse to travel?"

Mom was all about family. Harper totally understood that. But her mother hadn't met the Blodgetts, which was Cameron's real last name. It took Harper a while to understand why he'd changed it after he graduated from college. His family hadn't exactly cottoned to Harper the few times she'd been with them, including the intimate dinner party when he'd proposed to her last February.

Because of her mother's own health issues last year, Harper hated to get her stressed out. "Maybe they'll change their minds. You never know, and we still have a month to go." *Snowball's chance in hell.*

"Should I put a question mark next to their names?" In the background, Harper heard paper crinkle. She pictured her mother at the dining room table surrounded by lists, seating charts and menus.

"Sure. Fine." But it wasn't.

"Ok, let me just note that. So mother is a maybe, along with Cameron's sister Lily and her husband. The two brothers?"

"Oh, I doubt it." She imagined Fred and Henry plowing the fields in December, getting ready for spring planting.

"That really is a shame, Harper. A wedding is a family occasion."

Harper swallowed a groan. "I'm working on it." Talk about a fish out of water. She could hardly picture the stoic Blodgett family in Oak Park, Illinois, for the Christmas wedding. But they were Cameron's family. If they weren't at the ceremony, would they remain estranged? How could she ever build a relationship with them? Although she saw her mother's point, she sure didn't know how to fix it.

Maybe today was the day she couldn't fix anything. The light had changed to red at Johnny Mercer Boulevard, and Harper slammed on the brakes. The portfolios slammed the back of the leather seats.

More paper crinkling on the other end. "Now remember, McKenna and I are going to Facetime you this Saturday at two, so you can see us taste the food. I know it's the weekend before Thanksgiving, but we have to get things settled. Final run-through. Okay? You can probably tell from our expressions what we think of it."

"What were the choices again?"

"Tarragon chicken, french green beans and au gratin potatoes or beef stroganoff with asparagus and fingerling potatoes."

"What are those?"

"Oh you know, just those tiny little potatoes."

The light turned green and Harper floored it. Maybe she was just having trouble getting her mind around anything today. "Okay. Sounds yummy." But it didn't. Not really. It sounded standard. They were going to have a standard wedding, and Harper hated the thought. She loved food with color and texture, food that smelled and tasted wonderful, like her breakfast panini. Green beans? Really?

"You don't have to Facetime me, Mom. I trust you and McKenna, okay? This weekend might be crazy for me. I'm behind on my projects."

"Are you sure? You only get to do this once."

"No really. You handle it and I'm sure it will be fabulous."

"Well, all right. But then there are the flowers too. I'd like you to reconsider the pink poinsettias." Her mother never laid a guilt trip on her but this wedding? Mom was turning herself inside out to do it right, which meant her way. Harper had to remind herself that her mother just wanted her to look beautiful when she came down the aisle in the dress she herself had worn thirty-five years ago. The dress that was probably full of mold and would make Harper sneeze and itch all day.

"All right, Mom. I will reconsider the poinsettias. Thanks for all your hard work."

"Oh, sweetheart, don't mention it. Dad and I are so thrilled. But I have to put this to the side now and start on Thanksgiving dinner. The pies, you know how I always make them up ahead of time."

Harper smiled. "You could do that with your eyes closed."

"Sure. And the girls will all do their part."

"Yep, I know." Her sisters-in-law all stepped up to the plate, and everyone brought something to a family gathering. "Bye, Mom. Love you."

"Love you too, sweetheart. Give Cameron a big hug for me."

Well, that would be easy. She set her phone in the console.

When the road turned right onto Tybee's main drag, Harper sucked in a big breath of sea air. She loved this vacation town. How she wished she could develop more clients out here just to enjoy the beautiful drive. Maybe Julep Tucker would help her. She didn't know Julep that well. They'd met the couple at the Savannah Music Festival last March. All four of them loved Tab Benoit and were jiving to his Louisiana blues at one of the venues when they got to talking. Savannah could be like that. People in Chicago were a bit more guarded.

Since then, Cameron and Harper often had dinner with Julep and Tuck, as he was called. With the holidays approaching, she'd called for help "dressing the place up" for Christmas. But Julep *was* from Charleston. Would she be just as picky as the rest of them?

Driving along the beach condos made Harper remember the time she'd come out here with Cameron and Bella. That day she'd been Bella's new nanny, and Cameron's girlfriend Kimmy Carrington met them out here but soon left. Things changed that day. Was it when they were sitting at the North Beach Grille, and the waiter thought they were a family? Or was it Kimmy's rotten attitude that convinced Cameron she was never going to be a good mother for Bella?

Harper couldn't remember how long she'd worked for him before they both knew. Their first kiss had been cosmic. She fell so hard, like the time she jumped into the pool, forgetting she couldn't swim. Her big brother Connor had saved her. When it came to Cameron, she didn't want to be saved. He had become her whole world, which was totally terrifying.

When the relationship developed, she'd delayed any talk of marriage. Heck, it took her forever to even use the L word. But on Valentine's Day, Cameron had proposed when McKenna's good friend Selena was visiting, due to her own romantic dilemma with Harper's brother Seth.

Setting a date hadn't been easy. Harper had been the one putting it off. Between Cameron's business commitments and restoration business, she told people they had no time to organize a wedding. Then her mother took over and now they were just powering through the process. Destination: Christmas wedding.

Julep Tucker was lying in the hammock on her porch when Harper pulled up. Looking like a water lily in bloom, she gave Harper a desultory wave. Then she ran one hand over her tummy. Harper wished all her clients could be as casual and fun as this southern belle throwback. "Hey, girl," Julep called out as she approached, lugging her portfolio.

"Do y'all mind if I don't get up, Harper?"

"No, Mrs. Tucker." Harper teased, bounding up the stairs. "Not at all."

Julep wrinkled her nose. "Mrs. Tucker? I'm Julep, sugga. Y'all know that."

"I sure do. Thank goodness."

"I've got a bad case of the lazies is all." Looking splendid in her early pregnancy glory, Julep winked. "Do you believe this weather? Feels like September all over again."

The sun streamed through the palm trees over her sprawling beach home. Married to a man from Vidalia, whose family owned both cotton and onion fields, Julep preferred Tybee. Her own family was gone, so she didn't have any attachment to Charleston anymore. In fact, she spent more time here on the island than she did in Vidalia. "Such a little town," she'd once complained to Harper. "I told Tuck, you can't keep me captive here in Vidalia, darlin'. You just cannot." With her long, blonde curls and sultry blue eyes, who could say no to Julep? Of course, her husband adored her, and so did the rest of the world.

"Do sit down, Harper." Julep waved to the wicker settee.

Sitting down, Harper sure hoped the plan was something Julep would enjoy. The day was taking a toll. Of the three clients, Julep was her favorite, so she might take her disappointment personally. "How's that baby?" she asked, heaving her design portfolio onto the low table next to the hammock, careful not to spill the lemonade.

"Getting rambunctious." Smiling, Julep ran a hand over her bulging stomach. "Tuck swears it's a boy. Wants to get one of those imaging tests." She pulled a pretty pout. "But I don't want to know, Harper. Really I don't. Shouldn't I have a say?"

"Absolutely. I understand completely." But what did she know about pregnancy? Resting her head against the wicker rocker, she wondered if this would ever be her, dreaming about having Cameron's baby? Adding to the family. Her frustration with the day melted, and her body turned all soft and shivery, like one of those white jellyfish that floated along the shore at Tybee.

"Can you pour yourself a drink Harper, honey? The pitcher's right there. You look like you need it, and I am too damn lazy to get up. Lemonade okay? Stronger stuff inside. I cannot indulge, of course, so you drink for me."

Harper was sorely tempted. "I admit that so far, this has felt like a Cosmo day, but lemonade is fine. Want me to top off your glass?"

"Would you be so kind?" The rich scent of the ocean enveloped Harper while she poured. Glass cool in her hand, Harper sat back and sipped. The lemonade was just enough sweet and sour to awaken her taste buds and clear her melancholy. She looked up to find Julep giving her the eagle eye. "What's up? Huh? You are not looking like you're in a holiday spirit, Harper. Thanksgiving's next week, and then we roll right into Christmas and your wedding."

"I'm okay," she said cautiously. "Besides, I hate to complain." Tybee wasn't exactly Savannah, but these ladies all knew each other.

"So do we all. But Harper, clearly something is bothering you. Until you let that bitch out, she is going to tear you apart. Come on, honey. Tell Julep all about it." Her fingers beckoned.

Well, she just had to tell someone. "Two of my clients requested radical changes this morning—not that they aren't allowed to do that. It's fine, Julep. Really it is. I want them to be happy, but time is getting short. A lot of this is special order. And the decorations are supposed to go up the weekend of Thanksgiving. Thank goodness Cameron and I decided to stay in town for the holiday. We have so much to do."

"It sure as hellfire is not all right." Julep heaved herself up further so she was sitting in the hammock.

Harper leaned forward, concerned that the pregnant woman would lose her bearings and spill right out of that fancy, fringed hammock. "You're right. Christmas is just, what, five weeks away? If they keep changing things, Santa might not be able to fill their stockings."

But even as they chortled together, Harper knew it was serious. Knew her reputation was on the line. Didn't matter. The two of them shrieked raucously, one giggle bubbling over the other. Lordy, it felt so good. By the time they quieted down, Harper was wiping tears from her eyes. "I have to give them what they want or my reputation will be trashed. If that means changing orders, I'll do it. Pay the rush charges."

"Please, Harper. If you are going to trash your reputation, do it in a more colorful way. One I'll enjoy repeating." Julep wiggled her eyebrows, and they collapsed into laughter again.

For a little while, they lounged and sipped, the only sound the distant slap of restless waves and the cawing of seagulls. The sandy expanse came right up to the Tucker house. During low tide, you could walk out to Little Tybee Island from here. When the tide was high, well, that would frighten Harper a little. If you lost track of time, you could be stuck out there or be prepared to swim.

But she was here on business, and it was way too cool for swimming. Setting her glass down, Harper got ready for her pitch, snapping the elastic from the portfolio.

"Let's see what you got." Julep's eyes brightened. "I don't know if I'm up to entertaining this year, but I sure do want this house to look pretty." Of course, the sprawling two-story beach house was already fabulous.

For the next thirty minutes, Julep oohed and aahed as Harper spread out the sketches on the porch, using some of Julep's white rock collection to hold them down. How Harper had loved working with this plan. Julep had asked for a lowcountry, coastal touch. Boy, she got it. Seahorses, shells and starfish were intertwined with yards and yards of garland, the expensive kind that would be ordered in fresh. "I can almost smell that pine right now, Harper."

Turning to the sketch of the Christmas tree, Harper pointed. "And then I thought we'd take palmetto leaves, tie them just so. I'll spray them with silver and tuck them on the mantle and into your tree branches."

"Brilliant, Harper. Oh, won't Tuck be pleased?"

"This might please him more." Pointing to blowups of some of the ornaments, Harper called attention to the baby booties, bibs and teething rings, all presented in the right color combinations. "I tried to stay away from blue or pink...you know."

"So you chose aqua and green. I love it." Julep looked positively transfixed. The hurt that had dogged Harper since morning dissipated. As she explained the concept, she couldn't help thinking back to the beautiful lime green and aqua color scheme Georgina had kicked to the curb. "Could you just hold on one minute, Julep? Be right back."

Clasping her hands together, Julep giggled. "Don't keep me in suspense."

But it didn't take long for Harper to grab one of the other portfolios. "One of my morning clients didn't care for this..." As she spun the color samples onto the table, Julep snatched them up.

"Someone didn't want this? Oh, Harper." Holding out a length of shimmery aqua ribbon, Julep looked positively entranced. "Who, if I may ask?"

Harper sighed. "Georgina Darlington."

"Well, of course. Pay her no mind. Her loss will be my gain."

Yes, the day had turned around.

Then it was on to the mantles and doors.

Julep studied everything Harper had brought with pure appreciation. "You are a magician. What would I do without you? Just when I was having trouble getting inspired this year."

Driving back to Savannah, Harper felt soothed by Julep's approval. Her day had run longer than usual, and Bella would be home from school. She'd texted Connie, asking her to pick up Bella.

What had Cameron said about his schedule? Was he working late tonight? She sure hoped not. What she needed right now was a good hug with hopes of more to come. He'd put so many hours into the holiday plans for Broughton Street, plus trying to finish the renovation of the Buchanan house. The family wanted to be in by Christmas, but they kept making changes. Cameron would understand why her day had been so upsetting, and she couldn't wait to tell him about shifting the original ideas for the Darlingtons to Julep and Tuck. Her mood rose as she drove over the causeway near Thunderbolt, admiring the yachts moored there.

In so many ways, they were a team. Harper's body hummed when she thought about winding her arms around Cameron's neck and telling him about her day. He'd kiss her, rub her back and tell her everything would be fine. Would this crazy obsession with him ever get old? It sure hadn't for her parents. He was everything she'd never dreamed of— a southern gentleman so hot, she sizzled when he glanced her way.

Dusk was falling when she pulled into the garage. She was late getting home, so he should be there. After all the trouble they'd worked through with Bella and her eating issues, Cameron knew how important it was to be on time for dinner. But his car wasn't there. That wasn't like him. A shiver iced her spine.

Chapter 3

Leaving her portfolios for later, Harper dashed through the side garden and raced up the steps to the kitchen door. The summer flowers were gone, but Jack had planted some pansies and pink kale in the flower beds. The fragrant spring wisteria? Now only gnarly stalks twisted along the wrought iron railings that edged the verandas.

"I'm home," she sang out, coming through the back door. Connie was busy cutting carrots at the sink, and the smell of a roast filled the air.

"Cameron's not home?" Harper asked casually.

"Not yet." The housekeeper glanced over and smiled. "Busy day?" Connie had been Harper's ally from her first day on the job.

"Terrible until my last call." She hooked her purse on the chair. Banshee screams came from the TV room, and she exchanged a look with Connie, who merely shrugged. They'd never had any luck switching Bella over to Sesame Street. She preferred her Ninja shows.

Coming closer, Connie said in a low voice, "Ask her about school."

"Why? Did something happen?" An alarm bell sounded in Harper's head.

After wiping her hands on her apron, the housekeeper whisked a small, pink slip from the counter and handed it over. "You're supposed to call. One of you. The principal, no less."

Heart sinking, Harper studied the perfect Palmer penmanship. "At your earliest convenience, please call me," Mrs. Powers wrote. At the top of the note, she'd scrawled *Cameron Bennett* and underlined it. Oh, poor Bella. Now what? Tucking the slip into her purse, Harper sauntered toward the TV room. At least she could see what this was all about before Cameron got home. Sometimes news like this needed some diffusing before it moved on up the line. Although they'd made a lot of progress with Bella, Cameron still hit hiccups along the way. Harper liked to make them less painful.

"Hi, Bella." Trying to sound upbeat and failing, she asked, "Whatcha doing?"

"Nothing." Half hanging off the long kidney bean-shaped sofa, Bella was intent on the screen where two super powers warred with each other. Next to her lay Pipsqueak, their adorable mutt. Although the dog would lick Bella now and then, she was coming in a far second. The little girl loved the super heroes and gave him little response. Not a good sign. She adored that mutt. When Pipsqueak wriggled closer, Bella ran a hand lightly over her chocolate fur, but that was about it. "When will Daddy be home?"

Casting an eye back at the closed kitchen door, Harper felt her stomach wrench. Dusk was falling, which made the light over the back door even brighter. She had almost a psychic connection to the man and something felt off. Her skin crawled. But Bella didn't need to know that. "Soon, I guess. We're having a roast. Doesn't that sound good?"

"I'm not hungry."

"Connie's making those burned sugar carrots you like."

Another shake of the head. "Not for me."

The words sent Harper into free fall. *Please, not now when everything is so busy.* But their holiday wedding wasn't the little girl's fault. Perching on the edge of the sofa, Harper said, "Want to tell me what happened at school today?"

With an exaggerated sigh, Bella heaved herself up. In the process, she leaned on Pipsqueak's paw. With a yelp, the dog leapt down and, with an aggrieved backward glance, trotted toward the kitchen.

"Sorry, Pipsqueak," Bella called out in that nasal tone she had from all her allergies. The air felt heavy with dread. Or was Harper imagining things? Her family didn't call her the drama queen for nothing. Gnawing at her thumbnail, Harper wanted to clear this up before Cameron came through the door. Grabbing the remote, she turned the sound down. Bella swung her allergy-smudged eyes up to meet hers.

"Why did the principal send a note home?"

"I don't know." Bella pulled at the neck of her pink-striped shirt, a familiar nervous gesture.

"Bella, honey? What happened? Did you have to stay after school?"

A serious shake of the head. "Nope. I stayed in from recess." She studied her pink tennis shoes.

Harper's heart pinched. "Can you help me understand why the principal wants us to call her?"

"I don't know. Just because…" Her lower lip trembled.

The little girl's misery swept Harper back to a time she'd rather not think about. Bella had been a problem child when Harper signed on as her nanny. She had absolutely no qualifications, but it was take this job or go back to wintry Chicago a failure. Again.

At that time, Bella refused to eat, and Cameron was about out of his mind with worry. But they'd worked through it, giving Harper renewed hope in her own skills. Then a day like today would come, and she just wanted to shave her head.

What she really wanted was a hot shower, but she didn't want Cameron to be blindsided with a school problem. "Bella? I'm going to sit right here until I hear the whole story, no matter how long it takes." *Ease back, girl.* Even she could hear the threatening tone in her voice. This day had been rotten, but she didn't want to take it out on Bella. "Please? Please tell me about school."

Her eyes welling with tears, Bella gave a heartbreaking sigh. "I hid in the bathroom. They couldn't find me. Mrs. Davenport got really mad so she told the principal. They were going to call the police." Her eyes grew bigger. "Would they really do that, Harper?"

Smoothing one hand over Bella's wiry hair, she shook her head. "I doubt it, sweetheart." Wouldn't that be just great? That's all Cameron needed was to get a call from the school telling him Bella was missing. "You probably scared the daylights out of them, though. Why were you hiding?"

The troubled, dark eyes Bella turned on Harper held a day full of hurt. "I'm sorry, Harper. I didn't want to be bad, but the girls were mean to me." If she tugged any harder on that shirt, it would become a V-neck.

"Yes but hiding makes other people worry. What if your daddy had gotten a call?"

The tears spilled over, trailing slowly down Bella's cheeks. This called for some cuddle time. Pulling Bella back onto the sofa and into her arms, Harper spooned behind her while super heroes collided on the screen. Didn't take long for their breathing to sync. That was important with Bella since she also had asthma. Tucking Bella's head under her chin, Harper wanted to shield her from the world. Meanwhile, Pipsqueak pattered back into the room and bounced up to settle at their feet. A sense of calm returned.

So what if two of her clients weren't happy? So they hated her ideas. All that hardly mattered compared to the misery she held in her arms right now. "Want to tell me about it, sweetie?" She smoothed back's Bella curls that tangled no matter how much conditioner they applied.

"Tiffany said my hair was a rat's nest." *Well.* A tiny smile pried at Harper's lips. But this was serious. Gently working through the stubborn knots, she kept stroking.

"You know, Bella, we can't do anything about what people say, but we can control what we do." How Harper wished she could follow that advice. "When Tiffany said that— and it was really rude, don't get me wrong—what did you do?"

"I yanked her hair as hard as I could." Clenching her hands, Bella smiled. Harper fought hard to contain her chuckle. Kids were so open and honest. How she would have loved to pull Georgina and Brittany's perfect hair that morning.

But she had to stay in her adult world. And on days like today? Really hard. "Do you think that fixed anything?"

"Nope. The principal said I better think about consequences." Her head pivoted back. "Harper, what are consequences?"

Irritation prickled across Harper's chest. At least Mrs. Powers could use words small people could understand. "Things happen as a result of something else. You and your dad were such great people that I fell in love with both of you."

A small hand reached up to pat her cheek. "Oh, I like that consequence."

Harper gave a dry chuckle. "Here's another one. If I come up with an idea that no one likes, well, then the consequence is that nobody will buy it."

"Oh, Harper. Everybody always loves what you do."

Uh huh, right. Don't I just wish.

"Thank you, sweetie." By this time, Harper was rubbing Bella's back in a circular motion that always seemed to calm her. They were in a total mess here, and she felt the need to fix it. The truth was, she would have done the same thing when she was Bella's age, when her reddish hair stuck out all over. Talk about a rat's nest. She would have smacked that girl for her mean words and been glad to pay the price.

But Bella was more vulnerable. She didn't have the big, rowdy Kirkpatrick family to back her with older brothers. Mouth trembling, Bella whispered, "Do you think Daddy will be mad?"

Harper didn't even want to go there. Cameron thought his little girl walked on water. "I think Daddy might be concerned, Bella. He wants you to be happy. And we want you to get along with other kids. Sometimes that's hard. When I was your age, I pushed a girl named Marjorie off a swing one time."

Bella's mouth fell open in disbelief. "How come?"

"I wanted that swing." Harper chuckled, remembering. "Marjorie had it for over ten minutes, which was the rule on the playground."

"Did your dad get mad?"

How should she phrase this? Looking back, she remembered how Big Mike, as everyone called him, had laughed. Chief of the Oak Park Fire Department, her father was more an eye-for-an-eye type of guy. "My mother said I had to go over and apologize. That was hard. I hated doing it."

"Boy, I bet." Bella's soul-searching glance held respect. Even Pipsqueak seemed to be hanging on her words, panting. "Will you talk to Daddy for me?"

"Yep, you bet. He'll probably be the one to call Mrs. Powers." She was always careful when it came to roles with Bella. After all, she wasn't officially Bella's mother in the world's eyes, not yet. Cameron was the parent listed on all the paperwork. She handed Bella the remote. "Think I'll see how Connie's doing with dinner."

As she sat up, her ears strained to hear the sound of the back door opening. What time was it anyway? Outside the plantation shutters, everything was pitch dark. Oh, where was Cameron?

She was starting to worry as she slipped into the kitchen, where

Connie stirred the sugar-burned carrots. "Gee those smell good." Coming closer, Harper sniffed the steam rising from the large frying pan. Cooking had never been her strong suit, and she was always happy with Connie's efforts.

"All fixed?" Connie asked, pushing back curls that were more gray than blonde.

"Kind of. Some hair tugging going on at school."

"Little girls can be so mean." Her lips tightened in disapproval.

"Right. Once she started first grade, the group seemed to change. A different mix."

Connie's shoulders lifted. "Next year, let's invite the whole class to Bella's birthday party again."

"Great idea. We had such a good time last year." She lowered her voice. "Anything to help Bella. Her social skills need some tweaking." Harper knew all about that.

Going to the window over the sink, she pulled back the eyelet curtain and stared at the light over the garage. "Why hasn't Cameron called?"

Connie cast an eye on the clock. "It's not that late."

"But this isn't like him. He usually lets us know if he'll be late. He knows how important meals are." Taking out her cell phone, she called him. The darn phone rang for what felt like the longest time. With each ring, her stomach twisted tighter. When his voicemail came on, she waited. "Just me, wondering where you are. Love you." Ending the call, she pressed the phone against her lips. Her concern was probably silly, and she didn't want to alarm Bella.

"Dinner in ten minutes?" She turned to Connie.

"Right." But it wasn't right. Not at all. Harper set the kitchen table. No dining room tonight. She wanted to stay close to the door.

Connie's pot roast was one of Cameron's favorites, and Harper wanted him to be able to eat it hot. When Connie had everything ready, Harper and Bella sat down to eat. Jack came to the door, and Connie got her coat. The couple went to their cottage in the back. Every time Harper checked Bella's plate, she was just fiddling with the carrots. No serious eating was happening here.

"Hey, Bella. You haven't eaten a thing." The dainty pieces of meat were right where Harper had cut them. "Not even the carrots?"

"I'm not hungry." Resting her head on one hand, she wouldn't look up. No way was Harper reminding her to take her elbows off the table. The past came rolling back in Harper's mind. Weren't they past this? But tonight felt different. "Okay. I'm not hungry either." Picking up the plates, Harper rinsed them off and filled the dishwasher. While she tidied up, Bella went back to her TV shows, the louder the better. Tonight Harper didn't have the heart to lay down the law and ask her to turn it down.

Thanksgiving was one week from today. Cameron and Harper decided to stay in Savannah because they had so much to do. Cameron said he did not want to travel to Hazel Hurst to be with his family, about a two-hour drive away. Not with the wedding right around the corner, and his mother still on the wire about coming.

Hearing a car pull up, she pushed back the curtain. The white pickup belonged to Rick, one of Cameron's project managers. What the heck? Had the Bentley broken down?

"Is that Daddy?" Bella stood anxiously in the doorway of the TV room. Usually she ran to greet him. Her run-in with Mrs. Powers had put a cork in her bubbly personality.

Harper's attention went back to the truck. "Oh, my God." In the dim light, she watched Rick help Cameron out. His right foot was all wrapped up. Heart thumping, she watched Rick reach inside and pull out some crutches.

Next to her, Bella climbed up on a chair and peered out. "Is Daddy hurt?"

"We don't know, sweetheart. I'm sure he's fine." But her heart was thumping in her chest. Flinging open the door, she rushed down the back steps without pausing to grab a jacket. "Bella, stay inside," she called over her shoulder.

"Cameron, what happened?" He looked a wreck. Now, she never minded when the man was sweaty and rumpled. Just made taking a shower more interesting. But this was different. Cameron looked like he was way beyond a bad day. Torn slacks, rumpled shirt. Messed up dirty blond hair and stubble that went beyond dreamy.

But the thing he was wearing on his right foot concerned her the most.

"Just had a little accident. Nothing serious." Clearly not accustomed to crutches, he wielded them with a clumsy swing as he started through the garden. From beneath lowered brows, Rick shot Harper a cautious look. His expression was almost worse than

Cameron's.

Pipsqueak had escaped and trotted down to nip at the strange sticks Cameron wielded. Bella scooted down right behind her. Panting with excitement, the dog wanted to play with the guy who could toss a ball to the corner of the yard. Only it was clear they wouldn't be playing ball for a while. When Bella slipped two fingers into her mouth, Harper knew she was worried about her daddy. That habit had been left behind months ago.

"What happened?" Harper glanced from Cameron to Rick.

Opening his mouth, Rick quickly clammed up when Cameron said between grunts, "I was checking something out up on the scaffolding. My foot went through between two boards."

"Scaffolding? What were you doing up there?" The thought of something happening to Cameron, well, it cut her to the quick.

"Jed Buchanan ordered custom crown molding. The pattern is tricky. I wanted to see it." When one crutch sank through a patch of moss, he wrenched it free with disgust.

Since Cameron was a perfectionist, this wasn't a strange story. He liked to supervise his teams but scaffolding? They'd talked about him not taking risks. Matching her pace to his slow progress, she aimed for a lighter tone. He wasn't a man who would take well to a worrying wife. Truth be told, the depth of her concern amazed even her. She was used to him taking care of her. Suddenly the tables had turned. "I'm getting you a pair of binoculars for Christmas."

She could see from his expression that her joke fell flat.

"Yeah, right." He kept walking, but a grin teased one corner of his mouth.

"And you couldn't call me from the hospital? I've been, you know, waiting."

He slid her a guarded look. "I wanted to know what we were dealing with before I alarmed you. Rick took me to Memorial's ER, and things got kind of busy after that. Thought I'd make it home for dinner. Guess I'm a little late." The words came in choked groupings as he worked with the new crutches.

"Watch your step now." She felt like Pipsqueak, dancing along beside him. By the time they reached the stairs, his chest was heaving. Sweat beading on his forehead, he leaned back on his good leg and looked at the stairs leading to the back porch as if they were Mt. Everest.

"Hey Boss Man, why don't you let me help you?" Not waiting for an answer, Rick swept the crutch from under Cameron's right arm and replaced it with his shoulder. Harper wanted to hug Rick. While she stepped back, he half carried Cameron up the steps. Scurrying around him, she rushed to open the back door, calling Pipsqueak and Bella back inside.

"Daddy? You okay?" Eyes glued to her father, Bella edged backwards into the house.

"Just fine, darlin'. Nothing I can't handle." Always confident, he was putting on a good show. But beneath that bravado, Harper heard shredded pain. Saw it in the set of his jaw.

No matter, her dad's words worked miracles on Bella and that's what counted. After all, he was her hero. If Dad wasn't well, then nothing would go right. He was home and she threw her arms around his legs.

Cameron winced. "Hey, Bella, let's give Daddy some room," Harper said softly.

From where Harper was standing, this wasn't encouraging. His baby blues that always told her everything were hooded tonight. And here she thought she'd had a bad day.

"What did the doctor in the ER say?"

Cameron shrugged. "Just stay off it. Not much more."

Although she was tempted to wring the explanation from Rick, he'd never say anything in front of Cameron. He just helped his boss to a chair. A Christmas carol came on the TV, still blaring in the next room. "Bella, turn the TV down, sweetheart," Cameron said, his lips tight.

She disappeared and when she returned she kept her distance, unlike Pipsqueak squirming at his feet, tail just about wagging right off. Cameron let a hand fall, caressing the dog's head while his mind looked a million miles away. Disgust and pain contorted his features.

"Thanks, Rick. You can get home to your family." Lifting the hand from Pipsqueak's soft head, Cameron waved him away. "Maybe two of you can drive the Bentley back here tomorrow?"

"You left the Bentley out on the street?" Harper didn't like that.

"It's in the driveway at the Buchanan house." His eyes got blurry. "I think I locked it. Don't worry, okay?"

She bit her lip. This wasn't the time to trouble him about anything.

"Yeah, you locked it, Cameron. Here are the keys. Guess I'll be on my way. Talk to you tomorrow." Tossing the keys on the table, Rick couldn't get out of there fast enough. The door slammed behind him, probably a lot harder than he intended.

"Oh, Cameron. What were you doing up there?" Harper sank into a chair. Scaffolding was set up to work on high places. Since she had a pretty active imagination, scenarios ran through her mind. They all ended with Cameron a lot worse off than in this cast. The realization should have made her feel better but it didn't.

Lifting bloodshot eyes, Cameron shrugged. "I was just checking the crown molding. You know how particular Jed Buchanan is."

Yes, indeed. Harper did know. "We never should have taken on that renovation. His wife Kristie isn't any better. Remember the seven rolls of fabric I had to send back?"

The chair creaked when Cameron leaned back. "I just wanted to make sure, you know..."

"That the edges were crisp. That the swirls were soft." Did she know this man or what?

"But Daddy, what's a...." Bella's small hand went out to tug on her daddy's slacks.

"Bella, no." His entire body jerked back, which just made everything worse.

In a flash, Bella was out of the room, her shoes sliding on the marble floor of the foyer, Pipsqueak yipping behind her, glad that finally someone was doing something. Harper would go and find her. But not yet.

"Guess that's just one more thing I messed up today." Cameron stared after his daughter, looking totally disgusted with himself.

Moving closer, she rocked his head onto her chest, sweat and all. What did she care? This Boss Man was hers. She smoothed his damp curls, glad it wasn't any worse than this cast.

"Damn. Harper, I'm so sorry." He gave the cast on his foot a disgusted look.

"Is it broken?"

"So they tell me. Wasn't watching what I was doing. My foot slipped between two boards and caught. Grabbed a piece of railing but I still went down. Jerked sideways so hard, I snapped it. Of all the stupid things..."

Her heart broke just to look at him. He knew what this meant. How it would complicate everything. She massaged her fingers a little deeper into his scalp. "We'll get through this."

"But the wedding?" His words were muffled as he nuzzled deeper between her breasts, and lordy, it felt good. How perverse. The man came home broken, and she was getting turned on.

But Cameron could do that to her. Always.

"I'm saying, we'll get through it." Her fingers left his scalp to work down to his strong neck.

His hands found her waist and then skimmed up under her sweater. "You wouldn't think of just not..."

"Nope. Never. You know how my folks are. We are having this ceremony." She pushed away. His hands on her body felt way too good, and she had to find Bella. "Hungry?"

Heat smoldered in his eyes. "Yep. Always."

She tugged his ear lobe. "You know what I mean. No time to get creative. How about some roast?"

But he seemed distracted. Cameron's sigh filled the room as he ran his hands down her thighs. The tights were so soft; she practically felt his fingerprints. They were imprinted on her body, just as he was imprinted on her heart.

So. Hard. To break away. But she did.

"When did you start wearing black?" His brows drew together as she stepped back.

"This is my new mature look." She ran her hands over the black mini skirt. The sweater had enough color.

"Now let's not get too crazy. I like the wild colors." He grinned. "You never cease to amaze me."

She was trying to become a mother who wouldn't draw stares when she went to a parent-teacher conference. Rummaging around in the refrigerator, she found the roast, potatoes and the carrots. She arranged them on a plate and covered them with wax paper before they went in the microwave. While she punched a few buttons, Cameron asked her how her day had been. "You don't want to know."

"Yes, I do." He lounged back in his chair, eyes draped over her like a bed sheet.

"Well, since you asked. Honestly, babe, why does Georgina Darlington have to be such a bitch? And after I've ordered the inventory to make her centerpieces. Who else would want all the lime green and aqua ornaments?"

"High maintenance clients come with the territory," Cameron said when she whisked the plate from the microwave and set it in front to him. Sometimes this just felt so weird. Like she was playing house.

"Yeah, I guess. Thank goodness we aren't going anywhere for Thanksgiving. I have to work and..." She could hardly look at him.

"Sorry, darlin'. I know I said I'd help you with the setup." He put his fork down. "Isn't there any work I can do sitting down?"

"Don't even think about it." She took his chin in one hand. "We'll manage."

His slow smile usually promised trouble. The kind she liked. Bending over, she gave him a lingering kiss and tasted his salty sweat and the beef. When she drew back, he patted her behind. "Thanks. I needed that."

"Now eat." She pointed and he picked up his fork.

Not that she didn't want to fool around but they didn't have the time. Not right now, anyway. "Okay. Gotta run up and get Bella settled. I'll be right back."

Taking the steps two at a time, she shook herself out of the heat Cameron could ignite with one look, one touch. From the first moment she saw him, glowering at the foot of the stairs when she showed up late as entertainment for his bachelor party, she knew he was trouble she wanted to explore. Oh, that night had been entertaining all right.

When she reached the top of the stairs, she called out, "The Cookie Monster is coming to get you, Bella Bennett!"

Growling, she tromped into the room to find Bella tussling with Pipsqueak on top of her bed. The Ninja girl motif had been Harper's birthday present for Bella last year and suited the little girl perfectly.

"Aw, I'm too big for the Cookie Monster," Bella giggled, trying to keep a straight face and failing.

Wrapping her arms around Bella's slender little body, Harper tumbled back on to the bed. Delighted, Pipsqueak piled on top of them. Being with Bella had brought her so much happiness. Such a sense of purpose. And it had brought her Cameron, who was a young widower at the time.

But sometimes Bella could still be a handful. Pushing her dark, witchy hair from her eyes, she sat up, suddenly serious. "Did you tell Daddy?"

"What? Oh no, Bella. But I will." Harper wanted to think about it. The game plan had just changed.

"When are we going to put up the Christmas tree?"

Whoa, that caught her sideways. "But it's not even Thanksgiving yet." The thought of hauling that artificial tree down from the attic storage depressed her for some reason. Just one more thing they had to do before the wedding. She wasn't feeling the fa-la-lah.

"Everybody's talking about their Christmas tree at school. How their tree is the biggest and the prettiest." Harper almost laughed at Bella's huffy expression.

"Your dad and I will talk about it. How's that?"

"Soon, okay?"

"I'll do what I can." She remembered what it felt like to be Bella's age. "Right now, it's time for PJs and a story. Your dad's waiting for me."

Fifteen minutes later, Harper shot back down to the kitchen.

Just as she feared, Cameron wasn't at the round kitchen table. And somehow he'd put his dishes in the dishwasher. The rack was still pulled out. She pushed it in, filled the soap dispenser and started the dishwasher. He must be in the TV room.

"Cameron?" Football blared from the TV. But Cameron wasn't watching it. In fact, he'd nodded off on one side of the sofa that could fit eight people. One section was a sleeper sofa. Seeing how things were right now, that might come in handy. No way could Cameron make it up the stairs tonight to his master suite. Despite his objections, she still slept in her room on the third floor. After all, she'd gone to St. Edmund's and had her standards.

Oh, so carefully, she swung his legs up and onto the sofa very slowly. For a while, she sat and watched a game she didn't care about, afraid that he'd wake up if she changed the station or clicked the TV off. But looking at Cameron lying there, something stirred inside. One muscular arm thrown above his head, he looked so hot and adorable. Worn out by the end of the day, he always headed straight for the shower when he came home. But tonight he couldn't.

He'd feel terrible if he woke up like this.

Only concern for his comfort made her fill the basin with warm water. Really. She stirred it lazily with one hand and smiled.

Chapter 4

He'd really messed up. Thank God Rick got him home. Facing Harper? Pure hell. Maybe all girls from Chicago were this tough, but Harper could always handle herself. Tonight? One look at the shock on her beautiful face killed him. For a second, he thought she just might faint. And Bella? Poor little thing was so confused. He wanted to chase after her when she ran upstairs. But man, between the medications and the pain, no way. He felt hot, sweaty and sick—like he'd failed them. Not only did they have a wedding coming up, they both were crazy busy with work.

And now this. A compound fracture that hurt like hell. He was going to keep that "compound" part to himself so Harper didn't freak out. Sinking onto the sofa, he found the remote and clicked over to a game. But his eyes felt so damn heavy.

Later, a tickling feeling woke him up. The lights were low and the TV off. Sitting on the sofa where he lay stretched out, Harper had a pair of scissors in her hand. Holding out his shirt, she began to snip.

"Whatcha doing?" His tongue felt dry and thick.

"Nothing." But she had a wicked gleam in her eye. He knew that look. This was just how she smiled when she'd stepped onto his bar downstairs in her Catwoman suit for Beau's bachelor party.

This was her I'll-show-you look.

Bring it on. Kind of kinky, her cutting off his clothes. "So, Connie can't wash these?" he mumbled, drifting in and out. How he wished the damned meds would work. Maybe they were.

"Nope. These babies are gone." She kept cutting. Weird, but he liked the cool metal sliding across his skin. He was burning up.

"Can you turn up the air, sugga?" he whispered. But he missed her when she left with a soft rustle. Felt relieved when she came back. The metallic slide of the scissors started again. Felt good when the grubby shirt was somehow gently pulled from his body. "Shreds, probably shreds."

"Shredded. Right, baby."

Drifting in and out, he rode the waves of the meds. When she started on his face with a soft sponge, it felt so damn good. He hated to be grubby. Hated dirt. Reminded him too much of his folks' place back in Hazel Hurst, where his mother could hardly get his dad to wash his hands before dinner. His hometown might be only two hours away but his past? Worlds away.

"Feels so good, honey," he whispered. What a prize Harper was. Oh, those first days after he hired her had been rough. Some of the nannies only lasted three days. But Harper? She hung in there, putting up with Bella's crazy eating and tantrums. Helped him see how he could bring peace to his house. Simple things like coming home for dinner at a set time.

Whoa. Finished with his neck, she started on his chest. Just kept squeezing out that warm water onto his skin and then sponging it up. Swirled it. Her hand moved with a sexy rhythm that sent a shiver through his whole body. "Feels so good, babe. So damned good." She knew just what he liked. And she was being thorough, going over everything two or three times. "Should have been a nurse, Harper." But he sure didn't want her using this kind of dedication on any other man.

"Not gonna happen," she whispered, blowing a bit on his wet chest. "You know I love my work." The sponge skated across his chest again. She was so sweet and careful when she lifted his arm. Both arms felt like lead weights to him. What must they feel like to her?

"Darlin', you think I should be manscaped?" He and Rick had been talking about that lately, getting a good chuckle. But now the chuckle didn't come. Stayed in his head. Was she talking to him? "What do you say, Harper honey?"

"I say you're getting goofy. Don't you dare. I like it. All of you." Her nails slid up one arm and down over his chest. She chuckled as he drifted back out, enjoying this oh, so much. He was lucky, so lucky that her stupid ass boyfriend Billy had moved to California and left her heart-broken. She'd needed a job. A miracle when she showed up to interview for the nanny position, after she'd done a terrible job trying to be a stripper at the bachelor party.

Terrible but funny. Funny. Funny. The words echoed in his head that felt like one of those stills his daddy and brothers used to keep deep in the woods. The kind of crap he left behind him.

The activity on his legs brought him back out of it. The cool scissors inched up one leg with a cool, shearing sound. "Cost a small fortune." Could hardly get his fat tongue around the words.

"They're ripped, baby." And her fingers skated from his chest to his waist. "Just like your six pack. Ripped." And she laughed. Harper could be such a tease. Flirty and fiery. Should have known it from the red tint of her hair. A chill of excitement swept over him while she worked at getting the slacks off. She'd turned on the overhead fan. Glancing at the whirling blades made him dizzy. So he shut his eyes. Didn't have to see. Just feel. That sponge on his legs. God, she was hot.

Reaching for her hand, he fumbled until he felt his ring on her finger. "Oh, babe."

"Ye-ah-ess?" Only she drew it out, slow and sexy. Southern.

"Can't. Wait."

"Me too. Soon." But she sighed. He'd let her down. So much to do.

Now she was getting to the personal parts. His shivers worked deeper. Soul-deep where they damn near combusted. He loved her so much. Never knew he could. So very much. How she'd changed his home with her sassy ways. Her cute, crazy way of dressing. Bella adored her. He did too. Worshipped the ground that she walked on. Danced on. Loved on. On and on.

Words tumbled in his head while feelings washed over and under his skin. Even dulled the ache in his ankle. Dimmed the fear that he wouldn't be what he'd been, dancing with her, making love to her. When he squinted up, the dim light flickered over her face from the fan blade. Her hair had come loose from her braid. Cute smile on her face, Harper worked that sponge, dipping it into the warm water, squeezing it and coming back.

Always coming back.

Doing such a good job.

Then no more sponge. Just Harper. Settling herself over him. Smelling like Harper, feeling like Harper, loving him like only Harper could—just when he thought he couldn't be a man. That ankle hurt so bad. Then she made everything hurt so good. Better than he'd ever had it. "Watch the family jewels, okay?" he murmured. Or did he say that in his head?

"Oh, honey. I sure will." She was oh, so careful. Slow and careful.

~.~

Next morning, all hell broke loose. Harper tripped down the steps from her third floor bedroom to get Bella up. She could hear Connie banging pans around in the kitchen and the rumble of Cameron's voice.

Last night. She blushed to think about it. But those memories would last a lifetime. "Bella, you up?" She poked her head into Bella's bedroom.

"I don't want to go to school." Bella cowered under her blue Ninja blanket, and Pipsqueak peered out too.

Of course she didn't want to go to school. In all the fuss about Cameron, Harper hadn't gotten around to mentioning the pink slip or the problem. And she didn't want Cameron taking on more right now.

Time for her to step up to the plate. "Not to worry. But let's not bother Daddy, okay?"

"Okay." No questions asked.

Opening Bella's top dresser drawer, Harper pulled out some clothes and tossed them on the bed. Bella scrambled out of bed and into a pair of red leggings and a navy and red-striped top. Suddenly alert and aware that breakfast awaited downstairs, Pipsqueak scampered from the room, paws clicking on the hardwood. She was headed for Cameron, no doubt. Harper knew the feeling.

"You look good enough to eat," Harper teased Bella, helping her on with her tennis shoes.

"I want a ribbon in my hair. Can I have one?" Bella pointed to the lime green scarf holding back Harper's own hair.

"Hmm. Are you old enough for this?" Her wild ways were rubbing off on Bella, and she wasn't sure if that was a good thing.

"Harper. Pretty please?" Bella wheedled, but Harper was already pawing through a drawer and came out with a red headband. A few minutes later they were headed downstairs, Bella bouncing down the Oriental runner in front of her.

Harper's stomach turned squishy, just thinking about last night. Talk about making lemons into lemonade. Or love into making love. Or something like that.

At the kitchen door, she pulled to a halt. Cameron was sitting at the breakfast table, the *Savannah Morning News* in hand. He looked so cozy and casual in his gray tracksuit, the light jacket partially unzipped. This could be Sunday morning with toast and eggs, except for the cast on his right foot. The rings under his eyes indicated he'd had a rough night.

"Daddy, Daddy. Are you all better?" Bella looked ready to launch herself at her father when Harper grabbed her.

"We have to take it easy, punkin. Daddy's still healing."

Stirring something at the stove that smelled like oatmeal, Connie turned. "Such a surprise to see him on the sofa in fresh clothes." She gave Harper a knowing look.

"Amazing, right?" Harper wasn't offering any details. Connie would have been even more surprised if he hadn't been wearing the tracksuit. Sleep had almost claimed the man when she helped him ease it on. That cast wasn't easy. "Slit it. Rip it," he'd mumbled. "Woman you've worn me out. Just leave me."

"Okay, Boss Man." She kind of liked Rick's nickname for Cameron. Usually he needed to be the man in charge. But now? She might have to take on some things for him, not that she wanted him to know that.

"Oatmeal?" Connie held up a bowl.

"Just coffee, thanks."

Sliding onto her seat, Bella said. "Me too. Coffee, please." Then she giggled, wrinkling her nose.

Cameron exchanged a look with Harper and pursed his lips into a *pretty please*. Harper melted, although she was trying to diet to fit into her mother's wedding dress. "Yes, please Connie. I'll have some of that delicious oatmeal and so will Bella."

Smiling, Connie ladled oatmeal into two bowls. "Bananas and brown sugar on top?"

"Oh, yes. Yum," Harper said for Bella's benefit.

"Yes, yum," Cameron murmured. But those words were meant

only for Harper's benefit and had nothing to do with oatmeal. Her ears burned.

"Anything good in the paper?" she asked, pouring juice for herself and Bella.

"Not as interesting as what's right here."

"You rascal." She bent to kiss him. "Your face is scratchy. I may have to shave you later."

Shifting his jaw as if there were many things he wanted to say, Cameron smiled. "Later."

Patting her back, or thereabouts, he nuzzled her neck. "I'd say this is what interests me most right now."

"You two," Bella said with mock disgust.

Connie just smiled and the morning felt so warm and cozy. Why couldn't life always be like this? Filled with sweet moments. Just the two, well, three of them. Four if you counted Pipsqueak. She ruffled Cameron's hair. "Got a plan," she asked. "I'm taking Bella to school. I can drop you off. Maybe the guys can drive the Bentley back later."

"Sounds good to me. Thanks."

Harper felt Bella's questioning eyes on her and gave a little shake of her head that Cameron didn't see. This wasn't the time to bring up Mrs. Powers, the principal. Taking the seat next to Bella, she poured milk on her oatmeal and picked up a spoon.

Although Cameron did his best to negotiate the stairs when they left the house, she could see everything would be an effort for him. Cameron definitely would not be able to help decorate anyone's house next weekend. Maybe that had been wishful thinking anyway. She'd have to talk to Rick or maybe Adam, her buddy from college.

Once Bella was fastened into her seatbelt, they took off for the Buchanan mansion, where Cameron had been working. "Talk about returning to the scene of the crime," he murmured when they arrived. Jumping from the car, Harper helped him out and handed him his crutches.

"I can do this, darlin'." He started up the walk. Rick's pickup was already in the driveway, and he appeared on the porch.

"Have a good day, Daddy!" Bella called from the back seat. The crutches stopped thumping and Cameron turned, the sun catching his blue eyes. As Harper got back in the SUV, he threw a kiss and Bella sighed. "Isn't Daddy the most handsomest man?"

"Yes, sweetie. He sure is." But Harper had work to do, and she threw the SUV in gear. Time to go to school. She would talk to Mrs. Powers and explain the whole thing. If the principal didn't accept it, well then she would take another course. But she wasn't going to bother Cameron about this right now. When they reached the low, brick building that was Bella's private school, Harper didn't join the student delivery line. Instead, she pulled into the side lot and parked.

"What are you doing, Harper?" Bella leaned forward in her seat.

"Taking you into school." Jumping out of the SUV, Harper went around to open the back door. By that time, Bella had already unclipped her seatbelt. She was growing up, and Harper had mixed feelings. Sometimes she felt sad that the toddler she'd met at that first interview was becoming a little girl. Bella didn't need her quite so much. But today she did.

Hand in hand, they walked inside together, where it sure smelled, sounded and looked like school. A teacher stood primly at each door, greeting students.

"Hello, Bella." Mrs. Davenport called to them, and that was a good sign. Squatting, Harper looked Bella in the eye and handed her the lunch Connie had packed so carefully. "Now you have a good day, you hear?"

Uncertainty clouded Bella's eyes. How could she have a good day after yesterday? If she were truthful, the little girl reminded Harper so much of herself. She'd been a rascal in grade school. After the boys and McKenna, Big Mike and Maureen Kirkpatrick thought they could coast on this one. Hadn't they seen everything with their other children? Harper proved them wrong.

"Can I have a kiss?" Harper turned her cheek for the peck bestowed on her then grabbed Bella for a quick hug. "Bye, sweetheart. See you tonight."

"Later." Trying so hard to be a big girl, she trotted off. How could anybody be mean to this little angel? Taking the pink slip from her purse, Harper headed for the office door with *Principal, Mrs. Elaine Powers* etched on it in gold. When she entered the room, two other people sat on the wooden bench. Clearly, they were waiting and one older girl, probably in third or fourth grade, was having a heated conversation with the receptionist. But no matter how high her voice rose, the student got nowhere.

"You just wait until I tell my parents about this," she finally said. So young and such an attitude. Cameron still wasn't sold on the private school. Said they'd have to see. The receptionist's eyes remained glued to her screen. Looking down, Harper checked the nameplate. Lucinda Krebs obviously wasn't taking any guff from this girl. Turning, the girl stomped toward the door, her blonde curls bobbing.

The receptionist looked at Harper as if to say, *Do you believe this?*

"And what can I help you with?" Lucinda Krebs' eyes flitted over her lime green sweater and black miniskirt with lime and black-striped leggings. Too late, Harper realized this probably wasn't the type of outfit mothers wore. Not here. This school was more a country club, casual school. But this morning Harper had been preoccupied, and all her good intentions were forgotten. "Could I see Mrs. Powers, please?"

Making a great show of checking her desk calendar, the receptionist asked, "Do you have an appointment, Mrs..."

"No, not really." Did the pink slip in her hand count? She waved it. "But I do have this."

Stretching out a hand, the receptionist took the note and scanned it quickly. The waiting couple, probably parents, were all ears. "But Mrs. Powers has asked that you *call* at your earliest convenience."

"Oh, I know. But I thought, you know, meeting face-to-face would be better. More personal." The last part wasn't cutting any slack in the woman's eyes. Harper watched her eyebrows rise like bristling caterpillars.

"Please have a seat." The phone on the desk buzzed, and the receptionist motioned to the couple. "Mr. and Mrs. Vander Gann, you may go in now." Hmm. Were they the same Vander Ganns that owned the jewelry stores?

Sitting on the bench the Vander Ganns had just vacated, Harper felt her black miniskirt inch up. Thank goodness for the leggings. It didn't escape her that the receptionist was taking this all in. Picking up a magazine, she began to flip through the pages. Duller than dirt. No shoes. No fall fashions. Crossing her legs, she admired her new Jessica Simpson platform heels. Cameron had complimented the black she now wore, and she figured these shoes were a step in the right direction. Then she caught the receptionist eyeing them. Was there jealousy or contempt in that glance? Whatever. Harper was used to both.

She looked at the title of the magazine. *Education Today.* Yep, duller than dishwater, as Connie would say. So she checked her phone for messages. She had something from Adam, old friend and former neighbor, and she started to text. *What are you doing later this morning? I think I need an intervention.*

Adam's salon didn't open until eleven. Certainly by that time, she'd be finished here at school. *Name the time and the place* zipped back.

Her thumbs got busy. *Tied up now but I'll get back to you pronto. Tied up? Sounds like fun. I'm on pins and noodles.*

Harper smiled. She needed some time with Adam. She'd gotten a lot more than a cup of sugar from Adam when they were neighbors...some of the best advice ever. Her friend called it like he saw it. She glanced at the clock on the wall. Yikes, that couple had been in there for twenty minutes, which slowly turned into thirty.

She wondered what their kid had done. Keyed the principal's car? Gum on a teacher's chair? Not that she'd know anything about any of that. Giving in to one of her worst habits, she began to gnaw at a nail. After all, Lucinda Krebs was busy with her computer screen.

Time dragged on. Had that clock hand moved at all? She picked at her dark aqua nail polish. Once in a while, the receptionist would hit her with a self-satisfied look that said *we are so important in this office that you cannot expect to just get in without an appointment.*

Not that Harper was reading a lot into one glance. The woman sure seemed up tight, her fingers typing away on the keyboard. Maybe Lucinda just needed a bathroom break.

Phone still in hand, Harper went on her Facebook page. Took a picture of the magazine she'd pitched aside and typed... *For your Christmas List.* Added a smiley face or three. Then she shared some of the funnier videos her friends had posted. The cat and dog ones were favorites. A lot of her former SCAD classmates had interesting, creative jobs. That's just how they rolled. They'd had their act together and scored jobs in New York, hub of the fashion industry. She kept up with them on Facebook.

That wasn't Harper. She'd never even gotten an interview. Her resume had some holes, or so she was told. Something about those missed classes.

But the way things turned out, she didn't regret staying in Savannah. Not since Cameron entered her life. Holding out her left hand, she wiggled her fingers, enjoying the way the light hit her diamond. What fun that dinner had been when Cameron popped the question. Crazy, but fun. Selena Ruiz, who dated her brother Seth, had come to town for a break. Seth had messed up bad, so Selena had been there, along with Cameron's mother and sister, who just about slid under the table when he brought out the little box. But Bella got so excited. Harper had been over the moon. Happiness flooded her just thinking about that night, followed by a good dose of lust. Cameron just did that to her.

When the door to the principal's office clicked open, she slipped her phone into her handbag. Time to move this along so she could meet Adam.

The couple exiting wore satisfied smiles, as if the meeting had gone well. Maybe they'd softened up Mrs. Powers for her. "Thank you for coming in, Mr. and Mrs. Vander Gann," Lucinda stood as they passed. Yep, the woman was wearing enough gold to tempt a Brinks' guard. Hands down, they owned the jewelry stores.

"So good to see you, Lucinda." Mrs. Vander Gann breezed past, her perfume stinging Harper's eyes. Fumbling around in her bag, she grabbed her inhaler and took a quick whiff. Passing out in the principal's office? Not an option today. Although Harper expected to be shown back, that didn't happen. In fact, she sat there another five minutes before Lucinda motioned to her. "You may go in now. But Mrs. Powers has another appointment at ten." Oh, goody. That left five minutes.

Harper sprang up. "No worries. Short conversation." At least, she sure hoped so.

Mrs. Powers rose from her desk, a sharply chiseled woman who probably ate two crackers for lunch every day. Smiling, she extended a hand. "Good morning and thank you for waiting, Mrs...?"

"Miss Kirkpatrick." She shook the principal's hand. Dry as paper.

When Mrs. Powers tilted her head to one side, her short dark curls stayed put. "I don't believe we have a student with that name."

Harper hadn't expected this. "Oh, well, I'm...." What was she?

I'm engaged to Cameron Bennett, and soon you can call me her mother. But of course, she didn't say that. Instead, she dug the toe of one of her new heels into the deep plush carpet. "I, ah, take care of Bella."

"Won't you have a seat?" A frown appeared. "So, you're that nanny?"

That nanny?

"Yes, I was—am Bella's nanny." *Not that it's any business of yours.* But she didn't say that either. One more month, and she'd officially be Bella's mother. The thought stunned her. "I'm here to talk about this note. You need to know that the girls in Bella's class were mean to her. You probably don't know that." The words wouldn't come out fast enough and seemed to trip over each other, sounding ticked off and immature.

She was doing this all wrong.

Tapping the pink note with one index finger that could use a little nail polish, Mrs. Powers gave her a tight smile. "But of course I cannot discuss Bella Bennett with anyone but her father or her legal guardian." She blinked. "Have you been made her legal guardian?"

"Well, no. Not legally but..." Reading *Cat in the Hat* to her at bedtime probably didn't count.

The chiseled nose rose higher. "We pride ourselves on discretion. And we simply cannot talk about Bella's personality adjustment. Not to you, that is. Please ask her father to call me."

Personality adjustment? Each word ratcheted the heat higher in Harper's face. "I see."

"Yes, I'm so sorry..." But she wasn't. Mrs. Powers didn't look sorry at all. In fact, she looked pleased. Rising, she stood, waiting for Harper to leave.

I've really screwed up. Panic thudded in Harper's head. She'd told Bella she'd fix this. And she'd only made things worse. "But you'll make sure that Tiffany and the others won't corner her in the bathroom again?"

Mrs. Powers' mouth fell open. Her eyes deadened with disdain. "I can assure you we allow no hooliganism in our restrooms. Not with our children." Only *our* was pronounced *ahh*, floating in the air with stubborn pride.

Hooliganism? "I see." But she didn't. "Thank you for..." *nothing*. She had to get out of here. Fighting for breath, Harper stumbled from the office and flew past Lucinda. Sliding her bag from her shoulder, she rooted around for the inhaler. This school was probably full of poisonous cleaning products...and maybe poisonous people. As she hurried through the lobby with Olympic speed, a maintenance crew was erecting the largest tree she'd ever seen. It dwarfed the two-story lobby, and a pine scent thick as syrup closed her throat.

No wonder Bella had Christmas tree envy. This Jack-in-the-Beanstalk tree was big as the tree that graced Marshall Field's when she was a little girl. Every Christmas, her mother would take the girls down to have lunch under the tree. Now the smell and the tinny taste of her own failure made her want to hurl.

Back out in the sunshine, Harper leaned against a brick pillar and drew in a lungful of air.

She'd messed up. Plain and simple. Somehow, she made it to the car. Before she started the motor, she took out her phone and called Adam. "Five minutes. Foxy Loxy?"

"I'll be there. You okay? You sound funny."

"Tell you later."

Swallowing a sob, she started the car, punched a knob and blasted Adele's latest CD.

Chapter 5

When Harper reached Foxy Loxy, Adam was relaxing on the back patio with a steaming chai latte. Jumping up, he opened his arms. "Hey, fashion plate, what's up?" A big guy, he gave a good bear hug. She buried her face in his red cashmere V-neck and breathed in.

"Gosh you smell good." But her voice bobbled at the end, and Adam held her away, scanning her face. The man knew her way too well. "What's this?"

Sinking into the chair across from him, Harper tried to control her anger. "I just came from Bella's school where the principal put me in my place. No wonder Bella is having trouble there."

The waiter came. Pointing to Adam's drink, Harper said, "I'll have one of those, please." Just being with Adam helped.

He did one of those circling motions with his finger. "Now let's get this straight. I thought Cameron handled all of Bella's school issues."

Good friends always remembered stuff. No need to hold up cue cards with Adam or fill in the backstory. "Correct. But Cameron doesn't know about this. Not yet."

The frown on Adam's face deepened. "You're keeping stuff from Cameron? Your man?" He was almost shivering with indignation.

The drink was set in front of her. "You're right, and normally I wouldn't be doing this because he likes to take the lead with things that concern Bella. But he's had an accident."

She thought Adam would levitate right out of the chair. "An accident? Was he hurt? Total the car? Is he in the hospital?"

Taking a deep sip of the warm drink, she let the comforting spices ease her throat. "Down, boy. Your questions make me feel better because no, he is not in the hospital and he did not total the car. He broke an ankle."

Her friend's hand flew to his mouth. "I want it all. Dish, please."

Just remembering the moment when Cameron came though the door got her all jittery again. "Seems that he was up on a scaffolding, which I asked him never to do, checking out the work of the crew. His foot went through and he twisted. Broke his ankle."

Adam recoiled. "Sounds nasty. And inconvenient with the wedding coming up and everything."

"Exactly. Which is why I didn't want to put one more thing on his plate. But oh, Adam, I made such a mess of it this morning."

"It couldn't have been that bad." Reaching over, he squeezed her hand.

"Yes it was and I blew it. Bella is being bullied and that has to stop. Irritates me no end that I couldn't handle it just because I don't have that Mrs. in my name."

He expelled a breath. "Honey, you don't have the Bennett in

your name. Double mark against you."

"Just a technicality. Now I have to tell Cameron and he'll be furious. I can't let this hang out there because I promised Bella I'd handle it. This has to stop." Remembering Bella's anguish, Harper thumped a fist on the table.

"Bullying? Of course it has to stop. What kind of bullying?"

"Some girls said her hair looks like a rat's nest. Which it kind of does. And then Bella took matters into her own hands."

"Rat's nest? What kind of conditioner are you using?" Looking alarmed, Adam took a whole different avenue.

"I don't know. Baby shampoo?"

A finger wagged in her face. "Well, no wonder. I can fit you in tomorrow, ten o'clock."

"But your salon opens at eleven."

"For you, I make exceptions."

"You're such a good guy." The humiliation of the morning eased a bit. "What would I do without you?"

"Don't even think about it. The timing is bad, right? With Thanksgiving next week and the wedding, you both have enough on your plate."

"Right, basically this whole week has sucked. Georgina Darlington and Brittany Bedford have made me crazy." When she filled Adam in, he was predictably horrified. "If it weren't for Julep Tucker, I'd really be tearing out my hair. I've ordered everything in their individual color pallets, and now I'll have to rethink my whole plan."

"The SCAD design library. Perfect place to start for ideas."

"I was thinking the same thing." She started to work on her hangnails again.

"And don't bite your cuticles." Leaning over, Adam gave her hand a slight tap. "Just think of all those photos coming up. Your hand under Cameron's cutting the cake. Your hands clutching your bouquet. You could go down in family history for having chewed cuticles."

She looked at her hands in disgust. "Too late for that to be big family news, Adam. I chewed my fingernails all through grade school. It was hard to live up to McKenna's performance. She was an A student and I was, well, the youngest in the family."

"But certainly the best looking. Certainly the most charming."

Aw, and this is why he was a good friend. "No truth to any of that but it still sounds good."

"How is the wedding coming?"

"My mother seems to have it all in hand."

"Got your invitation and noticed all RSVPs go to your mom. The design was beautiful. I especially liked the holly berries. Your work?"

"Yes, glad you like it." She twisted a curl over her finger. "Somehow it all seems obscene to be trying to pull off this wedding at Christmas."

"Why not? Do it the way you want it."

"The way I want it?" Harper stared down her good friend. "You're kidding, right? My mother has talked of nothing but this wedding since McKenna got hitched in Santa Fe, which totally rocked by the way. But my mother didn't think so. Not that she'd tell McKenna that. No, Mom wanted an old-fashioned wedding in our hometown, but she zipped her lip and said nothing. My wedding? It's her last chance. I'm wearing her gown, you know."

Brows went up. "Good or bad?"

"Good if you like swirling meringues and loved Lady Di."

"Girls, mothers and wedding," Adam mused. "A recipe for disaster."

"Think you got something there." Harper stabbed a finger in his direction. "But I don't think boys, weddings and mothers are any better. Cameron's mother refuses to come to Chicago. I feel terrible. Not exactly the wedding I'd pictured. Families should be together, kind of bless the union."

"Really? You want that rag-tag group there? From what you've said, I thought he was estranged from the family over in Hazel Hurts?"

Her glare could have steamed his chai latte. "That's mean. It's Hazel Hurst. No matter what happens, your family is your family. Besides, now that his dad is gone—who was the main problem, mind you—Cameron feels closer to his mother and especially his sister Lily. They were at the Valentine dinner when he proposed."

Dramatic rolling of the eyes. Adam really had that down. "Don't want to mention that I wasn't invited to said affair."

"Adam, it wasn't a flash mob, it was family that night. Don't sulk. Did you buy your ticket to Chicago? You know I'll need you there to do my hair. The one thing I get to do my way."

"Done and done. Wasn't easy or inexpensive because of holiday travel but anything for you. I've always wanted to see Chicago in the snow. I'm bringing the bobsled and my pack of huskies."

"Okay, enough. But Michigan Avenue is magical with all those lights when it gets dark."

"We're going down there?" Hope glimmered in his eyes.

"No, probably no time. But I love your loyalty, Adam." Checking her phone, she found a message from Cameron saying that Rick had brought him home. *Nothing to worry about. Just thought I'd come home.*

That didn't sound right and she grabbed her purse. "Adam, I have to move on."

"And I should go open the salon. I'm doing Sissy Grantham's hair before she leaves on her honeymoon. They'll be throwing rocks through the windows if I'm not there."

"Guess I'll stop at the library and then run home to check on Cameron." They tossed their empty cups in the trash.

"Really? He's a grown man for God's sake."

How to explain this? "For probably the first time, I feel he needs me." And that tug felt good.

"Well in that case, we're out of here." Against her protests, Adam grabbed the check and paid it. Then they ambled outside.

Putting on her heart-shaped sunglasses, she watched him drive away in the shiny pickup truck that he'd loaned her more times than she could recall. The SUV felt pleasantly warm after being in the sun. After climbing in, Harper called Cameron. The phone rang and rang. She went back to her cuticles.

"Babe." Finally he picked up.

"Hey, why are you home?"

"Just thought I'd come home early." The glum tone told her just what he thought of that. She knew he had tons to do.

"How are you feeling?"

"I've had better days."

Her whole world seemed to shrink. This just didn't sound like Cameron. "I'll be home in about an hour, okay? I'm headed to the JEN library. Have to get my projects back on track for Georgina and Brittany."

"You don't have to babysit for me. Everything's fine here." The defensive note in his voice told her it wasn't. And it wasn't going to be fine when she told him about Bella and Mrs. Powers. But for Bella's sake, that had to happen soon. "One hour and I'll be there. Don't go anywhere, okay?"

"Right. I'd thought I'd jog to Daffin Park. Get some exercise." That familiar teasing tone made her smile. "Love you, Harper."

No matter how many times he said it, the words always made her feel squishy inside.

"Love you too."

Silence hummed between them, and she closed her eyes, imagining what he was thinking. The sofa pit and the scissors did come to mind. With some effort, she cleared her throat and her thoughts. "Okay then, see you soon."

Cameron was laughing when she ended the call.

Her stop at the library didn't take long. She knew just which magazines to consult and quickly took notes. When she left the building about forty-five minutes later, she hesitated. Across the street sat Leopold's, and she was sorely tempted to stop for a chocolate soda. Maybe that could qualify as lunch as far as calories went. They made an old-fashioned ice cream soda that reminded her of Petersen's back in Oak Park. But she had two more stops to make so she continued to her car.

Driving to Abercorn Street, she turned south and continued to JoAnn Fabric. A quick inventory of the ribbons told her she'd better move on this. The holiday plaids were already looking a little picked over. She bought a few rolls, and then drove on to Michael's where she did the same thing.

As she drove home, her thoughts turned to Bella and school. Somehow, she had to temper the news about Bella, and then Mrs. Powers, without Cameron going ballistic. The situation had to be fixed and fast.

Pulling in the garage, she saw the Bentley sitting there next to the red Porsche, which was clearly Cameron's favorite. Bags swinging from her arm, she skipped through the garden, passed the mermaid fountain and took the stairs. She could see Connie working at the sink and waved.

"Hey, what's going on in here?" she asked, swirling through the door.

"Not much." Crutches leaning against his chair, Cameron sat at the round kitchen table. Eyes shifting to pool blue, he looked up when she bent to kiss him.

She could feel his tension. "How's my patient?"

Wrong thing to say. His body stiffened further. Damn. How she wanted to reel those words back.

"Fine, little girl."

Okay, sometimes she liked him to think of her that way. But not today. Not when she'd failed so miserably this morning at school. Delaying this wouldn't be any easier. When she slipped into the chair next to him, Connie disappeared into the dining room. "Cameron, we have to talk about Bella."

"What now?" The smile slid right off his face. She felt him waiting.

"She brought a note home yesterday."

"Yesterday?"

"Yes, sorry. I didn't want to bother you because of...everything." And she waved a hand toward the crutches. "Thought I could handle it and I met with the principal this morning."

His frown gave her a chill. "But I'm the one who handles Bella, when it comes to problems."

"I know that but I just thought, you know, because of everything."

Man, she'd never been known for her silver tongue. This was just getting worse. "So I stopped...today to talk...to the principal." The words came out in breathless bursts. In gathering up her bags, she'd left her purse in the car with her inhaler.

"And?"

Oh, this was going to kill him. "She said...she could only discuss a student...with a legal guardian...and that wasn't me."

With a roar, Cameron shot up. The pain on his face when he stood on the broken ankle pierced her heart.

Chapter 6

"Cameron, are you all right?" Her heart hammered as she watched him struggle to stay upright.

"Of course I am." Clenching his jaw, he reached for his crutches. "Harper, honey. Can you just take me over to the school?" Crutches tucked under his arms, he stared at his right foot in disgust.

"Sure." Besides, she had to get to the car to retrieve her inhaler.

In silence, they made their way outside and down to the garage. Grabbing her purse from the seat before she climbed in, she took a couple draughts from the purple inhaler. Once they pulled out and were on the road, she had to break the silence that felt like a wall. "I went to the library today, leafed through some magazines. I think I've got some ideas for the Darlingtons and the Bedfords."

"Good. I'm glad to hear it." He was clearly preoccupied.

"Look. I'm sorry, okay?"

Looking over, he squeezed her hand. "Sorry, Harper. I'm not mad at you. I'm upset about school and the legal guardian runaround. I should have done a better job at explaining your position, that's all."

Oh, wow. "I thought I could take care of this for you. Isn't that what a wife does?"

But even as she asked, she heard a big no in her head. In the Kirkpatrick house, Big Mike made many of the major decisions. Or at least, he thought he did. But underneath, it was Reenie who orchestrated a lot. Harper had failed in that role this morning.

"Want to talk about your ideas tonight?"

Bless his heart. "If you're up to it." She pulled into the school driveway and parked in the lot.

"Of course I'm up to it. Don't worry, everything will be fine."

But as they slowly made their way toward the front door, she sincerely wondered how. The man could hardly walk, although he'd never admit he was in pain. Above everything else, he had his pride. When the glass doors of the school whooshed open, the distinctive smell of pine enveloped them. The staff had made a lot of progress since that morning with the decorating. The tree brought Cameron to a halt. "Isn't it a bit early for a tree?"

"For some people, I guess." The Christmas tree wasn't at the top of her list, although she knew it really mattered to Bella. With Cameron keeping a steady pace on the crutches, they made it down the hall to the gold-etched glass door where she'd made such a fool of herself only a couple hours ago.

Lucinda Krebs glanced up. The smile came when she took in Cameron's pink dress shirt rolled up on strong forearms. And no doubt, she noted the determination on his handsome face. Even when he was on crutches, he was a force to be reckoned with. Harper watched as he pulled himself together and became the self-possessed man that could sell the city on development strategies to move the city forward.

"Can I help you with anything?" she asked sweetly, refusing to look at Harper.

Cagey man that he was, his eyes swept the nameplate. "How are you today, Lucinda? I hope your brother's recuperation is going well?"

"You know Lee?" Her expression adjusted even more. "How sweet of you to ask. Of course he's doing much better since he got to the VA hospital."

"Please tell him Cameron Bennett asked about him."

"I most certainly will." She blinked. "And how may I help you, Mr. Bennett?"

"Would you ask Mrs. Powers if I could steal a few minutes from her day? I know she's so very busy."

Harper steeled herself for the excuses. Instead, Lucinda slowly got up, smoothed her ladylike navy skirt and said, "If you would just excuse me for one moment." And she disappeared from Harper's amazed sight.

"You know, Cameron," she murmured from the corner of her mouth. "I'd be really ticked about what I just saw, but I want this to go well for Bella."

His eyes swung her way. "Whatever are you talking about?"

"You know darn well what I'm talking about," she hissed, keeping her voice down. "I don't need you to tell me one more time that my Chicago ways can be more bricks than brown sugar."

Even though she was mad, it sure felt good to see that cheeky grin on his face. "Honey, I will take your sugar anyway I can get it."

Snatching a brochure from a side table, she fanned herself.

Cameron leaned so close; his hair tickled her cheeks, and his aftershave made her woozy. "And one more thing, darlin'. You ever buy an old-lady skirt like that and you won't have it on for long." His expression shifted. "Which isn't a bad idea."

She fanned faster.

Lucinda returned and they were ushered back to the inner office. Even with the broken ankle and crutches, Cameron Bennett carried himself as if he belonged. How a man from his humble background had perfected that carriage, Harper might never know. She could hardly believe the smiling woman behind the impressive, mahogany desk was the same person who'd put her in her place that morning.

"Elaine, how very nice to see you." His hand went out, and of course Elaine Powers reached for it.

"Cameron, it's been too long since we saw each other. Whatever brings you here when you obviously should be resting at home." A curious glance slid Harper's way, and she felt, once again, inadequate. As if she'd broken Cameron's leg herself, and then dragged the poor man down here. "Do sit down and make yourself comfortable."

"A minor inconvenience, but thank you." The man was a wonder. He eased himself into the chair with admirable grace.

Taking the crutches, Harper set them against the wall and sat on the edge of the chair next to him. This was definitely his show, and she was a bystander, not a comfortable feeling.

"We've been studying the sketches you provided for our library addition."

"I'm so eager to hear the board's thoughts on my suggestions."

Okay, Harper never heard him mention any involvement in school improvements, but they had been really busy.

"Such a good sense of our history." Then she folded her hands in front of her as if she were praying. "Now, how may I help you?"

"Elaine, I...*we* are here at your request. Apparently, Bella had a problem at school yesterday, and you wanted to speak to us?"

Her mouth twitched as if choosing her words very carefully. "Why yes, we were quite worried when we couldn't find her. Considered calling the police. I cannot tell you how concerned we were."

There's a difference between concerned and irritated, Elaine.

Legs crossed, Harper began bobbing her right foot.

"I can only imagine. Now, I do hope that if a situation ever arises again you would call me. The police have enough to do, and we wouldn't want to trouble them with something so trivial."

"You are so right, Cameron." Elaine hadn't looked her way since she sat down. Harper was invisible.

"And I know you will be appalled to hear about the physical bullying that went on. Harper, darlin', would you share what Bella told you yesterday?"

In halting speech, she retold the sad story about the insult, Bella's response and the bullying. The word *bullying* was dropped onto the principal's desk like a live bomb.

Elaine Powers flinched, her administrative composure showing signs of wear. "I'm sure we can straighten out the situation, Cameron. I will have a talk with Tiffany's parents and assure them of course that you have attended to this on your end. We want all students to feel secure in this educational environment." Nostrils flaring, she acted as if she were hearing this for the first time, which fried Harper's brain.

"Excellent, and I will check with Bella just to keep up on your progress. I'd like to think that the children in Bella's class have been taught to respect each other."

"Absolutely." Mrs. Powers' chin came up as her neck extended. "That is my goal as well."

"Yes, I so appreciate everything you do for the well-being of the students."

When had this meeting turned into a love fest? Harper felt the words flow back and forth like syrup on a warm stack of hoppin' Johnny cakes, the kind only Connie could make. Not content to leave it there, Elaine walked them out of her office, where she again told Cameron how wonderful he was and how lucky Bella was to have him for a father. The implication of course was that Harper was just an inept, incidental bystander.

But Cameron wasn't finished. "Oh, one more thing, Elaine. Feel free to discuss Bella's school progress or anything of a confidential matter with Harper. Our wedding ceremony is coming up, and very soon, Bella will be calling her mother."

The delight in the principal's eyes indicated this was the first time she'd heard the news. "Why, of course. Isn't that wonderful?"

Harper could hardly contain her laughter when they strolled out through the lobby. The men were placing a Christmas angel at the top of the tree, and she stopped to take full stock of their efforts.

At that moment, she could have soared to the top of that tree and joined the angel.

Then her professional nature took hold and she stood back. Sure, all the required components were on that tree. Red and green glass ornaments. Brilliant lights in all colors. Felt ornaments that looked handmade, with names of staff and students. All well-intended, but in Harper's eyes, standard.

She could do a lot better. She *would* do a lot better.

"Hey, babe." Cameron cocked his head toward the door that swung open when they hit the pressure pad. They walked through. The cold air outside felt welcome and overdue.

Resting one hand lightly on his back, she mumbled, "What a lot of horse pucky." They turned toward the parking lot.

"I knew something was smelling in that room." Chuckling, Cameron sniffed the air. He'd handled everything so well but at a price. The meeting had taken something out of him. Teeth gritted, he swung across the lot.

"How are you feeling?' she asked.

"Fine. Everything's fine." Of course he would say that.

"Are you taking the pain medication?"

No answer. "Cameron, the doctor gave you that medication so you would take it. How can you get better when you're tensing against the pain?" Taking his crutches, Harper opened the front door of the SUV. But when she went to take his elbow, he looked at her as if she'd lost her mind. "Harper, darlin', I can handle this myself."

She dropped her hand. "Of course. I'll, ah, just stick these in the back." Pushing up off his left foot, he managed to leverage himself into the front seat. Unable to watch, she walked around the back of the SUV and got in. By the time Cameron snapped his seatbelt shut, his forehead was beaded with sweat.

They hadn't gone far when Harper's stomach growled. The crisis past, she was starving.

"Have you eaten lunch?" Cameron asked.

"Not really."

"Me neither. Let's stop at Back in the Day for a late lunch. Get some of their rosemary chicken salad."

"Are you sure?" That would mean getting out of the car. Right now, she wanted to see him settled and comfortable.

"It's past the lunch hour so we should be able to get a seat."

He was only doing this for her because he knew she loved their chicken salad. Although it took a while, finally they were seated at one of the funky tables with mismatched chairs. The food was fabulous, the air always smelled of fresh bread, and she loved it. Slugging down some root beer, she started eating the chicken salad, savoring the crunch of the celery and currants, along with the tang of rosemary. Cameron did the same. The confusion and hurt of the past twenty-four hours faded.

"Wait until I tell Bella," Harper said between bites. "She'll be so relieved, and she's got a hair appointment with Adam."

"Isn't she a little young for a hair appointment?"

"When the kids at school say your hair looks like a rat's nest, it's time to call in the big guns. This was Adam's suggestion."

Cameron's laugh relieved the tension. For a second, things

weren't screwed up. For a second, it was just Cameron and Harper, not a holiday season that had become tense beyond belief. Smiling, she reached to wipe a dollop of mayo from the corner of his mouth, and he kissed her hand. It was as if a pilot light flicked on in his eyes, and suddenly she wanted him more than lunch.

"Everything okay at work?" she asked, just to get her wandering mind back on track. Cameron always had three or four renovations going at once. He usually barreled from project to project, checking plans and conferring with his onsite managers.

"Rick's holding down the fort. He'd call if there was an issue. What about you? You stopped at the library?"

"I did." And she took him through some of the ideas she'd picked up. "Those bags I brought home are full of a lot of stuff to work with. Now, I have to pull it all together and sell each woman on the revisions."

Made her tired just to think about it. But the food helped, although she couldn't finish the ciabatta bread.

"Maybe we should spread everything out in the TV room." Reaching under the table, he squeezed her knee. "Then again, maybe we should just spread out."

"We could do that." His hand warm on her thigh brought some options to mind. "But Connie will be there. And Jack."

Rolling his eyes to the ceiling, Cameron smiled. "Think I have a solution." Getting Connie on the phone, he asked if the two of them could drive over to Pace Lighting in Pooler to look at some lighting fixtures for the library. "Tell him we need some new cans in the ceiling, and I want to add a ceiling fan." His hand inched higher, and she squeezed her eyes shut, knowing what she wanted for dessert.

Thank God the ride home was short or she could have veered off into the live oaks that draped moss over Victory. When they pulled into the driveway, Jack and Connie were just leaving in their black pickup truck. They waved.

Like a couple of guilty teenagers, they hustled through the garden, crutches and all. Going up the back steps took some time. He absolutely would not let her help him. But impatience made her body thrum, especially certain lady parts. "Did I tell you how cute you look in your little black skirt?" he whispered once they were inside.

"No." She gulped. "Not yet."

"Slip it off, darlin'."

So she did. "And this shirt, Cameron?" She ran her hands up the placket of his Oxford cloth shirt that Lucinda had so admired.

"Yes, Ms. Kirkpatrick."

"History." As she unbuttoned the shirt, the warm musky smell that was uniquely Cameron washed over her. Every nerve ending in her body said hello.

But when she went to kick off her new shoes, his hands stopped her. "Let's leave the shoes. Just for now."

Yanking his shirt from his slacks, he grabbed the crutches. In no time, they were in the TV room where apparently he'd be sleeping for the next few nights. Fighting all those stairs was just too difficult right now. Jack had opened the sleeper sofa, which Pipsqueak thought was just great. But right now, the dog must be napping up in Bella's room, her favorite spot. The green sofa felt like returning to the scene of the crime. Heck. She'd never think of this sofa in the same way again.

The sun slanted through the plantation shutters in creamy bars. After peeling off her lime green top, he ran his hands down her body, sighing her name as if he'd just created it. "Harper, Harper. I can't wait until I can call you my wife."

"I know." Ever so gently, she pushed him back. "But maybe stuff like this will get boring. You know...we'll be old married people. We might get tired of…stuff."

"You think?" His eyes dropped while she settled next to him. "You mean this?" And he kissed the tender warm skin on her tummy.

She squirmed. "Nope, not that."

His lips trailed a damp path up to her collarbone. She thought she heard her skin sizzle. How could she be wet and hot at the same time?

"When does Bella have to be picked up?" he whispered against her ear.

In short tense gasps, she told him.

"Plenty of time," he said with satisfaction. "I do not like to rush things."

"Oh, I know." Arching her back, she gave herself. In her heart, in her soul, she was already his wife.

She'd never tire of his kisses, the way he fingered her hair, the way he paid homage to her body as if she were the most precious thing in the world. The cast made things a little tricky but they managed. "I always knew you were a creative girl," he whispered after a particularly inventive move.

"I make things up as I go." The story of her life.

He didn't seem to mind.

Somehow, her bag of goodies from the two fabric stores ended up under them. By the time they were stretched out thirty minutes later, sweaty and panting, ribbons were tangled in her hair, her notes and fabric swatches scattered on the floor.

She glanced at her phone. "Good grief. I've got to run." His eyes never left her as she scrambled into her clothing.

"Bye, darling.' " His eyes were flagging. "Give my best to Elaine."

"Nope. I've already got your best." Laughing, she threw some clothes at him. "Get something on before we come back."

All the way to Bella's school, she relived the afternoon delight. How amazing that she didn't run right over the curb.

Chapter 7

When Harper opened the door of Salon 5400 Saturday morning, Bella popped through under her arm and skidded to a halt. She couldn't blame her. Adam's salon was magical, and this was Bella's first visit. The little girl's eyes widened.

"Come on in, you two." Adam beckoned to them from the side coffee bar. Caramel mocha scented the air.

Eyes darting around the room, Bella was too busy taking in the decor to budge. Huge mirrors with hammered tin frames hung on the walls at each station. The floor was black, liberally marbled with silver. All the chairs and stations were a deep, sumptuous black, but every knob and pull was hammered silver. Five other hairdressers worked in Adam's salon, but the other stations were empty since the salon wasn't officially open. From floor to ceiling, the only other color was a splash of hot pink here or there.

Dressed in black dress pants and a gray mock turtleneck, Adam looked the epitome of cool. "Harper, he matches," Bella whispered, tugging on Harper's hand. "Adam matches the furniture."

"Oh, of course." One hand on her back, Harper gently propelled Bella forward.

"Want to have a seat, Bella?" Adam patted the black-cushioned chair, now holding a pink booster seat.

Harper gave another little nudge. "Go on, sweetie. Let's get this party started, right?"

Why hadn't she done this earlier, instead of struggling with Bella's hair and failing? Standing over to the side, Harper couldn't wait for the magic to begin. Adam had met Bella before, but she'd never been to his salon. "You can hit the coffee bar, Harper."

"Thanks, think I need a cup." But she hated to tear her eyes from the unfolding drama.

Giving Bella his full attention in the mirror, Adam asked, "Now, what would you like this morning?"

Scrunching her shoulders together, she whispered, "I don't know."

"Well, then. Let's consider our options." Like a magician, Adam grabbed a silver cape from behind his station, snapped it open and draped it over her. Pulling her hands out from under it, Bella patted the shiny surface the way she'd pet Pipsqueak.

Adam began to play with her hair. "Would you like bangs? How long do you like your hair to be?" Right now her hair had no particular style, and Harper felt a little embarrassed about that. Usually she braided Bella's hair, caught it up into a ponytail or let it hang loose with the headband, kind of how she wore her own hair. But maybe Bella's hair called for a different approach. She could see that from Adam's expression.

"You have naturally curly hair." Squeezing handfuls of the hair that had been dubbed a rat's nest, he let it spring back against his palm. "Did you know that?"

Yes, Harper definitely wanted to konk herself on the head. Bella did have naturally curly hair. What they thought was unruly was really her natural curls, allowed to get kind of scrubby.

"No, I didn't know that," Bella said in her timid, nasal tone. "Is that good or bad?"

Reaching over to his station, Adam grabbed a big-toothed comb. "Depends on how you look at it. Naturally curly hair can be a lot of fun. You just have to know what to do with it. This morning we'll learn that secret." Such a showman.

By that time, Bella had Adam eating out of the palm of her hand. Or was it the other way around?

"Want to do some experimenting after we shampoo and condition your hair?" Adam asked.

When Bella looked to Harper for her opinion, she shrugged. "This is the morning to try some new things, don't you think?"

Adam leaned closer to his new customer and crooned, "We'll never know until we step out into the unknown, will we?"

Yep, definitely a showman. Mesmerized, Bella gave a slow nod of her head. Adam had become the Pied Piper.

In two shakes, he had her down from the chair and walking with him over to the shampoo bowls where he also had a booster seat in place. "Hey, I didn't know you worked with children in your salon," Harper murmured as Adam pulled out several expensive-looking bottles.

His lips never moving, he shot back, "I don't. This is my special case."

Although Bella looked a little nervous when he lowered her

head into the niche of the black bowl, she soon relaxed under the warm water and Adam's skilled hands. Harper sipped the hazelnut coffee, glad to hand her charge over for just a while. Instead of closing her eyes, Bella stared straight up at the ceiling. "Are those sparkles up there?" she asked while Adam worked up amazing suds with shampoo that smelled like jasmine.

"Sure is, darlin'. I love sparkles."

"Me too." The bond had been established. Bella closed her eyes, safe in the hands of a kindred spirit.

Of course, Adam never stopped talking during the entire shampoo. He told her about the superb sushi he'd had the night before. Bella actually asked questions, screwing her face up when she learned sushi was raw fish. Then he launched into the reasons why he'd moved to Savannah. Harper had never heard that story, and she curled up in a soft, black leather armchair while he described his small hometown and a little boy who never fit in. While she listened, it hit Harper that Adam was treating Bella like an adult. The little girl seemed to sense the respect in his voice, her attention never wavering.

When it was time for the conditioner, he poured what looked like liquid silver into his palm. "This is very special stuff."

If Bella's eyes had been large before, they were now saucers. "What does it do?"

"It makes your curls beautiful."

"Oh, good," she whispered. "I need some of that."

Opening her purse, Harper was relieved to see the case with all her credit cards. She was going to need them.

When Adam wrapped a towel around Bella's head, all you could see were her delicate features peeking out between the enormous black turban and a wide silver cape. She looked like a regal swami giving audience to her subjects. After lifting her down, Adam led her back to his styling chair. Turning toward Harper, he mouthed "*So. Adorable.*"

"Bella, do you go to school?" Adam asked innocently as he wielded a hair dryer.

She nodded somberly before dropping her eyes. Adam exchanged a look with Harper, giving a barely perceptible shake of his head.

"Do you like your teacher?"

Harper felt relieved when the expression lightened a little. "Oh yeah. Mrs. Davenport's cool."

"It's always good to have a cool teacher. What about the other kids? Do you have friends at school?"

Bella heaved a sigh big enough to blow out birthday candles. "Nope. Not at this school. I'm new." This would kill Cameron if he heard it. Harper tightened her hold on her coffee cup.

"Ah, huh. I know just how that feels." Adam looked so crestfallen that Harper thought he might shed a tear or two. "Sometimes you have to work at making friends, Bella. A pain but that's the way it goes."

"I guess." Her eyes were on his hands, so efficient, so gentle as he worked with the tangles that had miraculously become silky.

"Because people don't always like you right away, you know."

The dark eyes flew to his face. "They don't?"

Shoulders lifted. "Not always, because they don't really know you."

Bella had to think about that for a minute. "I guess so."

"I mean, you've got to talk to them. You've got to do things with them." Here, Adam glanced over at Harper. "When I first saw Harper dashing in and out of the house next door, she looked like a pretty hot chick. I figured she probably had lots of friends and didn't need any more."

Eyes wide, Bella was hanging on his every word. By this time, Harper had moved to sit in the next station to see what he was doing.

"But everyone needs more friends," Adam continued. "Even Harper needed more."

Here Bella's eyes flew to Harper, and she nodded very seriously. Heck, this was the truth. After she started dating Billy Colton, she wasn't as available for her friends. So when things started to go south with Billy, who could she talk to? One day when she took the trash out, she ended up sobbing out her sad tale to Adam, who was stenciling his name on the garbage cans.

"Sometimes it starts with one smile, one word, one indication that someone really needs you." By this time, Harper knew the words weren't just for Bella but were also for her. And that was fine.

Turning the hair dryer off and hanging it on a wall hook, Adam grabbed a tall white can, the label scripted in silver. Yes, definitely good that she had that plastic in her purse. "And here is how we make beautiful curls out of your hair." With an air of expectancy,

Bella sat up straighter.

After shaking the bottle thoroughly, Adam squirted a small bit into his palm and showed it to Bella. "Why do you think they call this whipped cream?"

"Hey, it looks like whipped cream." She licked her lips. "Can I taste it?"

With a shake of his head Adam said, "Trust me. You do not want to eat this stuff. It's yucky." Then he cocked his head to one side. "Just like some people can look beautiful, but they're yucky inside."

Yes, Adam was waxing eloquent this morning. Harper restrained herself from hugging him.

As the session continued, Bella was gradually given pixie bangs, shoulder length hair that waved to her shoulder and a magical braid that Harper could pull over as a head band some mornings. Watching how it came together, she decided she might try this for herself.

"It's nice when you can do a lot of different things with your hair," Adam said, standing back and studying his masterpiece. "Harper does that all the time, right?"

Bless Bella's heart, she nodded. But the truth was that Harper had been so exhausted trying to get her business going, she hadn't had time for this kind of fun. That had to change.

"Wait until Daddy sees you," Harper said as Adam swept the silver cape away. She gave Adam a big hug. "You are the wizard," she whispered in his ear.

His brows arched. "Oh honey, was there ever any question?"

Bella studied every different angle of her hair in the large three-way mirror in the reception area. Stepping up to the desk, Harper took out her wallet.

After popping products into a silver bag with Studio 5400 scripted on it in black, he handed the bag to Bella. "An early Christmas gift, my dear."

"Thank you, Adam." Bella looking so pleased holding her beautiful bag.

"Oh no, Adam," Harper protested quietly after Adam pushed away her credit card. "I can't let you do this."

"Of course you can. Now get out of here. I've got clients coming." And he shooed them from his shop. "Have a wonderful day."

Of course when they got home, Bella burst through the door, searching until she found Cameron in his library. "Daddy, Daddy," she screamed at the top of her lungs, grinding to a halt when she saw him engrossed at the desk.

"What is it, sweetheart?" Looking alarmed at first, Cameron broke into a smile when Bella pirouetted in front of him.

"Am I pretty, Daddy?" Everything hinged on Daddy's reply. That would never change.

"You are the most gorgeous girl in the whole world." The love in his eyes said it all. And that was one of the reasons why Harper had decided to marry Cameron Bennett.

Not totally satisfied, Bella pointed back at Harper. "Except for Harper, Daddy. She's pretty too."

And in this case? It felt great to come in a close second.

Chapter 8

After Bella had spun herself dizzy just to feel her ringlets bob, they all had lunch. Then it was out to the yard where Cameron tossed a Frisbee to Bella and Pipsqueak. It was hilarious to watch Bella try to hold her curls in place while she ran. At the end, he was tossing the toy just for the dog.

Harper had sequestered herself in the dining room, and he couldn't resist wandering in there. All her rough sketches were laid out on the table, along with fabric swatches, a ton of ribbons, plus other stuff like pinecones and oyster shells. Pretty colorful and definitely looking creative. Those uppity women were lucky to have Harper working on their houses. It made Cameron's blood boil to think of how Georgina and Brittany had treated her. Enjoying the sight of her leaning over her work, dressed in black tights and an oversized shirt that looked like one of his, he pulled out a chair.

"Like the shirt." Setting the crutches aside, he settled into a chair.

"Thank you." Then she looked up and blushed because, yes, it was one of his.

"What do you think, Cameron? I have appointments with Georgina and Brittany Monday, so I have to get this right." She pushed her hair back with the flat of one hand as if testing herself for a fever.

Coffee mug in hand, he tried to concentrate. Really, he did. But when Harper fluttered her hands as she did to make a point, Cameron got distracted. Those copper-tinted curls swayed with her. With an aggravated sigh, she'd swat at them, so serious and impatient. He wanted that long hair draped across his chest again, and he had to shut his eyes against the memory. Didn't seem to matter. Prickles still danced across his skin. This session might lead to nothing but frustration.

"So it's that bad?" Harper stood, hands on hips and frowning.

"Not at all. Where do you come up with all this?" His contrite smile must have sold her.

"Here and there. I went to the library to page through some magazines."

What Harper didn't realize was that a lot of people could search some books and magazines. Being able to put the elements together set her apart. His admiration growing, he listened while she dove right back into her plans for Georgina and Brittany. They better be pleased with her efforts.

What a mess he'd made of the coming week because of his carelessness. Man of the house, but he couldn't help her set all this up, which had been their original plan. Somehow, he'd cover it. Of course, Rick had agreed to help, and he'd bring two of the younger guys. The ones who weren't married yet and didn't have children commanding their time on the weekends, especially a holiday weekend like Thanksgiving.

Now he pulled his attention back to Harper, and his shirt

creeping up her thighs when she reached for something. Too bad about the tights but the weather was cold. Not that he needed much to recall how her soft skin felt against his. He'd probably never be able to wear that shirt again without getting turned on.

Damn. Get it together, Bennett. He was supposed to be helping her, not sizing up her assets, and she had quite a few. "What do you think, Cameron?" After she finished telling him what both women had objected to, Harper looked to him for his opinion again. He felt flattered.

"So Georgina wants something deeper. Darker colors. Vintage, is that what she called it?" Lordy, southern belles had a way with words. They had to have the latest styles but when it came to their decor? Either coastal or vintage. At least, that's the way it ran in Savannah.

"Classic," Harper said with a hopeless look on her face. "I figure the lime green and aqua? That all goes to Julep. She was crazy about it when I mentioned it. Suits her."

"Sounds like a plan." Julep was a kick, and he liked her husband Tuck too. Used to having it all, she still didn't seem to carry any hang-ups. Surveying her samples, Harper rearranged stuff as she talked. She was a bright woman, and he was proud of the way she'd taken hold of her interior design business. Sure, she'd started with him when he was working on the Winston House, but the rest was all her. Her skills had helped develop her own client base, no matter what the ladies might tell her. Bringing the pragmatic touch of the Midwest to her work, she also met deadlines, adding to her success rate.

Holding up what looked like a brass bugle, she smiled. "Maybe, just maybe Georgina would like what I've planned for Brittany. Deep mauve red, with a rich forest green. Lots of shiny brass tones."

Sipping his third cup of coffee, he settled back, trying to forget the dull ache in his ankle. "And Brittany?" Harper's hands were full of ribbons, mostly green and red plaid, plus all kinds of designs. "My sketches aren't finished yet, but I think she'll love these." She made one of her funny faces. "Guess I'll find out Monday."

When she tugged nervously on her hair, her large gold hoops caught the sunlight streaming through the windows. Puffing out her cheeks, Harper collapsed into the chair next to his. "Honestly, Cameron, I don't know what I'm going to do if they turn this down. I'm out of time." Suddenly, she was that uncertain girl again, the one he'd rescued at the bachelor party before she bravely tried stripping. Her kicks had done enough damage, and he'd called a halt.

"Don't let them turn it down. Tell them it's all their idea and how brilliant they are."

"But they're my ideas." She looked crestfallen.

"I know, darlin'. But with these two? Let the ladies lead." Then he stopped. Not the time to give away all his secrets.

Her eyes slid to his. "Is that what you do? Let me think you lead?"

This felt about as safe as wading into the marsh when the tide was rolling in. "Aw, darlin'. You know that's not true."

Being so careful, she got up and rotated to set her tiny tush on his lap. He welcomed the warm weight of her curves and took her hips in his hands. "Oh, isn't it?" She was playing with his curls. Probably time for a haircut.

"Didn't I give into you when you insisted we not share a room until we are properly married in the public eye?" he murmured low enough so Bella wouldn't hear. He could hear her romping through the house with Pipsqueak yapping behind her. So much for her new hairdo.

Her hands stopped. "You know how I feel about that. Propriety and everything. After all, my family goes to church every Sunday. They're pretty understanding but let's not poke the bear."

"I know, I know. I'm just teasing you." She'd threatened to move out completely and that would have been more than a mere inconvenience. For all intents and purposes, Harper still slept and worked on the third floor. Bella often camped up there with Pipsqueak, leaving him alone on the second floor in a master suite that seemed way too big for one person.

Harper continued to fret, plucking at the neck of his T-shirt. "Who knows what people say in their own homes. About us, I mean."

"Harper, sweetheart? The War of Succession is over. And I don't give a rip what people say and where they say it."

The ripe strawberry she created with her lips looked so tempting. "Easy for you to say. And it was the Civil War, not the War of Succession or War of Aggression." She sighed as if she'd just been defeated by her own words. "Anyway, this will all be straightened out once the wedding takes place."

"Right." But there was one situation the Chicago wedding would not solve, and it annoyed him no end. His own family had become a problem.

Skimming a cool hand over the stubble he hadn't bothered shaving today, Harper murmured, "You don't think your mother and sister will change their minds? Or your brothers?"

"Sweetheart, trust me. This is not personal. I'm sure they'd like to be at our wedding, but that just might not be in the cards. They don't have the clothes or the heart for the frozen north."

Bending closer, she teased him with her lips. Inflamed him with her tongue. "Sure you can't convince them? I know how persuasive you can be. You persuaded me to stay more than once when I tried to leave this job." Her voice lowered at the end to a rough murmur that conjured up all sorts of images. Harper Kirkpatrick was bad to the bone.

"Actually it was your cooking skills that attracted me," he murmured between kisses. "The way you brandished that meat fork. Who could resist?"

"Daddy..." Bella appeared at the door. Bounding in behind her, Pipsqueak skidded sideways on one of the Oriental runners and slammed into the credenza. When Bella fisted her hands on her hips, she looked for all the world like Connie...or Harper. He was outnumbered. "Are you two at it again?"

When did his little girl become his keeper? Springing from his lap, Harper began arranging her samples in three piles.

Looking up at Harper, Bella tugged on his borrowed shirt. "Harper?"

"What, sweetheart?" Squatting, she swept the dark hair from Bella's face.

"Can we play badminton today out back?" Sunlight beckoned from the window. "Daddy says he can't play because of his foot."

Now that stung. Talking about him as if he were an invalid. He hated not being able to join in their fun.

"Sure. You bet," Harper said, pushing her work aside. They'd agreed that they would spend more time with Bella, or the problems would just come back. During the excitement of the last few months, her eating had become irregular, and the doctors had stressed the importance of a schedule.

"I'll keep an eye on you from the porch." Cameron waved a crutch. "Last one out there is a rotten egg."

Bella whirled from the room and Pipsqueak followed.

"Kids," Harper said, giving him a kiss. "What would we do without them, right?"

Grabbing his crutches, he pushed up with a sigh. "Oh, I can think of lots of things."

While Harper gathered the badminton set from the garage, he settled onto a rattan chair on the first floor verandah. The weather continued to be mild but with a refreshing cool edge. He'd been slow to take the badminton set down this fall, and water still splashed from the mermaid fountain. Now he was glad. What fun to watch Bella and Harper whack the birdie around until they both were tired and winded. The winded part concerned him, and sometimes he had to call a halt.

Some of the leaves were down but the live oaks were still green, as were the pines and palms. Contentment settled over him as he cheered for his ladies. His ladies. How he loved the sound and feel of those words. Just as he enjoyed watching Harper run around the yard, shirttail flapping, allowing a teasing view. Good thing the garden was enclosed or there might be a traffic accident.

"Did I do good, Daddy?" Bella asked, cuddling up against Cameron after Harper had let her win numerous times.

"You did great, but I think you're growing up too fast. When did your legs get so long?" She glanced down at her jeans with the pretty patch pockets as if she didn't know what he was talking about. Where had the years gone? He'd been so busy working after he became a single father. Sometimes he wondered if he'd spent enough time with Bella.

But he tried not to let thoughts like that ruin his day. Watching the two of them play had been a pure joy, even when they argued with each other about who had won.

After putting the racquets in the garage, Harper climbed up the steps. Looking winded, she sat down in the chair next to his, and he handed her the inhaler, which she'd refused earlier. "Penny for your thoughts."

"Nothing. Everything. Just thinking about how the two of you mean everything to me. Does that sound sappy?"

Harper grinned. "Yes, and I've always like sappy. Especially from you."

~.~

They spent a lot of time together that weekend. Harper had grown up in a rowdy household with five older brothers and one sister and thrived on activity. While she continued to work on her presentation, Cameron taught Bella to play checkers in the family room. And when he got tired, Harper encouraged him to stretch out on the couch and let Bella choose a movie. Since he'd already seen *Jungle Book* about a gazillion times, he nodded off. By the time Harper joined them, he was fast asleep with Pipsqueak draped over his good leg, as if she were protecting it.

When Sunday evening came, Harper could hardly wait to talk to McKenna. Her older sister was her sounding board, and they talked just about every Sunday. McKenna was the voice of reason whenever Harper was about to take a leap of faith...right into a fiery pit. That's just the way her life rolled.

"How did the food tasting go?" she asked.

"Um, fine." McKenna sounded less than enthusiastic.

"No, really, how was it?" The last thing she wanted was a hiccup with the catering, although she herself probably wouldn't eat a thing. What bride did?

"It was food, okay, Harper? The chicken tarragon was tender. The beans weren't over cooked. The red potatoes were roasted. Really, it was good."

Sighing, she sat back in the wicker chair up in her bedroom. "Sounds about as exciting as a grilled burger, although the burger might taste better. McKenna?"

The silence on the other end of the phone had Harper worried.

"So what's the problem, McKenna? Was Mom happy with it?"

"I think so. She's doing what she always wanted to do...plan a wedding."

Harper chuckled. "Is this sour grapes, dear sister?"

"Nope. Logan and I did it the way we wanted it. I'm a mature woman who doesn't care at all that her mother is making herself crazy over this wedding."

So that's how it was. "Do you think this might be too much for Mom?" Since McKenna was a midwife, everyone in the family referred their medical questions to her or her husband Logan Castle, an OB/GYN. The fact that the questions might not relate to the more private area of a woman's anatomy didn't seem to matter.

"I'm not sure. Mom's getting on. They both are, although they don't want us to know it. She'll offer to babysit for Connor and Amanda but Dad has to be with her. Three babies are a handful for anyone. The wedding has just added to what's on her plate."

"Hmm. " Guilt descended on Harper like a cloud of Savannah gnats. Had she been wrong, letting her mother take charge? "Here I thought she'd love doing this. You know, the excitement of it."

"She's thrilled about you getting married, Harper. Don't get me wrong. She's crazy about Cameron and Bella. In the beginning, she probably thought she could dig right into this. I just see her tiring under the stress. But I didn't call you to complain, just wanted to give you the food update."

"Yes, but I don't want to dump all this on you either." Harper studied her ring. How could getting engaged feel so exciting when planning a wedding was totally exhausting? "How are you feeling, McKenna?" Her sister's baby was due in about three months.

"I'm fine. Sure it's a little tricky leaning over my laboring mothers in the birthing pool, but the baby is getting firsthand experience, know what I mean?"

"I suppose so." They chuckled together. Some days Harper really missed McKenna.

"Has Cameron's family changed their mind about the wedding?"

Pulling at the worn slipcover on the chair, Harper frowned. So much in the house needed to be redone. Cameron didn't seem to see that. "Nope. They can't handle a Chicago winter. I guess I understand but it sucks. Just doesn't feel right. Know what I mean?"

"That's such a shame. Logan only has his Grandmother Cecile. She's in her eighties, but she came to New Mexico. This may sound ridiculously old-fashioned, but having family there helps seal the marriage."

How those last words bothered her. "But that was last spring, and the weather was nice. Chicago can be brutal in the winter. Down here, December might be forty degrees if that, and we don't have snow. I guess the Blodgetts have never even experienced snow. That's what worries them most of all, and frankly, it would worry Cameron too. Especially since he might still be in a cast."

"What? When did that happen?"

Good Lord. Harper had been so busy that she hadn't brought everyone up-to-date. "He slipped on a scaffolding at one of his jobs and broke his ankle. In two places." How furious she'd been when he finally admitted he had a compound fracture.

"Oh my God. No wonder you sound so wiped out." How

Harper craved her sister's sympathy.

"Yep, and then there's my interior design business. I have some very picky clients who would like to complain." That was putting it mildly.

"And here I thought your work sounded like fun. At least my clients are always delighted to have a baby." McKenna was a midwife specializing in water birth.

Harper laughed. "Right. Well, you're lucky. The holiday season doesn't necessarily bring out the best in people."

"Look, don't dwell on that, okay? Everything will turn out the way it should."

"That's helpful." Yep, Harper definitely missed the sisterly concern.

"Okay, I'll keep an eye on Mom's stress level. You tell Cameron to ease off that foot."

Harper snorted. "Right. Like that's going to do it."

"You'll have to remind him. That's a wife's job. Help take care of your man...because heaven knows, they don't do such a hot job of it themselves."

Hanging up, Harper sure missed her family. She dragged herself back to her drawing board. Bella was in bed and Cameron was downstairs watching TV. She'd rather be there but she had to finish this up.

The next thing she knew, Cameron was kissing her neck, his lips soft and persuasive. Somehow they were stretched out on her bed and oh, she needed him so bad. "How did you get here?" she asked, puzzled. All those stairs. But his warm kisses were the only answer. And those hands? They knew all her secrets. He was exploring them one by one.

The love inside her ran so strong and deep for this man. Now it consumed her, licking her body like flames while they turned, twisted and pleased each other. "You are everything," she whispered. "Everything to me."

"You are more, sweet thing," he said, so faint she had to lean closer to catch his words, recapture the feelings.

She woke up with a jerk, her neck sending shooting pains into her head. How had she ended up head first on the floor at a really uncomfortable angle? Feeling groggy, she dragged her feet down. Above her on the drawing board, the presentations sat in neat packets, ready for tomorrow. What a dream. She pulled herself up on shaky legs and rotated her neck to get the kinks out. But her bed looked so spartan and unappealing.

The house was dark and silent as she crept downstairs, pausing at Bella's door to peak in. But her charge was curled under the comforter, a slight smile on her lips. "Sweet dreams, Bella," Harper whispered.

The only light in the family room came from the muted TV screen. Stretched out on his left side with one arm flung up behind his head, Cameron clearly was favoring his right ankle. Poor guy must be in such pain, although he'd tried hard not to show it all weekend.

She enjoyed studying him while he was totally unaware. How did he ever get those broad shoulders with that impossibly tiny waist? He looked so cozy in his gray track pants, and right now, she needed cozy. Being oh, so careful, she climbed onto the creaky mattress and slipped down behind him. His heat pulled her to him like a powerful magnet. With a contented sigh, she eased one arm around his waist and buried her face in the soft T-shirt. She'd know that scent anywhere.

"About time," he mumbled, tugging her right hand over his tummy. She sank into sleep. Only one more month.

Chapter 9

Facing Georgina across the dining room table, Harper struggled to read her client's expression. Her stomach stopped clenching when Georgina smiled. "Why, Harper, you have outdone yourself. The colors are so rich, so classic. Monte will love it!" She held one of the blue-green spruce garlands. "Fantastic next to my cream door moldings. You've done a wonderful job. And these bugles!"

Remembering Cameron's suggestion, Harper said, "Oh, the suggestions were all yours, Georgina." The words tasted like marsh mud on her tongue. "Why, if it hadn't been for you... I appreciated you pointing me in the right direction." She hoped to heck that Georgina and Brittany would be too busy exchanging holiday pleasantries to recognize each other's color schemes and decorations. Brittany might pick up on the bugle touch, though. Of course, by that time it would be too late. Harper would make sure the execution of both plans would be so outstanding that neither woman would mind.

And as Cameron had known, Georgina was preening, secure in the knowledge that she'd inspired all this. "Well, I guess *I* know what this historical home needs. These classic touches make it come alive. You know, I studied history in school." While Harper gagged, Georgina flitted from room to room, explaining what her thoughts had been when she'd made these suggestions. Harper thought she might try to blow the hunting horn on her way to scatter few huge fragrant pinecones on the side tables.

Somehow, the smile stayed pinned to Harper's face as if Santa himself had nailed it there. She left the Darlington house as soon as she could, after making an installation appointment for that Friday.

While Harper was driving over to the Bedford home, Adam called. "How is Bella's hair holding up?"

"Oh, Adam. You were wonderful! She couldn't wait to show Cameron. This morning, I tried that braiding thing in the front of her hair." No need to mention it had taken three attempts.

"Have I caught you in the middle of your appointments?"

"Yep, on my way to see Brittany right now." Then she brought him up to speed on the switch she'd pulled.

"You are one resourceful girl," Adam told her. "So proud of you."

"Appreciate your support more than you'll ever know."

"Early lunch later?"

"Hate to say no but I have an appointment with Julep when I finish with Brittany."

"Okay, another time. I'm going home to Illinois for Thanksgiving."

"Have a good one, Adam." She pulled into the circular drive in front of the Bedford mansion and said good-bye. Buoyed by her earlier success, she sprang from the car, grabbed her portfolio, and then followed Hazel to the sitting room. Yes, this mansion actually had a room called the sitting room.

Smile pasted on her face, Harper took Brittany through the spools of ribbons and bright green and gold beading— that was just for starters. To her relief Brittany seemed as pleased with the changes as Georgina had been. All that work over the weekend had paid off.

"Oh, Harper, this is more like it. Look how these sassy plaids lighten the room." Brittany spun around in the sitting room.

"Such a great idea on your part." Once again, Harper was prepared to eat humble pie. She just wanted to get through this. It didn't matter to her who took the credit, but Brittany surprised her. With a tiny frown on her finely arched brows, she turned, gold beading swinging from her hands. "Oh, but *you* were the inspiration for the ribbons. I just mentioned plaids. At least, that's what I recall."

Amazement took Harper's breath away. She played with the green and red plaid headband worn for Brittany's benefit. "Really? In all the rush, I guess I forgot."

Laughing, Brittany gave her a tight squeeze. "You better take credit when credit is due. Trust me. Doesn't matter if it's Savannah or London, people are similar in lots of ways. After all, what is a designer selling but her time and her talent? Others can be quick to claim a good idea, so jump on it."

"Why, thank you." Caught off-guard, that was all Harper could get out.

Smiling, Brittany ran one hand over her sedate pearls. "I appreciate your handling this for me, Harper. Really I do."

"Glad you like it. I'm glad you called me for this job." And there was some truth in that. Harper had never appreciated the beautiful variety of plaids before now.

"Trust me, I'm the lucky one. Now, will you able to put this up Saturday or Sunday? I will clear my schedule."

Harper was practically skipping when she left the Bedford home. Brittany had brought her a different perspective. It made her feel better about Savannah…and heck, the whole lowcountry region. Clicking on the radio, she sang along to "Frosty the Snowman," fast becoming Bella's favorite.

Now for some fun. Relief had left her ravenous. Julep had promised lunch, and Harper took off down Highway 80 toward Tybee, making it through the noon traffic at the Truman exchange without losing much time. The marshes stretched wide on either side when she took the overpass near Thunderbolt. This area was so beautiful, even though the green marshes of summer had turned to mauve and brown.

Private piers stretched out into the water, ending at a dock or a huge boat. The docks were designed to rise and fall with the tides. Maybe life was like that. Some days, Harper felt she still had so much to learn—about this area and life in general. And she had Cameron to help her with that, although he'd never take credit. She flushed, remembering the intimate details of her latest dream about him. If only she didn't have such a vivid imagination. But it was time to concentrate on the road.

When Julep met her at the door, she was swathed in a flowing white caftan patterned with aqua and peach coral. Her blonde hair was caught up in a fashionable off-center topknot, while coral earrings dangled from her ears. The woman was so darn pretty and utterly feminine.

"Now I want you to come right in and tell me all about it." Laughing, she laid one cool hand across Harper's brow. "Have those city women got you all hot and bothered?"

"You wouldn't believe it." Following Julep to the sun porch, she filled her in on the earlier appointments. As they passed through the kitchen area, Harper hoisted a waiting tray of lemonade and cucumber sandwiches so her pregnant friend didn't try to carry it. Taking seats in the sunlight, Harper didn't mention that she had let Georgina claim credit. That wouldn't sit well with feisty Julep. Setting the tray on the glass-topped coffee table between them, Harper plopped down in the rattan chair across from her friend.

"Well now, didn't you just show them a thing or two!"

"Julep, I am so relieved. I cannot tell you."

Nibbling at the crustless cucumber sandwich, Julep gave her a speculative glance. "And how's the invalid husband?" In a private weekend conversation, Harper had shared her bad news.

"Chomping at the bit. What man likes to be incapacitated? Especially right before his wedding." But still, Cameron managed to do a lot even with his cast. Amazing. Her grin wasn't lost on Julep.

"So, sugga, is that smile saying that your fiancé isn't *that* incapacitated?" Julep's hearty chuckle was rich with unspoken innuendo.

Cheeks flaring, Harper took a long, cool gulp of her lemonade.

"Let's just say some parts of Cameron are definitely not broken."

They both laughed until Harper was wiping tears from her eyes. Glancing around at the coastal paradise the Tuckers had created, she said, "Oh, Julep. I could stay here all day. Your place is so peaceful. All ferns and tropical flowers."

Julep looked around with satisfaction. "Tuck and I did it together. That's what made it fun, at least for me."

"You haven't been to Cameron's house yet, but it's very Old South, at least to me." She wrinkled her nose.

"Why? Has the furniture been in Cameron's family for years?"

"No. Not at all. As it turned out, the furniture is from shops. I guess the pieces represent what Cameron thought he should have. All very stiff and formal." How did she explain Cameron's need to belong and his chaotic first marriage? Maybe because they were both so young, his first wife had an affair with his best friend. "Cameron lived on the outskirts. Tuck grew up part of the inner circle and it shows."

"Landed gentry, my dear," Julep drawled. She could pile on the southern charm when called upon. Their chuckles morphed into hilarious laughter. How Harper needed Julep's high spirits and her friendship. Sure she had McKenna, but she was far away. And Adam was invaluable, but it felt good to have a woman friend about her age and just starting out.

When they quieted down, the more serious issues replayed in Harper's mind. "Oh Julep, he hates the whole broken foot thing. And my guess is, he's not following the doctor's orders. When I'm not right there, he probably doesn't use his crutches. With the wedding and everything... We just have so much to do."

"How's that coming?" Slinging her feet onto the hassock, Julep sat back.

"Fine, I guess." She tried to sort through McKenna's message. "My older sister feels that my mother is getting older. Letting her handle the wedding details might not have been the best idea. She did have a bout with cancer last winter."

Choking, Julep sat up. "A bout? Jumping Jehoshaphat, Harper, what the heck?"

"I know. Don't get too excited." Harper held up one hand. After all, Julep was having a baby. "Because I have firemen and healthcare workers in my family, we deal with serious stuff all the time. My mom's doing great, but I'm not there to help. At first, her offer made a Chicago wedding workable. But now, I don't know."

Grabbing her tall glass, Julep settled back against the palm-patterned cushions. "A wedding can be draining. Don't suppose you'd consider eloping?"

"My mother would never forgive me. McKenna was married in Santa Fe. Seth came as close as possible with his church wedding in Oak Park last summer. But he's a son. I'm the second and last girl. I'm just doing what's r-right."

There she was. Crying. And for no reason.

"There now, sugga." Whisking over to her side and settling like a deflated air balloon, Julep rubbed her back. "Do you think she'd use a wedding planner?"

Harper shook her head. When she thought of her family's modest brick bungalow in Oak Park, she almost laughed. "That's not quite our lifestyle. My folks want to take care of this themselves. My dad's very old-fashioned that way."

Julep gave her shoulders a little shake. "Oh lordy. From what I hear, weddings have gone through the roof, and Savannah is not a town that takes to moderation. I imagine Chicago is even worse. I have to admit, I wish I could be there. Just hate to miss seeing you walk down that aisle, looking so gorgeous." Rising to her feet, she ambled back to her chair.

Actually, Harper felt the same. Her friends here had become so important. And her marriage to Cameron was rooted in Savannah. "I know. Adam made his flight reservation but that's about it. Cameron's own family can't or won't come." A frown found her face. "The snow, you know. Chicago can be beastly cold in December. If it does snow, it's often a major storm that paralyzes the city."

Julep's eyes widened until they resembled the spearmint leaves floating in her seltzer. "Sounds absolutely terrifying."

"Right. It can be. I haven't dealt with it in years," Harper said, thinking back. "But when I was growing up, our sidewalk always needed shoveling. The cars had to be dug out. The boys took care of that. When we took Bella home for Christmas last year, we had a major storm. Cameron couldn't get over it. Driving was hazardous on those snow-packed roads. I think he was glad we had a rental car and not one of his darlings."

Sitting in the sun on Tybee Island, such wintry chaos didn't seem possible. December might bring a low of forty-five degrees in Georgia, and the wind could whisk across the marsh and nip your ears. But you'd never need boots or a heavy coat and scarf.

Julep's chuckle bounced off the windows that glassed in this lovely porch. "So tell me again, why are you getting married in your hometown? You're a grown woman now."

Her stomach twisted. "I know. Crazy, right? Maybe Cameron's family has a point." She slid her plate onto the glass coffee table.

"I know how in-laws can be. Why, Tuck's mama can really dig in her heels. She wants us there for Christmas but I just don't know."

Somehow, it felt comforting to hear that other women had family trouble. "We'll talk to them on Thanksgiving. Hopefully they'll reconsider."

"Maybe so. I mean, after all, this is a wedding."

"I know. Almost seems like bad luck, getting married without both families there." Harper checked the time on her phone. She had to get going.

"But they are his family." Looking thoughtful, Julep circled her rounded tummy with one hand. It looked like she was stroking her unborn baby, and something warm unfurled in Harper's own stomach.

"How are you feeling, Julep? Everything okay?"

Her full lips tilted upward. "Just dandy, darlin'. At least I'm past the morning sickness and that tired feeling all the time."

"Yeah, my sister said the same thing. She's expecting in February." The whole pregnancy thing was a mystery to Harper. "Can you feel the baby move?"

"Oh, you bet." Wiggling closer, she took Harper's hand and

guided it to her stomach.

Curious, Harper waited, fingers stretched over Julep's warm rounded tummy. And then it came—a little bump under her hand that startled her. "How precious."

"The baby's been active this morning. Maybe it's excited about your wedding too." Eyes wide, Julep waited, smiling when another bump came.

"I'll be darned, Julep. I sure felt something. Thank you." The moment felt so intimate. Feeling humbled and privileged, she settled back in her chair. Julep sat there soothing her unborn baby, or so it seemed.

"What about you and Cameron, Harper?" Julep asked. "Are you hoping to have a family?'

"Oh, we have Bella." Jumping up, Harper began to gather up her samples. "So you don't mind the lime and aqua color combination?"

As she got to her feet, Julep pressed a hand into her back. "Not at all. Love it, and I'll gladly accept any other ideas you have floating around in that creative head of yours that Georgina or Brittany don't want."

"Done. See ya. And have a wonderful Thanksgiving."

Rolling her eyes, Julep said, "Yeah well, I'm going back to Vidalia. My one concession to his family. Since mine is long gone, I'm short of good excuses." Harper found it so sad that Julep had lost both her parents when she was in college. Leading the way, Julep strolled through the sunlit kitchen and into the wide hallway leading to her massive front door.

"How long will you stay? After all, we're decorating our clients' homes this weekend, and I did promise everything would be up for the holidays."

"Don't be ridiculous, Harper. You have your hands full with those two Savannah hellions. You just bring your holiday cheer over after I get back. How does that sound?"

"Girl, you really are a friend." Hugging Julep's motherly wonderfulness, Harper realized this was why she stayed in Savannah. The majority of people were laid back and generous, like Julep. Unfortunately, she lived a half hour away. "Wish you lived closer. I'd like to have you right over my back fence."

"Me too." Julep hugged her back. "But at least I'm not in Vidalia. Then we wouldn't even have met."

Backing out of Julep's driveway, Harper waved goodbye. She hated to leave her. But all the way back to Savannah, Julep's words about the family stayed with her. Granted she didn't know Esther, Cameron's mother, well at all. The crotchety woman had been terrible to Bella at Cameron's father's funeral. But since then, Esther and Lily, Cameron's sister, had come to visit. Mostly short stays, but they'd come.

"How did it go, sweet thing?" Cameron greeted her when she came through the back door, dragging her portfolios with her.

"Great. We're set to decorate at Georgina's on Friday and Brittany's on Saturday. And don't get up."

But he was already teetering onto his feet. And she sure wasn't going to turn down that hug.

Checking a list she'd set on the counter, Connie said. "Now,

I've ordered your Thanksgiving dinner from Publix. You just have to pick it up."

"That I can handle." Kind of embarrassing. But with everything that was going on, Harper couldn't even think of cooking a turkey, whipping up mashed potatoes—everything that went into a Thanksgiving dinner. She'd never learned how to do that. Queen of the kitchen, her mother always took care of meals, especially the holidays.

Looking up, she found Cameron watching her. "Hey, what's going on?"

Crooking a finger, she led him into the TV room. Bella was still at school, and Harper would have to leave in a few minutes to pick her up. As they sat down on the sofa, Harper couldn't help but think how absolutely darling Cameron looked in those soft but sexy track pants and T-shirt. She thoroughly approved of his new uniform, glad he hadn't scheduled any meetings at City Hall. "How was work?" she asked, putting her own concerns aside.

Facing her with his right leg propped on the coffee table, Cameron began to play with her fingers. "Fine. Now let's talk about you and why you look so worried."

That was so Cameron. Always putting her first.

"Cameron, it's about your family."

The finger play stopped. "What have they done now?"

"Oh no. Nothing." She cupped his hand with both of hers. "It's just that, well, I hope we can convince them to come for the wedding."

The mixed feelings Cameron held for his family flickered across his features. "But why? I'm sorry, darlin'. But why is that so dang important?"

At moments like this, it felt like they were from two different countries, not two different cities. "Because they're family and we're getting married. We need to bring our families together." The sight of Julep in her maternal bliss unfolded inside her like a peony in spring, rich and fragrant.

His features had set, rigid as the stone ledge around the side yard. Sometimes her man could be stubborn. "But I'm not a Blodgett."

"Oh, come on, Cameron." His denial was about as blasphemous as her declaring that she wasn't a Kirkpatrick, which would never ever happen. "You may have changed your name, Cameron, but you are your family until the day you die. At least, that's how I see it. And families stick together. Celebrate together. Go through hard times—"

"Together, I get the picture. You're sounding like a Hallmark card."

Laughing, she caught that stubborn chin in her fingers. "Cameron, you look just like Bella when you pull that face." Capturing her hand, he brushed a kiss across her fingertips. One touch of his lips, and she was a goner. If Connie hadn't been in the other room, she'd be stretched out on that green sofa, and they wouldn't be watching TV. For now, she just snuggled closer and brought one knee up onto his lap.

"Please," she whispered against his lips.

His eyes swung to the door. "Oh, sugar, I would but Connie's in the next room."

Coasting the back of her hand across his stubble, she smiled. "Not that and you know it. Please encourage your mother and sister to come celebrate our wedding. Okay?"

Cameron brought her hand flat onto his chest. She felt his heart beat strong and steady. Breathed in the heat he exhaled. Then he nodded. "Okay. Whatever you say, darlin'."

But although Cameron tried and tried when they spoke to his family on Thanksgiving Day, his mother would not budge. "Now son, I wish we could accommodate you. I really do. But that's a long way for an old woman."

Since Cameron had the call on speakerphone, Harper could watch his face flush with frustration. She jumped in. "Mrs. Blodgett? We'd really like to have you here to witness the wedding." Now, that sounded lame but Esther had never said, "Call me Mom."

Harper's mother Maureen had told Cameron to call her Mom last spring when they were at McKenna's wedding. Esther? Totally different story. It might take ten years before she ever made that request of Harper. No use waiting for it. Esther was Mrs. Blodgett and that was that.

"Harper, I'm sure there will be many witnesses. No need in us dragging ourselves up to the hinterlands just to sit in a cold church." Stern and disciplined, Esther lacked warmth. Maybe the stark conditions of her life did that to her. Cameron had told Harper that their father had made life hard for the whole family.

Blinking back tears, Harper drew in a shaky breath. She couldn't even look at Cameron. *Hinterlands?* Was it worth it to try to bring families that were so very different together for their Christmas wedding? Running one hand up Cameron's arm as they bent over the cell phone, Harper felt the tension in his body. Watched him try every verbal tactic to sway his mother. But Esther was immovable, and Harper sure hoped this stubbornness wasn't hereditary. By the time they said goodbye, nothing had changed.

"Sorry, darlin. I tried." Cameron kissed her, wiped the dampness from her cheeks. "Are you crying? Please don't."

"Your mother just makes me crazy." She reached for a tissue.

The disappointment stayed with her all weekend. Thanksgiving passed quietly, nice but uneventful. Friday was her day to spend at the Darlingtons. Even while she arranged pine branches and candied red apples on the mantles, and Cameron's crew strung garlands over arches in the Darlington home, her heart remained heavy. But the work kept her mind occupied, and the Darlingtons were more than satisfied.

The cheerful plaid theme at the Bedfords the next day didn't even lift Harper's spirits. Brittany's effusive gratitude pleased her, and it was hard earned. The home did look spectacular by the time Harper left with the crew. Every door, mantle, banister and bathroom could have been plucked from a department store window. Brittany Bedford had tears in her eyes when she waved good-bye. But Harper still had a heavy heart.

Christmas was bearing down on her, bringing the wedding with it. This was the day every girl wishes for, the day she'll marry the man of her dreams. Cameron Bennett was all that and more. But something was missing. Something just was not right.

That weekend, Cameron insisted on taking them down to Broughton Street to see the decorations. He had worked so hard on this area with his fellow developers and the city council, and he was rightfully proud. Harper tried to smile. Oh, he said it was for Bella, but in her heart, Harper knew he was trying to lighten her spirits. He'd rather be on the sofa, leg up on the coffee table. Crutches under each arm, he really shouldn't be walking. For his sake and Bella's, she tried to be appreciative. But she knew the circles shadowing Cameron's eyes darkened her face as well. How she wished it was one month from now. The Christmas season would be behind her and she would be Cameron's wife.

That Sunday night her mother called. And that changed everything.

Chapter 10

"I'm afraid I have bad news," Harper's mother began in a hesitant voice. This sure didn't sound good.

Harper's chest tightened. Her resilient mother wasn't sounding like her cheerful self. "What is it? Is it Dad?" Sitting next to her, Cameron clicked the TV off.

"Oh no, dear. We're all fine. It's just that a pipe broke at the Weatherby Mansion over the weekend. They didn't find it until this morning."

"Oh no." This was absolutely the last straw. The Weatherby Mansion was a dream house. Dating back to the 1800s, it had been redone in classic furnishings and was fabulous for special occasions.

"I'm afraid it's out of the question now. The poor owners. We're one of many weddings that were booked for this month. Worst of all, a lot of the water froze and ruined the period furniture, of course. It's devastating from what they told me. I'm so sorry, honey."

"Oh, Mom. What now?" Seemed like they just solved one problem and another one reared its ugly head.

Cameron's arm tightened around her. "Whatever it is, we'll manage," he said in an undertone.

"Your father and I will start phoning tomorrow," her mother continued, swinging right into her practical Reenie mood but sounding a bit frayed at the edges. "Of course, many places will be booked. But maybe there will be a cancellation. All is not lost. McKenna is taking part of the list and so is Selena."

"But it's Christmas. The busiest time of the year."

"Plans change. Let's just see what we can turn up."

"All right, Mom, but I hate to put you to all this work." She felt absolutely helpless. Luckily, Cameron's arm around her shoulders let her know she wasn't alone in this.

When her mother had gone full steam ahead on this wedding, they sure didn't envision all the hurdles that would be thrown in their way. Cameron's accident, his family's resistance and now this.

After the conversation ended, Harper felt bleak. "So with one hundred and twenty of my parents closest friends and my family, we're left without a place for the reception."

Cameron studied the cast on his foot. "And all for a ceremony."

Blinking, she looked up at the man she wanted in her life forever. Good grief, she was the one dragging him to Chicago in December for this ceremony.

Bella appeared at the doorway, rubbing her eyes. "Daddy? Harper? I can't sleep. The TV's too loud." That was always her excuse when Bella was restless. No way could she even hear the TV up in her room.

Casting a concerned look at Harper, Cameron pushed himself up. "Come on, darlin'. I'll take you back to bed."

"No, no. You stay here." Jumping up, Harper held out a hand.

"Come on, Bella. Up we go."

"Will Daddy be better soon?" Bella asked as they climbed the steps to the second floor.

"Of course he will. He'll be his old self before you know it. At least, by Christmas." Harper knew Cameron was hoping he'd have his cast off for the ceremony. Otherwise, the trip might be difficult. But she couldn't even go there. Her imagination spun into overdrive, conjuring up stacks of lost luggage that wound up in Tahiti. That's just the way things were going right now. At least her wedding dress was safe in Chicago, along with the dresses for the wedding party. That hadn't been too hard to manage, with McKenna and Selena the only bridesmaids, with Bella as flower girl.

After tucking Bella into her high four-poster bed, Harper kissed her goodnight. "See you in the morning. It'll be back to school, and you'll get to show off your new hairdo."

The little girl peered up at her. "My throat kind of hurts."

"It does? Oh, honey, maybe it's the dryness in here." The temperature had dropped to forty-five that day, and the heat had kicked on. The old pipes shuddered in protest.

"Maybe." Clearing her throat, Bella settled back, her eyelids already looking heavy. "Good night, Mommy," she said in a sleepy voice.

"Mommy?" How Harper looked forward to officially being Bella's mom. The little girl deserved it after all she'd been through. Cameron had done the best he could as a single father, but every little girl needs a mother. Bella was only two when her mother

Tammy died in that crash.

A tiny smile tilted the corners of Bella's lips. "I'm practicing."

"Oh, that deserves another kiss." When Harper leaned over to kiss her forehead, Bella smelled like Adam's wonderful shampoo. But her forehead felt a little warm.

"Night, Harper."

"Good night, sweetheart."

Leaving the nightlight on, Harper made her way downstairs. Sometimes all the love in her life made her feel full to bursting. How did she get so lucky? If this was a dream, she didn't ever want to wake up. She skimmed one hand over the shiny banister. This staircase could have been in a movie of the old South, except that etchings of the Savannah squares hung along the wall.

When she'd come for her interview that first day, she'd concentrated on these pictures, not the nervous tremors in her stomach. There had been so much to take in that day. The marble foyer. The dark, antique furnishings. The huge vase crammed with droopy, pink tulips that had her holding her breath. She'd been so relieved to learn they were artificial. Her asthma couldn't have survived that pollen blast. But like many things in this mansion, the flowers were fake.

Now in the foyer, she glanced around. Why, this house was every bit as grand as the Weatherby Mansion in Chicago. But the more time she spent in Julep's home, the more Harper wanted to make changes here.

Cameron looked up when she returned. "Come here." Arms lifted, he pulled her to him for a comforting kiss.

This man was so very precious. She framed his sweet face with her hands. "When you kiss me like that, I can't think." His lips felt so soft, and she sensed his smile. Felt his excitement swell under her.

"You are something else," he whispered, gently tugging the purple scarf from her hair. "What did I ever do to deserve you?"

"You had a little girl like Bella. She's perfect."

"She's trouble," he murmured, his kisses heating. "Just like you."

With his hands traveling to her waist and then up again, she lost her concentration. Desire rippled through her in deep, hot waves. Cameron's lips tickled their way from her chin to her breast bone. And he took his time, leaving her waiting. Wanting. When he unzipped her hoodie, she felt the slow slide of the metal teeth, felt the cool air disappear under his warm palms.

The wedding and all the problems faded. Nothing was as important as this man and what he'd brought to her life.

In the morning, Bella had a full-blown fever, and Harper could hardly talk. With Julep's house to decorate that week, she just couldn't be sick. No way could she go over to her house in Tybee and risk giving the expectant mother her germs. After taking Bella to her pediatrician and getting advice and a prescription, she took her home to Connie and continued on to her own appointment with Dr. Cohen. "I just cannot be sick this week," she croaked to Dr. Cohen. "Too much to do."

"I'm seeing a lot of this lately." After giving her a thorough exam, the pretty blonde handed her a slip. "That should knock it out. Save your voice. Hot soup. Rest. All of that."

"Thanks." Harper tucked the script in her tote. "As if things weren't bad enough, Cameron broke his ankle last week, and he's hobbling around on crutches."

"Crutches?" The doctor wrinkled her nose. "Get him one of those knee walker things. You might be able to pick one up or order it at the pharmacy."

So while Harper waited for the two prescriptions, she found and bought the scooter. A handy little contraption, it might save Cameron's arms, not that he seemed to have any trouble with them. She smiled, remembering last night. When she reached home, Bella was asleep with Pipsqueak cuddled in her arms. Crawling onto the four-poster bed, Harper joined them. Her head felt like a pumpkin. When they both woke up two hours later, they took their medicine, sipped some soup and fell back to sleep.

By the time Rick dropped Cameron off in the late afternoon, the two of them were all slept out and back downstairs. When Cameron came through the door, the first thing he saw was the knee walker. "Something for Bella?"

"Nope. You. Saves your arms."

Looking skeptical, he nudged it aside with his crutch.

"You kneel on it with your injured leg," Harper said. "Steer with the handle bars. It's like a scooter." His puzzled frown didn't look promising.

Connie had left lentil soup in the refrigerator, and Harper heated it in the microwave. But she didn't feel like eating and neither did Bella. This was one time when Harper wasn't going to make a big deal out of it. Besides, she herself felt like a limp rag.

"Let me clean up the kitchen," Cameron said when they finished. "Maybe you should watch a little TV and then early bed for both of you."

"You read my mind." Harper pushed back from the table.

The following day she felt better after a good night's sleep but not completely recovered. Bella stayed home with her that Tuesday, and together they watched all the Avengers movies they could fit in. Bella was such a Ninja princess. But while they watched the super heroes exchange blows, Harper was scribbling on her yellow pad.

"Whatcha doing?" Bella asked, leaning over the list during a down time in the action.

"Just making a list." She had to get on this tonight. Three weeks, that's all they had. But first, she had to get her energy back. Digging in her purse, she took out the antibiotic and chugged one down. Even though she felt a little better, she knew enough to take all the medication and made sure Bella did the same.

Although Cameron should probably have been at home too, he'd gone in to work. The man was so stubborn. He refused to slow down. Didn't want his men to think he was a "sissy." That's how he put it. The knee walker still sat in the kitchen, just where Harper had left it. Cameron had started using it as a coat rack.

For lunch, Connie made one of Harper's favorites, chicken noodle soup with lots of celery. Sitting around the kitchen table, Harper sipped and doodled. There was so much to do.

"You better eat your soup, young lady." Bella's teasing cut

through Harper's busy thoughts. She was mimicking Harper, with the words her nanny had always used.

"Yes, ma'am." Tearing her attention from her notepad, Harper picked up her spoon.

By that time, Connie had finished her own lunch and was clearing off the counters.

But the soup had made her sleepy. When Connie cleaned up, Harper popped a Kung Fu Panda movie into the DVD player. The animated film hadn't been playing long when Bella crawled into Harper's lap. Stretching out on the pit, Harper cuddled up with Bella. They both needed it.

When she woke up, Cameron was kissing her forehead. Smiling she stretched, feeling refreshed but groggy. The TV was off.

"Wake up, sleepy heads." He moved on to Bella.

"What are you doing home so early?" Yawning, Harper looked at the time on her phone.

Taking a place next to her, he propped his right leg on the coffee table. "Hate to admit it but I'm exhausted."

"I'm not surprised." She glanced around. His crutches were leaning in the doorway. "Where is that knee thing I brought home? Under your jacket?"

Looking sheepish, he dropped his eyes. "Look, I appreciate the thoughtfulness, but that thing makes me feel foolish, honey. Besides, I can't take that onto a work site. Too many levels."

"Cameron." How exasperating. And he thought she was stubborn.

"Come on, Harper. What would the guys say?"

"That you were doing everything to speed your recovery?" But she couldn't mess with this now. "Okay, whatever. We have too many other things to worry about." Reaching over she snared her yellow pad.

Chapter 11

Looking at Harper's notes and doodles, Cameron felt exhaustion flatten him. That yellow pad made him feel worse than the pain in his ankle.

"We have things to do." She tapped her pen on the pad. Then her eyes softened. "Please?"

When Cameron grabbed her hand, her fingers felt so delicate. "Can this wait until after dinner?" He hated to see her looking so down.

Her lips pursed as if she were swallowing bad medicine. "Sure. Is Connie gone?"

"I think so."

"Are you hungry?"

"Yes, but not necessarily for food."

She tipped her head to one side. "Nothing I can do about that right now, mister." Her eyes slid to Bella.

Easing out a frustrated breath, he stood and pulled her up with him. Standing wasn't easy but he wanted her body against his for just a second. He breathed in her apple shampoo and nuzzled the warm curve of her neck. "Lord, you smell good."

Pulling back, she chuckled. "Like I said, not now." She gave him a playful kiss on the nose.

Turning from the TV, Bella rolled her eyes. "Are you at it again?" But her smile told them she was kidding, and they dissolved into laughter.

Leaving the dreaded list behind, he hobbled out to the kitchen, Harper with him. While she heated up something that sure smelled good, Bella set the table. The silverware looked huge in her hands. Harper was teaching her where to place the spoon and how to turn the knife blade in. "That's so you don't goof up at prom," Harper told Bella.

Bella wrinkled her nose. "What's prom?"

"It's a dance and you're way too young." Panicked, he raised a brow at Harper. His little girl going to a dance with a boy? The thought terrified him.

With a frustrated sniff, Harper looked from him to Bella. "Trust me, the last thing you want is to go out for dinner on prom night and not know which fork to use. Every girl needs to know some basic stuff." Bella gave a solemn nod.

This conversation never would have happened in his home. Growing up, he'd been lucky if his brothers Fred and Henry even used a fork, much less the right one. Bella attacked her chore with new appreciation, and Cameron smiled to see her concentration. She always wanted to please Harper.

Catching his eye, Harper winked. He made a quiet kissing motion with his lips. In his mind, he was doing a lot more than that. Her lilac colored tracksuit clung to her body in all the right places. Sometimes his love for her almost felt painful. The primal need to share it made his breath tight, along with every other part of his body. Picking up a spoon, he began to drum it on the table until Bella shot him a glance. "Daddy."

Laughing, Harper poured oyster crackers into a bowl. "Dinner's ready."

But while he was finishing his second bowl of the best soup he'd ever tasted, Harper cleared her throat. "I've been thinking..."

Those words always spelled trouble. He put his spoon down. "Yes?"

"Why don't we have the wedding here?"

"What?" It felt like someone had socked him in the chest. Harper began ticking off reasons on her fingers. He tried to follow her, but inside he was appalled. "What will your parents think?"

Harper pushed her soup bowl away. "I'm sure they'll go along with it. Who wouldn't prefer Savannah over Chicago in the winter?"

"You mean, we'll have a wedding right here." Bella glanced around as if she expected guests to pour through that back door any minute.

"What about *your* family?" Harper's chin jutted out and Cameron chuckled. She'd gotten that move from Bella.

"This is *our* wedding, Cameron. McKenna didn't call for a vote when they decided to be married in Santa Fe."

Well, she had him there. Cheeks pink, Harper grabbed the damn pad of paper from the counter. "First, we have to call my parents and your mother."

"My mother." His mind just couldn't get past that. What would her response be? "You're not doing this because of her, I hope."

His relationship with his mother had come a long way. Still, he wasn't giving in to her now. There would be no end to concessions if that were the case.

"She'll come then, won't she?" Harper's features tightened. How he hated to see her disappointed, especially by his own family. How could he help her understand? He'd spent time with the Kirkpatricks, and they sure weren't the Blodgetts.

"I really don't know, sweetheart. My mother's a mystery." They'd been estranged for such a long time, but his father's funeral had helped close some of that rift. His mother and sister came to Bella's birthday party. But this?

He was still enlightening her about his family. They liked Harper, especially his sister Lily. Thought Harper was a lot better for him than his first wife Tammy. But Esther Blodgett, his stern mother, could really dig her heels in when she wanted to, and sometimes he suspected it was a power play.

"I hope they'll come, darlin'." But he wanted them there mainly so Harper wouldn't be disappointed. Glancing over the pad, and then at the calendar on the wall, he said, "I guess we should get started."

Frowning, Harper studied the list. "Should we run this past my parents first?"

Knowing Harper's family as he did, Cameron hesitated. "Maybe McKenna."

Harper's redheaded sister had been a huge ally. If anyone could tell them how Mike and Reenie were going to feel about the change, McKenna would be the one who knew.

Damn, this was feeling more like a military campaign than a wedding.

"Oh, Cameron, you're always so right." Leaping from her chair, Harper flung her arms around him and landed a sizzling kiss. One that he wanted to follow up with something a little more personal.

"How are you feeling?" he asked, wanting to test the waters. Bella would be in bed soon.

"Much better." And she wiggled her brows. *Game on.* "Later?"

"Okay, you two. I'm gonna tell Connie." Bella tapped her spoon on the table, but she was smiling. Reluctantly they pulled apart. Cameron mouthed *later* while Harper straightened her purple headband. With a wicked smile that he adored, she dug her phone from her handbag. She had McKenna on speed dial.

"I think it would be fun to have a wedding here," Bella said, eyes round as pie plates.

Harper didn't have her phone on speaker, but McKenna's screech could be heard clear across the room when she heard their suggestion. Cameron's own reservations faded. After all, he wanted Harper to be happy. Eyes sparkling, she pressed the speaker button, and McKenna's voice came through loud and clear. "Just tell Mom I'll take care of everything...letting the florist know, and so on. Word is the caterer has overbooked, so he'll be thrilled to cross the Kirkpatricks off his list."

"Looks like we're going to pull this off," Harper said after she'd ended the call. Then she zeroed in on him. "What's wrong?"

"Nothing, sweetheart. I'm just getting used to the idea."

"Good, let's call my parents. I don't want Mom to hear about the wedding from McKenna."

Just as her sister had predicted, Harper's mother didn't need much persuading. "Are you sure you feel all right about this?" Reenie asked.

"More than all right." Sure sounded like Harper meant that with her whole heart. After the call ended, Harper turned to him. Cameron knew this was coming. "Now, your mother?"

But he didn't want witnesses for this call. Happiness filled the air. No way was he going to spoil that. "Maybe we should put Bella to bed first. Is she going to school tomorrow?"

"Yep. I'm bored," Bella announced. Cameron exchanged a glance with Harper, who shrugged.

"I think the medication has kicked in for both of us." Harper stood. "You stay right here, mister, while I take Bella up to bed." He wasn't going to argue. Those steps were killers. "Come on, Bella. Up we go. Bedtime." Harper reached out a hand.

"Can I have a story?" Bella wheedled.

"Fine with me as long as you read me the book." Although Bella was learning to read, she mostly paraphrased the stories.

Cameron heard them chatter as they went upstairs, Harper sounding so excited by this latest turn of events. Only, they still had hurdles in front of them. He eyed the phone. If she would just let him handle the call to his mother, everything might be fine.

In a few minutes Harper was back, handing Cameron his phone and taking the seat across from him. "Why don't we put your mother on speaker phone. That's okay, isn't it?"

No. "Of course it's all right." He set the phone between them and pressed the button.

His mother picked up on the second ring. "Hi, Mama. It's Cameron."

"What's wrong? We just talked on Thanksgiving." Nothing like a warm hello.

Crossing her legs, Harper began to jiggle her right foot. Her feet were bare, and the pink polish caught his eye. Even in a situation like this, she could distract him. "We're calling with good news."

"Ye-ah-ss?" One word sounded like three put together and ended on a down note.

"Harper and I have decided to get married here. At the house."

~.~

Silence. Harper should know better than to expect excitement from Esther. Cameron's mother was a woman who gritted her teeth and endured life. Harper found it amazing that Cameron had come from this family.

Wanting to help, she jumped right in. "Mrs. Blodgett, this is Harper. We felt so bad that you couldn't come to the wedding. After all this is an important family occasion." Cameron was frowning. Was he upset that she'd taken over the conversation? "My family is so eager to meet you."

"And why would that be?"

"Mother." The one word from Cameron completely changed the tone of the conversation. "Of course Harper wants you to meet her family. The mansion where we were going to have our wedding in Chicago, well, some frozen pipes broke and flooded the place. So for a lot of reasons, we're having it here."

The last thing Harper wanted was to railroad her new mother-in-law into something she wasn't comfortable with, but darn it, her family was beginning to think this was very weird. Heck, the Kirkpatricks got together for Nascar races and football games almost every Sunday. "We certainly hope both families will come," she interjected. Cameron wouldn't even look at her.

"Well then," his mother finally said. "I'll check with Lily. She may be able to—"

"Mother?" Cameron's voice cut through her meandering excuse. Harper understood his frustration but didn't want his mother to feel backed to the wall.

"Now, Cameron. We'll do the best we can but things are very busy here in Hazel Hurst and…"

"You haven't even asked us the date of the wedding."

Her sigh could have inflated a hot air balloon. "Well it was Christmastime as I recall."

"Yes. Christmastime."

Cameron looked at Harper for help. Jumping up, she grabbed the calendar from the refrigerator and stabbed her finger at Christmas Eve.

But they weren't finished, and the conversation was agonizing. During the next ten minutes, she listened to Cameron lay one guilt trip after another on his mother. Sure wasn't pretty. Esther offered one flimsy excuse after the other. Couldn't she see how much this hurt Cameron?

Tears welled in Harper's eyes. When Cameron looked up and saw her running her fingers under both eyes he brought the conversation to a quick halt. "Well, Mama, you check with Lily and I will get back with you in a couple of days. How would that be?"

"Fine, I guess. Can't promise you anything."

Big eye roll from Cameron. "I'll call you back in two days."

By the end of her conversation, Cameron was hot and sweaty. His shirt was sticking to him, and you would have thought it was July. She didn't want him getting sick. "Why is she like this, Cameron?" Harper could not understand his mother. But if the marriage was to be successful, she knew enough from her own upbringing that the two families had to get along. They had to enjoy and appreciate each other.

"Don't take this too seriously, Harper." Cameron pulled his hair back tight with one hand. "She's doing just what she did with my father all those years. Stonewalling us. My mother is a passive-aggressive woman. If she doesn't want to do something, she will find a way to get around it by doing nothing."

Harper nibbled at the corner of her lips. "How can anyone be so stubborn?"

When she looked up, Cameron wore a knowing smile. "Just like somebody I know, Ms. Kirkpatrick."

Grabbing the dishtowel, she snapped it at him, the way she'd whipped it at her brothers when they were doing dishes in their Oak Park kitchen. "Stop right there, Mr. Bennett."

While she straightened up the kitchen, they talked about how they'd cover the bases of the changed wedding plans. "Are you sure we can pull this off?" Cameron finally asked. "I mean, we need a priest or minister. We need music and we need food."

She squeezed her eyes tight as her fiancé ticked off all the projects that lay ahead of her. But she was not backing down. Never in a million years would Harper Kirkpatrick admit she'd bitten off more than she could chew. After putting the last soup bowl into the dishwasher, she began to work on the soup pot. Thankfully, there were some bits fried on the bottom, so she got to take the Brillo pad and really scrub it out. There was nothing like a dirty pan to work out a woman's worry. At least that's what her mom always said. "Of course we can do this. Why, Cameron, we have four weeks."

"More like three and a half. And it's the holidays."

"What of it? Connie can work on the caterer tomorrow. And I'll talk to Adam."

Coming up behind her, Cameron gently took the Brillo pad from her hand. "Darlin', you are going to wear a hole in that pan. How does Adam fit in all this? Does he play a musical instrument?"

"Don't be such a smarty. He's got some kind of certificate that makes him an officiant at marriages. Said he wanted to be able to help his friends get married." She stabbed one finger into his chest. "I'm his friend and we're having a wedding ceremony."

She was passing Cameron to hang up the dishtowel when he pulled her down into his lap. "Didn't we say something about fooling around later?"

Her smile came slowly. "So I did and I'm a woman of my word."

"How are you feeling?" He put a hand on her forehead. Sometimes his simple caring gestures just about turned her inside out.

"My forehead's not the part of my body that's heating up," she whispered close to his ear.

His eyes turned smoky. "And I aim to please." Burying his lips in the hollow of her neck, he worked his way up to that ticklish spot behind her ear. She felt like warm butter melting on a biscuit. Their worries eased away.

"Now if I can just get you off my lap," he said. "I'd pick you up and carry you but..."

"Nope." Jumping up, she handed him the crutches. How he hated them.

But by the time he lowered himself onto the sofa, the light had returned to his eyes. Taking her hand, he tugged her down. "Remember that night I came back from the hospital?"

"Of course." How could she forget? Scared her half to death.

"That was a really special night, babe. One I'll always remember."

"Really? Whatever for?" She tried to play dumb.

But he wasn't having it. "Remember how hot and sweaty I was?"

"Yep. Sure do." Resting an elbow on his shoulder, she played with his hair.

"I'm burning up right now."

"I can feel it." She brushed his lips with hers. "Maybe you'd like a little cooling off, huh?" Her lips moved to the stubble on his jaw. She liked the texture. When her tongue flicked out, he sucked in a breath with a searing sound.

Loving how he squirmed, she whispered things in his ear she could never say out loud. Things that any red-blooded American boy would give his eyeteeth to hear. But the truth was, just whispering those words turned her on too. She helped him off with his dress shirt. "No way. You're wearing a wife beater T-shirt?"

A chuckle rumbled low in his throat. "Don't take it personally."

"Trust me. I'm not." Oh so lightly, she traced the arc of the armholes with her forefingers. He shuddered.

"Feels like this could get serious." His eyes fluttered closed when her hands drifted south.

"What do you need, Cameron?" She was a girl who liked to please.

"The warm washcloth." No hesitation on that one.

"Oh, really?" This was going to get fun.

Didn't take long before she held the wet cloth, the bowl of warm water within easy reach. While she was gathering her supplies, he'd stretched out on the green sofa. "We might just wear out this out," she whispered, lowering herself next to him.

"We could replace it, but I'm getting kind of attached." He ran a hand over the green armrest.

"To the sofa?"

His eyes narrowed. "No darlin'. To *you*...on the sofa."

Chapter 12

While Bella ate breakfast Wednesday morning, Harper crammed the back of the SUV with big plastic tubs full of decorations for Julep. She had a lot to accomplish today. Standing in the cool, dark garage, she glanced over at Cameron's Porsche and his Bentley. Warmth spilled through her body, as welcome as freshly made coffee. Last night would be on her mind for a long time. Feeling deliciously dazed, she closed the back hatch and scampered back through the garden to get Bella ready. Using Adam's products, she spent time on Bella's hair. No way was she screwing this up. At Bella's urging, she went heavy on the whipped cream foam until the curls danced, full and saucy. Adam would be proud.

After dropping Bella off at school, Harper headed straight for Foxy Loxy, where Adam was waiting for her. The man always had a surprise, and this time he'd changed his hair color. "So the trip was that bad? You're going older?"

"Right and hopefully wiser." He threaded his fingers through his newly-whitened hair. "You've got to have something to do in Paxton, Illinois, besides watch Jeopardy with your mother."

Stopping at the coffee bar, she grabbed a chai latte and took the seat across from him. This time they sat inside. "And how's your mom?" The past few months Adam's mother hadn't been doing well.

"Fine when she remembers to take her medications." A frown appeared between his brows. "Problem is, she never remembers."

"What does your brother say about that?"

Grabbing some pink sugar packets, he ripped two open and dumped them into his coffee. "Well, Brutus—my own personal nickname for my brother—says it's time to put mom in a home."

"No way."

"Exactly. More like, over my dead body—or his."

"Do you think she'd want to move to Savannah?"

"I'm not sure what she thinks." He adjusted the scarf around his neck. As soon as the weather got cooler, Adam pulled out his considerable array of scarves. They were alike like that. They both adored color.

"But enough about me. How was your Thanksgiving?"

She chuckled. "Publix came through for us big-time. But the dinner wasn't our focus. Our wedding was the topic of the weekend."

"What's the latest news?"

Where to begin? "It's really cold up north right now."

"No kidding? Let's remember I just came from Illinois." Tightening his scarf, he shivered.

"It seems that the Weatherby Mansion, where we were supposed to have the wedding, had a problem with frozen pipes."

"Oh. My. God." Adam's eyes grew as wide and brown as the coffee he was stirring.

"Split pipes. Water everywhere."

"Your poor mother. How is she handling all of this?"

"She assured me they would somehow find a new site for the reception, but Adam, I'm over it. Sure, Mom did want a traditional wedding, and I will wear her gown,"—Harper shivered involuntarily—"but the wedding might not be, you know, the old-fashioned kind."

Adam snorted. "Didn't you tell me that Selena wore a wedding gown designed like a flamenco dancer's?"

"Well, there is that." Selena's gorgeous gown with the flounces seemed to be the only thing anyone remembered about that wedding last summer. "And there were other problems about having it in Chicago."

An eyebrow went up. "You wouldn't be referring to the Blodgett contingent, would you?"

"Okay, have fun with Cameron's real last name. I think everyone has the right to shape their own future. That's all Cameron did with that name change." She admired him for deciding he'd rather be a Bennett than a Blodgett from Hazel Hurst. There was a reason behind that, and it had to do with his father, not that she'd ever discuss that with anyone. She drew her eyes down to her coffee cup. "So I'm thinking of having the wedding here."

The gasp was epic. "No way."

Glancing up, Harper could see his mind working.

"That means I wouldn't have to worry about the airlines losing all the hair products I'm packing. Not that this ever happens."

"Right, you can have all your products and equipment around

you." For the past month, Adam had done nothing but groan and worry.

While the cafe continued to fill up, her friend's mind continued to wander. "No freezing my butt off in Chicago. No slipping on the ice and breaking something. What's not to like about this plan?" Their guffaws made more than one customer turn.

"So, does this news mean that Cameron's family might actually show up? I can't wait to meet them." His eyes brightened. "I get to meet the problem family."

"Okay, have your fun but this is serious." She ignored the queasy feeling in her stomach. "Wish I could say yes. But after a conversation last night with his mother, things are still uncertain. Do you believe it?"

"Hold on there." Adam pushed back in his chair. "What else could she ask for? Prodigal son is getting married practically in her backyard. Two hours is too far to come?"

"Right, I don't know what the problem is."

Her headache throbbed again. She'd been feeling pretty good since she started those antibiotics, but didn't seem to be totally over the bug, or whatever it had been.

"Let me know if I can help. I mean, more than hair." He rubbed his hands together. "Your dress will be sent down here, right?"

"My mother is still waiting for the storage company to deliver it. Should be any day now."

"Maybe you'll get lucky and they'll lose it."

"Adam!" She hadn't even tried it on, and already she hated it.

"You have a point."

Looking all innocent, Adam said, "This is the dress that resembles Princess Diana's. Isn't that right?"

"Correct. The damn dress does look like a puffy meringue, but my mother adored it. McKenna told me I didn't have to take one for the team but I did. What could I say when my mother offered her own wedding gown? She'd had it in storage for her daughters for years. This being the youngest girl is a bitch." She sank further in her chair.

"Okay, maybe they won't be able to find it. Maybe you'll have a second chance." Dear Adam, always wanting the best for her.

"Oh and Adam, one more thing." Heck, she almost forgot this. "Remember when you told me you were going to become certified as a wedding minister?"

He sniffed. "Not a minister, Harper. A wedding officiant. And you want to know because…?"

"Because I need someone official or my family will never go for this wedding at home. I don't really know any ministers or priests down here. Besides that, Adam, you have been so instrumental in bringing us together. You're the one who told me not to wait for Billy."

Adam looked so pleased. "I'd be delighted, sweetheart. The best news I've heard all day."

"Thanks. Means a lot to me." Glancing at her phone, she got up to leave. "Gotta run. I still have to decorate Julep's house. I put it off because I had some bug and didn't want Julep to get it." Gathering up her keys and purse, she gave Adam a parting hug.

"Well, if we've got to worry about our mothers," he said while his Burberry scratched her cheek, "at least we can worry together, right?"

"Right but I'd rather not. I'd rather plan a wedding. We'll have fun." She backed away.

Looking delighted, Adam shook his head. "And that is why I adore you. You can always see the sunny side of shit."

As she drove down toward Tybee Island, Harper chuckled about their conversation. Adam had been a bright spot as she struggled through college.

Driving along the flat expanse of marsh, she enjoyed the sunlight flickering through the open sunroof of the SUV. She loved this ride. Always felt like she was taking a day at the beach. Sometimes she even wished she lived out here. Then she could feel the ocean breeze all the time. Maybe they'd rent a condo here for a couple of weeks some summer. Bella would love it, although Julep said the town was getting a little commercial. Sometimes Harper didn't mind commercial, especially for a vacation.

Passing all the shops, she smiled at the bold signs and displays holding colorful balls, surfboards and beach chairs. At Christmastime and New Year's, families might come, but this wasn't as warm as Florida. She came around the bend onto the main drag of Tybee; her mind circled back to the wedding and the long list in her notebook.

After she'd driven through the small commercial area, she turned right onto the upscale street where the Tuckers lived. Pulling into the driveway, she parked. Although the back porch offered plenty of space to relax, the two-story verandah ran along the front of the house that faced the ocean. The house was just perfection. Getting out of the SUV, she heard the snipping of shears and found Julep stooping over bushes, a basket of dead flowers over her arm and a floppy hat on her head.

"You should be in a gardening magazine!" Harper called out.

Turning, Julep giggled. "Yes, but which one would run an article entitled 'Pregnant Woman and Dead Peonies'?"

Opening the back hatch, Harper dragged out a Christmas tub while Julep peeled off her gardening gloves. In a flash, she was next to her with her big stomach, reaching for another tub.

"No, no." Harper pushed her hands away. "I haven't been pregnant so I don't know how this works, but my mother never likes to see pregnant girls lifting anything." Closing the back of the SUV, she lugged the tub toward the house.

With a laugh, Julep followed her. Inside, she took off her hat and left it on the hat rack in the foyer. "Why don't you leave this stuff here, and we'll head for the back. Let's sit down and have some sweet tea before we start. I want to hear all about your Thanksgiving."

Heaving the container onto the foyer floor, Harper agreed. "Sounds good, even though I just finished having coffee with Adam." Following Julep into her spacious kitchen, Harper sat on a stool, pivoting so she could see the yard.

"Did Adam go home to see his family?"

"Yes, I guess the holidays mean families." Feeling a bit bereft, Harper stared out through Julep's wall of windows and onto her perennial garden, neatly sectioned off with pavers.

Pouring sweet tea over ice cubes, Julep gave her a commiserating smile. "Missing your family, Harper?"

Her head was such a jumble. "I guess so. Oh, Julep, everything seems to be such a mess right now."

Sitting down next to her, Julep pushed a frosty, tall glass her way. "Anything you care to share?"

Even though Julep was a new friend, Harper let down her guard. "We've decided to have the wedding here in Savannah, and of course there's a ton to do."

Clapping her hands together, Julep squealed, "Oh, yippee! Can we come?"

That was another benefit of the change. "Of course you can. It makes me feel good that someone actually wants to attend our wedding. Do you believe that Cameron's mother still refuses? Cripes, it's only two hours away. And here I thought this change would solve everything."

"It didn't?"

Harper shook her head, her throat swelling. "Nope. Granted we didn't make the decision just because of her. The mansion where we were originally having the ceremony was damaged when the pipes froze and split open. Up north that happens."

"Mercy." Julep pressed one hand to her ample chest. When the sun hit her ring, the sparks were enough to set off a campfire.

"Just seemed like a perfect solution to have the wedding here. But it's not." She couldn't stop the disappointment that crept into her voice. "Mrs. Blodgett still won't come."

Wearing a thunderous frown, Julep held up a hand. "Pardon me. Mrs. Blodgett?"

"Right. I told you Cameron changed his name after he graduated from college."

Shaking her blonde curls, Julep said, "Yes, you did tell me that. But I'm more concerned about the Mrs. part. Do you really call your future mother-in-law Mrs. Blodgett? We may be formal in the South but not *that* formal."

Feeling like such a failure, Harper shook her head. "Is that a bad sign, Julep? As a southern girl, please tell it to me straight. All my brothers' wives and McKenna's husband call my mother Mom or Reenie, her nickname. I just haven't been, what, invited to the club."

Julep's eyes narrowed. "Sometimes I think the War of Northern Aggression still smolders in southern hearts."

"Shucks, Julep. Can't I just marry into the South and become one of y'all."

They both had a good laugh, one that Harper desperately needed. Then they sipped more tea and sized up the situation. "So I have this perfect opportunity to move my wedding to Savannah where it probably should've been in the first place, but my future in-laws still won't come. This wedding is turning into such a mess." She didn't want to cry but the tears came anyway.

Clucking, Julep looked at her with concern. "Girlfriend, you are one hot mess. But I know what you mean about in-laws. Mine are always screaming bloody murder about some imagined slight and my husband—well, he wants to accommodate them." Julep's lips thinned. "I might have to go to Vidalia for Christmas."

"Oh no. Does that mean you won't want all these decorations? Your place was going to look so beautiful."

"I know. Tuck and I would sleep in and then come out to have coffee while I opened up the gift that he'd chosen for me. You know, the one from One Fish, Two Fish, where I place my order."

They both giggled and Harper completed the picture. "You would take your gift from under the tree adorned by oyster shells, starfish and palmetto leaves. But now, who knows?" The two of them stared glumly at the adjoining family room that had been robbed of a memorable Christmas.

"But wait." Julep's face brightened. "What's the plan for your house? You know, for Christmas and the event?"

Another weight had just been added to her shoulders. "Oh, Julep. I haven't even thought about it. Poor Bella. She's been telling us how the other kids at school have been bragging about their trees."

"Not that you haven't had other things on your mind, like Cameron's broken leg..."

She waved a hand. "Ankle. Doesn't matter. Just as bad."

Wearing a mysterious smile, Julep gazed down the hallway toward the foyer. "Good thing you only lugged in one of those containers."

"Why? What are you thinking?" And Harper's eyes flicked to the green plastic tub that held a gorgeous wreath decorated with shells and tree garland festooned with starfish. Magical decorations that she'd worked on for hours.

"Take them home. They are yours. Merry Christmas." By this time, Julep was clapping her hands with delight.

The idea felt wickedly appealing. "But how can I steal your Christmas? You must want something around to remind you it's the holidays."

"This is how I look at it. I don't need to be fussing about decorations this year. I'll have to dust around the mantle pieces...or Patricia will." Eyes dreamy, she rubbed the top of her tummy. "After all, I'm a lady-in-waiting. But you, my friend..." She wiggled her brows. "...are in dire need of the decorations you planned so perfectly. What do you think of this aqua and lime color combination?"

"Love it. Always have."

"Will it go with your dress? The one your mother has tucked away for you?"

Harper made a face. "How do I know?"

Julep drew back. "That doesn't sound like you."

"The dress is my mother's. My mother loves it so..."

"Do you have your mother's taste?"

"Oh, not at all." Harper let her own words sink in. "You know what? It just hit me that we're planning the wedding my mother would've liked. Not one that's mine. And I'll never have another one."

Julep's eyes sparkled wickedly. "Not if you play your cards right. So, terrific, consider this your one chance to set everything right. After all, Georgina and Brittany are all set. I believe you mentioned you didn't take on any more clients before Christmas because of the wedding. You can spend your time decorating and get your gown down here. I stand ready to assist you in any way."

The sun beamed through the glass panes, and for a second, everything seemed clear. The wedding sounded bright and beautiful and could be everything Harper's heart desired. Then the sad truth came back to haunt her. "You know what? I still won't have Cameron's family there to bless our wedding. His sister might come, but she'll be standing in for the whole Blodgett contingent."

Julep rubbed her forehead. "Now tell me again. Your mother-in-law wasn't attending the wedding when it was in Chicago because of the weather. Now it's been moved to Savannah and she's still hesitating?"

"Crazy, right? Cameron's furious. But it won't do any good to call her again."

A devious expression formed on Julep's face. "Not unless you ask for her help."

"Her help?" Asking Esther Blodgett for help seemed ridiculous. "That's crazy."

"That's how it's done. What kind of wedding are you having? Are you thinking that you're going to drag this Chicago wedding down into that southern mansion? Are you going to serve roast beef and browned potatoes, God forbid, to your guests?"

Harper blinked. "I hadn't thought that far ahead. I think we were going to have tarragon chicken and green beans."

Bringing the back of her hand to her forehead, Julep closed her eyes. Such a drama queen. "The very idea gives me the vapors."

"Okay, Scarlett. You're too much."

Harper had a lot to think about on her way home.

Chapter 13

Harper waited until Bella was in bed before bringing up the issue that had been bothering her since visiting Julep. She wanted to choose her time. In the past, Cameron would charge through the door at the end of each day, eyes snapping and humming. Not anymore. With clients breathing down his neck and the ankle cast slowing him down, he dragged in, exhausted. He hated any sympathy, so she gave him time to recharge, extra hugs and casual kisses.

Her idea percolating in her head, she returned after reading Bella a book. He patted the sofa next to him. "Hey, sweet thing. How was your day?" The stress lines bracketing his lips were new, and even the grin looked tired.

She sank down next to him. "Hey, Boss Man. My day was fine. How about you?"

"Not bad."

Taking one hand, she smoothed his forehead. Sweet move but she was really checking for fever. If he got whatever had been bothering her and Bella... Well, she didn't want to think about it.

"My clients want to be in by Christmas. Imagine that." He rubbed bloodshot eyes.

"Any chance of that happening?" She did feel for the family.

"With overtime, sure."

Turning, Cameron tunneled one hand up under her hair. Smelling like a working man at the end of the day, he looked rumpled and weary. Even then, he was smoking hot. As his fingertips massaged her scalp, she let her head fall to one side. Man, this felt good. "I love it when you do this. Such talented hands."

"Wish I could put them to better use tonight, but I'm beat, babe."

What had they ever been thinking when they scheduled this wedding for Christmas? At the time, it seemed like such a good idea because people had vacation time around the holiday. But it created all kinds of scheduling problems for her siblings. Coming to Savannah might complicate things even more. Still, she pressed on.

"You're tightening again, sweetheart. What's up?" In the gray T-shirt that showcased his biceps, as well as a chest that was her favorite resting place, he looked hot...and concerned. Would she ever get used to him caring this much for her? She snuggled down into the crook under his arm, loving how she fit there.

"I've been thinking."

"That can be dangerous. Good thinking or bad thinking?"

He sounded so serious, as if he couldn't take one more bump in their road. Harper almost burst out laughing. "Oh, Cameron. You poor guy." Yep, she had put him through the wringer, but not intentionally.

The bristle defining his chin tickled when she brushed it with a kiss. "Just trying to make this whole wedding thing easier."

His eyes crinkled when he smiled down at her. "Got a magic wand? That is not going to happen. From what my friends say about weddings, that train already left the station." He gave her a tight squeeze.

"Were we crazy to try to pull off a Christmas wedding? Sometime I wish..."

But he pressed one finger softly to her lips. "Stop, darlin'. We agreed and we're trying to do it right. Now, if we can just decide what 'right' is." A chuckle rumbled in his chest, and she laid one palm against it. "We've kept our families waiting long enough."

She blew out a breath. "I just wanted everyone to enjoy themselves."

"It's a wedding ceremony not a party."

Swinging upright, Harper pressed both hands to her ears. "Oh, I don't want to hear that. I want a great party everyone will enjoy, especially our families."

Cameron tugged her back into his arms. The man was just too persuasive, and she melted against him. "It's *your* family I'm concerned about. They're the ones who jumped into the planning with us." The finger he traced down her nose tickled. "You're cute when you frown, know that?"

Batting the hand away, she tried to stay on track, never easy when Cameron was this close. "Funny. *Your* family is the one on my mind."

Drawing back, he gave her that are-you-kidding-me look. "Harper, we've been over this a million times."

"I know, I know." Hazel Hurst was two hours away, but it might as well be a thousand miles. And dang, he seemed satisfied having it like that. His life had been so different from hers.

Time and tragedy had weathered Cameron. Aged him somehow. How she wished she could erase those years. She'd hoped planning the wedding and this Christmas together would bring them closer. Nothing could be further from the truth. And his broken ankle hadn't helped one bit. No way was she going to bring that up. "I stopped at Julep's today."

"I'm glad you two are friends. She seems like a lot of fun."

"And a proper southern girl, who knows how to have a good time."

"That too." He twirled a strand of her hair around his fingers. Seemed as if she couldn't be within Cameron's reach without him touching her. How she loved that constant contact.

"Julep thinks we should ask your mom for help with the wedding. You know, maybe give us some suggestions for the food. Lord knows, I'm no good at cooking." She'd nearly poked Cameron's ex-girlfriend with a meat fork one time when she tried to cook a pot roast and failed.

The scowl brewing on his face told Harper just what he thought of her idea. "But what about Connie? Won't her feelings be hurt? She's pretty protective about her kitchen."

She'd expected this. "But don't you think a wedding is too much for one woman? Connie had to call in extra troops anyway."

"My mother isn't a troop, she's an army. And she's on the other side." His frown cinched tighter. "Lily might be the only member of my family at this wedding. You've just got to accept that."

Her throat closed. "Oh, Cameron, that just can't be. Have you talked to your mother or Lily again without me?"

"No, I haven't. I just know them." Palming her chin, he pressed his lips to her forehead. "I'm giving it to you straight, darlin'. Besides, why would you ever want her involved with the food? Remember my father's funeral? That's the kind of gathering they're used to. Plain food heaped on platters with grease dripping onto the floor."

Thinking back, she remembered that day so vividly. She'd felt totally out of place at the spartan, white house set in the wilds where they fought a constant battle with creeping kudzu. But time with his family helped her understand Cameron so much better. "Everybody brought something. Friends helped with the cooking."

"Exactly. Can you just see Julep arriving in Tuck's classic Lamborghini with her favorite casserole?"

Well, that was a stretch and she laughed. "It's not going to happen. But you have a point. We'll have to get right on the food. Connie can call caterers tomorrow."

That wasn't the solution she wanted.

With a groan, he readjusted his foot on the hassock. The darn thing must be bothering him. "We have to send out new invitations with an explanation. Have you thought of that?"

"McKenna's taking care of it." But Harper had been so busy with decoration plans. There were probably more ends to tie up. Still, Julep had a point and Harper wasn't a girl who gave up easily. "Will you at least call your mother and kind of run this by her?"

Cameron blew out a breath. "You don't understand, sweet thing. There's only one opinion that matters to my mom, and that's *her* opinion."

Time to button her lip. He was tired. But she wasn't giving up. Not by a long shot.

When Cameron nodded off on the pullout sofa, Harper sat in the library and came up with a daunting list. If she hadn't been so totally drained, all these bullet points would have kept her up all night. But her eyes flagged. She could hardly drag herself to the third floor. That night she tumbled into bed with the list clutched in one hand.

All the way to school the next day, Bella babbled on about their Christmas tree. When were they going to put it up? Where would they put it this year? Did they have enough ornaments?

Harper had to get with the program. "When you get home, I'll show you the bins with all kinds of magical things we're going to set around the house." Just thinking of it made her arms ache, but Jack and Connie would probably be around to help. And they would take their time. Last year she'd tried to throw everything up in one day. Not this year.

"Bye, Harper!" Bella gave her a wet smooch before she dashed into school. Elaine Powers stood outside in a tailored navy cape, greeting the students. As Harper edged past, she actually waved. When the principal bent to say something to Bella, Harper's hand tensed on the gearshift. But Bella's smile reassured her and she pulled away. Cameron had done such a great job of putting everything right. Her turn now. She'd do the same with this dang wedding.

When she reached the house, Jack was outside, trimming the bushes. She pulled into the garage and walked over on her way through the garden. Although winter had brought an end to the lush fuchsia and orange hibiscus that bloomed all summer, the garden still held plenty of greenery. A huge live oak shaded the area, along with smaller trees and bushes. And in the center, stood that mermaid fountain. Cameron and Harper found it soothing to sit on the back verandah while the water splashed below. How he'd laughed when Bella announced she wanted to be a mermaid when she grew up.

"Hey, Jack." Headphones in place, he moved smoothly over the shrubs. Not wanting to startle him, she waited until he turned slightly and saw her. Stripping off his head gear, he turned off the trimmer. The faint smell of gas hung in the air. "What's up, Harper?"

"Christmas is up, Jack. Do you believe it?" She hadn't told Connie or Jack yet that the wedding plans had been changed. In fact, she had to cancel those flights to Chicago as well as their own. "The back of the SUV is filled with tubs of Christmas decorations. Could you bring them inside when you have time? No hurry."

"Sure thing. I'll get right to it. So you're having Christmas here after we return from the wedding?"

He deserved an answer. Usually she left things up to Cameron, but he was always encouraging her to step into her role in the household. "There's been a change of plans, Jack. We're having the wedding here."

He cocked his head. "Well, that's nice. Guess I won't have to drag out my winter suit then, will I?"

She laughed. "No, no you won't and neither will Cameron."

Well, that felt amazingly easy. Satisfaction and relief filled her as she walked away. Of course, that was a man's response. She sprang up the back steps.

The kitchen smelled of toast and bacon. Warm and homey. And yet, was this mansion her home? Sometimes she still couldn't believe it. But enough of the grandeur. Right now, she wished it felt more like a home.

"Connie?" Stepping into the spacious marble hall, she looked around but no sight of the housekeeper. She must be upstairs.

Nothing much had changed here since she'd interviewed for the position of nanny. Running a hand over the side table Connie kept dusted, she chuckled. She'd been terrified when she arrived that day. Only two nights earlier, she'd pranced in wearing her Catwoman costume to entertain at a birthday party for kids. Instead, she'd run smack into a bachelor party. The guys hooted and howled for their stripper, which sure wasn't her. Back then, she needed the work so bad. Heck, she'd always needed a job, and she thought she really blew that gig. Cameron dismissed her. After the mix-up, she quit working for her sleazy boss and looked for another job, only to discover that Cameron had been impressed by her.

"You were gutsy," he told her later. "All Chicago and feisty. My daughter had already run through an embarrassing number of nannies. I needed a woman of steel. That was you, darlin'."

Not exactly flattering but his confession explained a lot. At first, she couldn't stand his arrogance. Harper never would have taken the job if it hadn't been for Bella. The tyke stole her heart. Hair snarled and wearing mismatched socks, she so obviously needed a woman's hand. Harper didn't have a great track record for finishing things, well unless you counted dark chocolate Milky Way bars. But she'd succeeded with Bella. How she loved that little girl...almost as much as she loved Bella's father.

Hand on the shiny banister, she glanced around. Yep the place hadn't changed much but she sure had. Maybe Christmas would be the start of a new life, a new home. But she would have to make it happen. She couldn't wait for Cameron to cover all the bases. The poor man had enough on his plate right now.

"Harper? Sure looks like you've got something on your mind." Connie appeared at the top of the stairs in her sensible shoes and the white apron she chose to wear. A pile of clean towels filled her arms.

Might as well get things sorted out. Walking upstairs past the historic etchings, Harper said, "Connie, there's been a major change in the wedding plans." And she watched Connie's jaw drop as she told her. The poor woman became as pale as the peach towels. "Don't even think you have to handle everything, Connie. We're getting people in, but we'd like you and Jack to identify the staff we'll need."

"So the reception also will be here?" She pointed down.

"Yep, right here. The decorations will mostly be holiday decorations that are in the car. I'll have more to tell you later."

First, she needed to make that one call.

Looking totally rattled, Connie looked like she might just drop the towels. Then her customary common sense kicked in. "Maybe we can contact that company who does Bella's birthday parties. Have them put up a tent." Harper loved that about Connie. She was a problem solver.

"Great idea. It'll be okay, Connie. We can do this."

But Connie didn't look convinced. "Well, I just don't want you to wear yourself out, Harper. After all, it's your wedding"

Her wedding. *Their* wedding.

As Connie came downstairs, the wonder of it caught Harper like a rogue wave at Tybee that grabs your ankles and upends you. Her throat closed with emotion, and she blinked furiously so Connie wouldn't notice. If she said another word, she'd bawl. This was supposed to be the happiest day of her life, and she wanted to do it right. But seeing Connie's reaction, the wedding seemed like a huge task. The kind she'd never been much good at.

Then she thought of Bella. Her thoughts stopped tumbling. Yes. Yes, she could definitely handle this. The little girl deserved a proper Christmas, just as she deserved a caring mother. Harper would be the woman who could give her both.

Setting the towels on the side table, the housekeeper took her hands. The nice thing about Connie's hands was that they were roughened by work and always warm. If she wasn't baking biscuits, she was cleaning the silver. "Now, don't you worry about a thing. Your wedding day will be the best Christmas wedding ever. Jack and I will do everything we can to make it perfect."

"Aw, Connie." She took the older woman in her arms. Breathing in the fresh scent of soap, Harper didn't know where she'd be without her. Wiping her eyes, she drew back. "Let me just make one call. Then I'll know where we stand."

"Just tell me what you need me to do." The quick kiss on the cheek surprised Harper. Then Connie went about her business as if it hadn't happened. Slipping into the library, Harper closed the pocket door behind her. Feeling like a small child misbehaving, she sat in the high-backed chair at Cameron's desk. She was saving him time. That's all she was doing. Running her fingers around the edges of the massive desk, she sized up her task. Right now, the wedding felt like a runaway train bearing down on them. Outside the library doors, she heard the slip and slide of the tubs Jack was dragging inside.

This Christmas wedding was happening, and she had to do her part to steer it in the right direction.

Thank goodness, Cameron kept his address book right on the desk. No way would she feel good about going through his private drawers. She flipped the cordovan cover open and began paging through. His mother's number wasn't under Blodgett. What? Okay, she kept going, smiling at all the names and numbers scratched out. Especially Kimmy Carrington's. Hmm. And then there was an Anne, Bethany, Diane. She liked the decisive, final crosses.

Here it was. How like Cameron to alphabetize his mother under Esther, not Blodgett. In two shakes, she copied the number onto a slip of paper so she could add it to her phone later. The Blodgetts still had a landline, and if she remembered correctly, Cameron had it installed. His family would have been perfectly fine to live without anyone calling them. Did Fred and Henry have cell phones? Probably, and their mother no doubt disapproved, so they kept them in their pockets. What was Lily's married name? Nothing came to her.

It embarrassed her that she still knew so little about his family. Her heart pounded in her ears when she tapped in Esther's number. The phone rang and rang. What now? Harper let her head fall into her hand. Just when she thought the answering machine would never kick on, Esther picked up.

"Mrs. Blodgett?" Startled, Harper sat up straighter, as if her mother-in-law could see her.

"And who is this?" Imperious as always.

She gulped. "Harper. How are you?"

"I'm fine. And yourself?"

Butterflies churned in her stomach. "I'm...I'm struggling." Time to let it all out.

"Well, for goodness sakes." Cameron's mother sounded as surprised as Harper felt with her bald admission. Remembering Julep's advice, she pushed on.

"It's just that it's Christmas and the wedding's coming and I'm at a loss. Just at a loss." Then she shut up. Let Cameron's mother do some work on her end of this conversation. Harper knew how much Esther loved her oldest son, although she'd never admit it.

"Whatever is it? You're having the ceremony at home, are you? I believe that's what Cameron told me. In Savannah?"

Was she playing dumb now? Fishing?

"Yes, we are. But I just can't get anyone to help...with the food," she finally blurted out. "Because of the holiday, every caterer is booked, and I just don't know what I'm going to do." Harper crossed her fingers, an old habit when it came to fibs. Oh, she knew they could get someone to handle the food, like Extraordinary Celebrations, who'd taken care of Bella's birthday party. But she wanted her future mother-in-law to think she was desperate.

"Yes, that would be a problem, I suppose."

"And I want everything to be right. You know, for Cameron's sake. "

"Yes, of course." Still that flat, dull intonation, like a stick dragging across a brick.

Get them saying yes. Hadn't Cameron taught her that about business meetings? "I suppose you have a lot of Christmas dishes and maybe even wedding recipes?"

"Of course I do." Outrage lifted Esther's voice. "Not written down of course. Why everyone knows how to make shoofly pie."

Well, not everyone. For a second Harper felt suspended, like she was clinging to the gnarled wisteria vines twined around the wrought iron railings. Hanging on for dear life but about to plummet into the bramble bushes.

"Well, I just don't know what to do about the food. I do want this to be a celebration." *One that you're going to attend.* "A special day. A wedding to remember." She tugged clichés out of her ear like silken scarves, bound to tempt and tantalize.

"Of course, of course." Esther Blodgett sounded huffy, not

happy.

But she hadn't hung up, and that was a good sign.

"What about Connie?" Esther asked. "Why, I'd think she'd help you. Cameron always seems to like her cooking well enough."

Oh. So there were hurt feelings here?

Time to think fast. "She already has so much to do with the house and everything."

Esther's breathy sigh rippled with frustration. Like a stubborn cow at milking time, she balked. Harper refused to take this personally, but for a second this felt like a lost cause. She'd bared her soul and now...

"I'd like to think on it," Esther said. "I have the recipes and all, but they're in my head."

Harper sucked in a tight breath and took a moment. Never would she let this woman know she was about to lose it.

"Harper, I just have to think about it, is all."

"That would be wonderful." The words exploded in a relieved burst. "Whatever you could do would be great. Otherwise we'll probably be eating TV dinners and store-bought cake." That was a stretch and Esther knew it. Maybe she thought Harper couldn't hear that snort.

"I will call you back. I have Cameron's number."

"Oh, let me give you mine," she said quickly.

Silence. "I'll have to get a pen."

Harper said nothing. No way was she letting Esther Blodgett off the hook, and no way did she want her calling Cameron. When she returned to the phone, Harper gave her the cell number, repeating it twice.

After they said goodbye, Harper slid down in the chair like a wet noodle. The tense conversation sure hadn't been a yes, and yet she felt victorious. Wiped out, she studied the dust motes that floated in the sunlight barely allowed by the heavily draped windows.

When the library doors slid open, Harper thought she might pass out.

Chapter 14

Leaning on the damn crutches he'd like to throw out a window, Cameron had trouble opening the library door. Connie must have closed it when she was cleaning. Three in the afternoon and he was beat. Why the hell did he climb up on that scaffolding? With the wedding coming up and all, he was disappointing Harper. He could kick himself from here to Forsyth Park. But he wasn't kicking anything these days.

Finally, he got the door open. "Hey, sweetheart." What a surprise to see her sitting there at his desk. When her head jerked up, the guilty expression was a total tell. She was up to something. Ducking his head and flattening the grin, he hobbled into the room. "What's going on? You hiding?"

Behind her, dim sunlight shone through the long library windows. He'd have to remind Jack to line up the window cleaners. Still, the light set fire to her hair, making her look almost angelic, with the emphasis on the *almost*. He knew better, but man, how he loved this woman. The fact that she quickly closed what sure as hell looked like his address book didn't change that.

This room had a lot of memories for both of them, and they all flooded back. She'd upended his life, just as she'd upended the bowl of pretzels she accidentally kicked off the bar downstairs with one of her cheerleader kicks that night. "What are you doing in here, all shut up?"

Rising from his desk, she quickly passed a tiny piece of paper behind her back. His suspicion grew, and it was hard to keep a straight face. Moving forward slowly, he tried to psych her out. "So I guess whatever it is you're doing, you don't want me to know about it."

She pulled her who-me face. "Just checking a few things."

"Ah huh. With the door closed?" Her creamy throat worked as she swallowed hard. "A few things that you don't want me to know about?"

Harper lifted a shoulder, the color burnishing her face like a bad sunburn. With a lime green scarf tied around her hair and a turquoise and lime Harlequin printed sweater, she was a walking billboard. But she'd always been like that and he wouldn't have it any other way. This girl would probably never wear the sedate clothes he saw on other women. No matching sweater set or modest string of outrageously expensive pearls. There were trade-offs and that included a warm washcloth.

Now one hand fidgeted with her scarf. "I was just, just..."

By the time Cameron reached the desk, he couldn't hold back his chuckles. Laying the crutches against the leather wing chair, he took her in his arms. She settled with a sigh, so warm and willing. But her hands were still behind her back. Tilting her chin up with one hand, he looked deep into those hazel eyes. "Now Harper, do you expect me to keep asking you questions until I hit the jackpot?"

"No, no." But her arms weren't flung around his neck. Easing a hand behind her, he tugged the paper from her grip. "Or will this give me the answer?"

She glanced down at the slip as if it were a gun. "Maybe. Cameron, I was just working on the wedding. So many things still..."

He glanced down. *What the hell?* "You called my mother?" But the doodles on the paper made him laugh. She'd written Esther and had lightning bolts shooting out of each letter. "Whatever for?"

Her moist lips opened and closed. It took two tries before she could force anything out, but he enjoyed watching that full mouth. "I just wanted to talk to her. A little."

Uh huh. "Right. Darlin', this is a little." He held his forefinger about a quarter inch from his thumb. "But my mother? She's more like this." And he flung his fingers open, the paper fluttering to the floor. His mother was a walking head case. Living with his father had done that to her.

"Oh, Cameron." Tilting her head to the side, she brushed his lips with a kiss, tantalizing and irresistible. With a groan, he covered her lips with his, claimed them until they parted with a sigh. Enough conversation. Their tongues did the talking.

Her chest rose and fell against his, and he felt the stirrings of their contact. This could easily become more than just a kiss. "Cameron I was just..." But she couldn't get her breath.

"Do you need your inhaler?"

"Oh, no. I need you." She held him tighter.

"I like hearing that."

She kissed his chin, carefully swinging one leg around his good leg and cinching him closer. Pressed her curves closer until he thought he'd lose his mind. Putting all of his weight on his good leg, he leveraged her onto the desk and looked deep into those eyes that gave him all kinds of ideas.

"Now you know what I would do if I could walk back to that door and slide it closed?"

Her eyes widened and her chest rose and fell.

"Where this whole thing might go if I could lay you down on this desk and slip off that sweater?" He glanced down. "And the black jeans?"

Her breathing became uneven when he slid both hands under the soft sweater, where the skin was even softer. When she shivered, he squeezed his eyes shut and just felt. One touch of the lace and he froze, mind shifting through ways he might make something happen. But the clunky cast mocked him. *Walking cast, my ass.*

Limping across the floor to shut that door? Not the manly thing to do and painful. While he hesitated, the moment passed.

"Connie might see us." She hitched her sweater down as if she recognized the barriers. The moment drifted away. Pulling her up, he buried his face in her sweet-smelling hair.

"Cameron," she whispered.

He lifted his head.

"I want your family to come to our wedding ceremony. I want them to come so bad." She was trembling in his arms, and his heart turned over. Why was this so damn important?

Pulling away, he studied her face, every precious line now twisted into a frown. "Oh, sweet thing. What you do to me. Does it really matter that much to you?" Why in heaven's name did she want the Blodgetts here when they didn't want to come? He'd spent so much of his adulthood trying to forget his upbringing. He just could not picture Fred and Henry in their coveralls fitting in with the Kirkpatricks from Chicago.

Were those tears shimmering in her eyes? His gut clenched.

"It most certainly does matter. At least, to me." Her eyes turned steely, and he hoped to God she didn't stamp her foot in those boots. He edged his injured foot away. "And Julep helped me think of a way to—"

"Julep?" Maybe he'd been wrong to think that Tuck's wife would be a good influence on Harper. "Go on. I'm just thinking."

Moistening her lips with her tongue, Harper motored on while his mind stayed right there with her plump, ripe mouth. "Anyway, she suggested I ask your mother to participate."

"Participate? How?"

"Remember your dad's funeral?"

He sucked in a breath. Hadn't they been over this? Cameron remembered way too much about his father, more than he'd ever tell Harper.

Hands fluttering, she continued. "An important part of the funeral was the food. Why not involve your mother? Then she'd have to come. All the family would come with her and we'd have...everyone...here." Harper worried him when she got all worked up like this and ended up gasping.

"Hold it. Hold it, darlin' or we will have to call the EMTs. I want to be the only one to give you mouth to mouth." He waited until her breathing settled. This wedding had her so riled. Cameron just wanted it over and done.

"Does Connie know that you want her to work with my mother? You know, we can't afford to lose Connie and Jack."

"Oh, Cameron." She socked him playfully in the arm. "Your mother's not that bad. Is she?"

"She's not exactly Miss Congeniality. So you called her and…?"

Hands on his chest, Harper fisted his shirt. "I think she turned me down." The surprise in Harper's voice made him roar. Pushing back, she fixed him with a look that could double as an ice pick.

"Go ahead. Laugh at me. Laugh at the fact that your mother might not want to bring her special recipes to her own son's wedding."

"Recipes?" His mind flipped through the past. "Harper, I don't think I ever saw a cookbook or a recipe card in our house. My mother threw stuff together, and it came out right. I mean, if you like okra and black-eyed peas. That's all I can recall."

"Shoofly pie." Her eyes glimmered.

"Right. There was that." He licked his lips, remembering the texture and the taste so sweet it made his teeth ache.

"Okra. Black-eyed peas." Harper repeated the words as if they were sacred. "Oh, Cameron, how perfect."

Perfectly awful. But his lips were closed with super glue once he saw her rapt expression.

Her delicate brows pulled together. "She must have written

something down, right? Even my mother had a binder where she stowed clippings. She never used them, but she cut things out of magazines and threw them in there."

"So your heart's set on this?" The more he dug in his heels, the more he reminded himself of his mother. And he hated that.

Rolling her eyes his way, she gave him a doleful look.

That settled it. "Let me give Lily a call."

"Your sister?" She blinked.

"Of course. Who would you call to influence your mother?"

He could see the wheels turning. "McKenna. Right," Harper said slowly. "Lily might be able to fix this."

Why hadn't he thought of this earlier? "Don't get your hopes up, but she might be able to help. However, this will be a private call. That all right with you?"

With a little hop as if she were Bella, Harper jumped down from the desk and snatched the paper with the phone number from the floor. It made him nervous to imagine what she might do with it. "All right. You'll let me know?"

"Of course. Could you close the door behind you?"

"Sure. No problem." The library doors were almost shut when that lime green scarf floated back in. "And Cameron?"

He lowered himself carefully into the desk chair and turned. "Yes, darlin'?"

"I love you."

The intensity of her gaze lasered those words onto his heart. "I love you too, sweet thing. Now scram, okay?" He shooed her away with his hands.

The door slid shut and silence settled. With a sigh, he sat back. Cameron didn't understand where Harper was going with this but he better get used to it. When she wanted something, she got it. He was marsh mud in her hands. He hit speed dial for Lily, and she answered on the second ring.

"So how are the wedding plans coming?" his older sister asked.

"You think I can't hear the laugh in your voice?"

"I just had a short conversation with our mother." Amusement danced in her words.

"And?" He just couldn't wait to hear this one.

"She thinks your intended bride is crazy."

He grinned. "She is. Crazy about me."

"Oh, Cameron I like to hear that. Harper's been so good for you, a lot better than Tammy."

That sobered him up quickly. He didn't even like hearing the name of his first wife. After all, she died in a car accident trying to leave him when Bella was just a baby. And she was setting out to meet one of his college buddies when she hit that tree.

But enough of that. "Lily, we're changing the wedding to Savannah. There's a lot of reasoning behind the decision." He hoped Lily didn't ask what.

"And like any man you're just going along with it, right?"

"Exactly. And I also can't tell you exactly why Harper would like to have Mama involved in this food thing. God knows, we could get someone to do that."

For a second Lily was quiet. She was a woman who thought things through before she spoke. He'd always appreciated that in her. "I think I understand Harper's strategy, and I totally support it."

Strategy? This was definitely a female thing. He knew when to butt out. "So you'll talk to Mama? You'll see that she cooperates?"

"Won't be easy but yes. Tell Harper she can count on me."

Relief poured through him. "Thanks, Lily. You just don't know." Forget surprised. He was downright amazed. His sister was going to make him look like a hero.

"I think I do. Talk to you soon."

As he tucked the phone in his pocket, he heard a ruckus in the hallway. Grabbing his crutches, he swung across the floor. Pushing the doors open, he hardly recognized the foyer. Green tubs were stacked everywhere. The tops were off some of them and Pipsqueak was cavorting down the hallway, a bright lime green ribbon trailing from her teeth. Harper came hurrying from the kitchen.

Waving a hand at the chaos, he asked, "What is all this?"

"This?" She grinned. "This is our Christmas."

Chapter 15

A string of starfish garland in her hand, Harper asked, "What did Lily say?" Her heart was in her throat.

"She said she'd help."

"Oh, that's wonderful." She nearly dropped the starfish. That's all she needed, shattered starfish on the floor. Her mind whirled. "I wonder if I should ask for a list? Should we have her meet with Connie?"

But Cameron was too busy checking out all the decorations to answer. She'd have to weasel it out of him later. "You mean all this stuff is going up?"

"Of course. Julep doesn't need it because they're going to Vidalia for the holiday. She was generous enough to let me borrow her Christmas, remember?"

Glancing around, Cameron looked worried. "I'd ask Rick and some of the guys to help but they're already working overtime."

"No, they're too busy. And those men work for you, not me."

Cameron had the funniest way of rolling his eyes at her. "Trust me. Those boys would rather spend a few hours with you than with me. But they're busy right now, meeting our deadlines."

She recognized that tight set of his chin. The last thing Harper wanted was to cause more stress. "You all have to keep moving ahead with those three projects. I understand." She looked around. "Since I'm finished with the Darlingtons' home and the Bedfords, I can take this on. I always like to decorate the house at Christmas time." *But not a big-ass mansion.* Of course, she didn't say that out loud.

But Cameron might've been thinking it. "Right," he said. "But you have so much to do."

She worked her bottom lip with her teeth. Cameron was right. How would she get this done? With the help of the antibiotics, when she remembered to take them, the virus had faded. She was feeling a lot better, but she was only one person. Of course, Bella would help and Connie would pitch in. Adam and Julep were other possibilities. But it was Christmas season. Everyone had their own parties and other responsibilities.

Glancing at her watch, she saw that it was time to pick Bella up. Off she went. On the way to the school, she blasted the Christmas music, even tried to sing along. When Bella climbed into the SUV, she was waving a white envelope. "Christie is having a birthday party next weekend, and all of the girls are invited."

"That's wonderful, honey." And it really was. But it was just one more thing. She had to pick up a gift. Mentally, she added that to her list. By the time they reached the house, Bella's attention had turned back to Christmas. She was all about it. And she couldn't wait to decorate the Christmas tree. The tree they didn't have yet. From the time Harper closed the garage door to when she took her jacket off in the kitchen, Bella babbled about what Christie, Joelle and Marceline had said about their own trees. Harper felt as if the stop watch had clicked, and she was seriously behind in the race.

But when Bella caught a glimpse of the tubs stacked in the hallway, she came to a halt. "What's all that?"

"Well, why don't you go and see?" The wonder in Bella's eyes made everything worthwhile. "All this beautiful stuff is for us?"

"Sure is. For Christmas and for the wedding." The little girl's excitement was infectious. For a moment Harper forgot all about the trouble she was having with Esther. This was all about Christmas and celebrating her marriage to the most wonderful man in the world.

The library door slid open. "What's all the commotion?" Cameron said with mock gruffness.

"Daddy, look!" Bella swung a hand over the green tubs, shining with glittery aqua and lime.

"Has Santa come?"

"Oh, Daddy." The disgust in her voice brought a smile.

Seeing the two of them together like this made Harper feel all mushy. She loved them so much. Cameron brought his attention back to Harper. "What can I do?"

Well, why not get started right now? Connie had dinner well in hand. "You can sit right there. And give us your advice." And she pointed to the same bench where she'd waited for her interview.

"You got it." So while Harper and Bella clambered up and down the staircase, twisted the garland here, working with glittery ribbon, Cameron made suggestions. But by the time Connie had dinner ready, they'd only finished half the banister. Oh, it looked glorious, glittery and wonderful. "What do you think?" She turned to Cameron.

"It's beautiful, just like my girls. But it is dinnertime and one of us is hungry." He patted his stomach. His eyes traveled up the partially decorated staircase. "And from what I see, we're going to need a lot of energy."

As Harper set the table with Bella, she couldn't help but be filled with the wonder of Christmas. Bella's exuberance had awakened so many Christmas memories. Today they'd felt like a family, decorating the house. And that felt wonderful.

All through dinner, Bella chattered happily. The problems at school seemed to be resolved, and all she could talk about was Christie's birthday party. What a relief, one she shared with Cameron.

Connie had cooked ham with scalloped potatoes. In her excitement, Bella hardly knew what she was eating. With gratefulness in her heart, Harper watched that fork scoop up the potatoes and go back for a bit of ham. She sure didn't care if some fell off the fork. Bella was eating. They were back on track.

At Bella's bidding, they went back to work after dinner. But by the time bedtime came around, they had only finished the banister. Skipping up the stairs to her bedroom, Bella's hands flitted across the garland while she hummed a weird combination of "Oh Little Town of Bethlehem" and "Silent Night."

As Harper tucked her in that night, Bella smiled up at her. "I think we will have the most beautiful Christmas wedding ever."

"Aw, sweetheart." Who could argue with that? Harper gave her another hug.

After Bella had been dropped off at school the next day, and Cameron had left for work, Harper took on the fireplaces. Starting with the living room that was really a formal parlor with Victorian love seats, she cleared the mantle of the bronze clock, candlesticks and figurines that Cameron had no doubt picked up on Bull Street. Her mother's rule was to put everything you took down into the box you were pulling decorations from. Harper followed that custom.

She just wished she could work faster. The weekend came and the three of them kept steadily working. Harper found a station on the radio that was playing the Christmas songs and that helped set the mood.

Since this house had a fireplace in almost every room, more than Julep's lowcountry beach house, Harper soon realized she'd run out of angels, elves and snowmen. Since they'd told the Bedfords that she was still nursing a virus, they did not go to the Christmas party. Oh, how Harper had wanted to see people's expressions, but no way.

After taking Cameron to work on Monday and dropping Bella off at school, she threw herself back into the decorating. She would have worked through lunch if Connie hadn't come into the parlor with a plate.

"You'd better stop now," Connie said with a warning shake of her head. "You look plumb tuckered out."

"Aw thanks, Connie." She tucked her red bandana tighter around her forehead and slumped onto a loveseat to eat. The ham sandwich was the best she'd ever tasted and so was the cold pop.

Everywhere she looked there was more to do, mainly because her ideas would not stop. After lunch, back to work she went. Connie left to pick up Bella and when they returned, Connie and Bella took on the dining room. McKenna called around four o'clock, and Harper was glad to take a break.

"How are people taking the switch in Chicago?" she asked. McKenna was a much better judge of all that.

"Everyone understands. They love you, Harper, but they realize your life has taken a different turn. The family will be there in full force for the party. But as for Mark and Malcolm..."

"I know. All the children and plans with the in-laws." For a second, guilt threatened to make a comeback but McKenna made short work of it, as if she knew how Harper was feeling.

"Not to worry. They are looking forward to having a party next spring. We think the snow should be gone by then." McKenna's hearty chuckle loosened the muscles knotting in Harper's neck.

"But I do have some bad news."

Her sister's sober tone put a cold hold on Harper's heart. "What's that?"

"Mom got her dress from the storage place to send to you. Something happened with their process. Maybe their air conditioning went out or something. Whatever. The fabric has rotted in spots. You won't be able to wear it."

"At all?" Harper struggled to get her mind around this.

"I'm afraid the dress is ruined, Harper." McKenna, the stinker, could hardly get the words out. What Harper had interpreted as distress in McKenna's voice was really pent-up laughter.

And then it hit her "Oh, McKenna. This opens up all kinds of possibilities."

"I figured you wouldn't be too broken up about it. But when you talk to Mom, sound disappointed."

"I'll be just crushed." But what was she going to do about a dress? There was always the SCAD costume department. She'd tapped that once for a gala with Cameron. But somehow, she didn't think that the college collection would hold a wedding gown. Then it hit her. She'd call Julep. "I have a resource that should be able to help me find one."

For the next few minutes, McKenna and Harper went through the list, checking things off. Florists, the caterers, the photographer—their Chicago resources had all been notified about the cancellation. Most were relieved because they had more work than they could handle due to the holiday and wanted their own family time. "Are you able to line up people down there?"

"Working on it." She wasn't about to go into the trouble she was having with Cameron's family. The situation would be so difficult for any Kirkpatrick to wrap their heads around, and she didn't want it to reflect poorly on Cameron. "My friend Adam has talented friends he can call on. He'll be doing everyone's hair, by the way."

"Okay, and Selena and I have our dresses. But what about yours?"

"You caught me off guard. Nothing comes to mind." The excitement revving in Harper's chest surprised her. "I have a friend who will probably help me."

By the time the call ended, Harper had a whole new list. But Bella was tugging at her hand, "Come on, Harper. You said we could decorate."

In the dining room, Connie and Bella had done a good job with the credenza. "It looks beautiful." She'd bought three different crèche sets at various sales. Bella had a great time arranging one on the credenza while Connie tucked garland and pine cones around the family. The lambs, of course, were especially fun to play with. But it was almost dinnertime, and Harper called a halt. Connie left to heat up the ham leftovers.

Bella's chin jutted out. "Why do we have to stop? I'm not hungry."

"Because we need more stuff. I don't know how many of the decorations in the tub will be used on the tree."

Bella's lips fell open. "The Christmas tree." The year before they had an artificial Christmas tree. It just seemed like a good idea at the time. But it only took visiting a couple of homes to realize that their southern friends preferred real live trees that provided a head-reeling pine smell.

As she stood there deciding, she heard Cameron thumping down the hallway. "Can I help in any way, crippled as I am?"

"Oh, Cameron." But he didn't look as tired as he had one week earlier. "I'll be so glad when you're off those crutches."

"You? What about me?" She cuddled in his arms, while his eyes circled the room.

A perplexed frown appeared. "Don't you like it?" Harper asked. He looked so uncertain, and they'd worked for hours.

Bella stamped one little foot. "Daddy. You have to like it or Harper will cry." She loved how Bella looked out for her.

Ruffling his daughter's dark curls, Cameron said, "Now don't go jumping to conclusions. The decorations look wonderful. It's just that the place looks so different." He turned to Harper. "Doesn't it? I mean the decorations all look so sparkling new. Great color combination, by the way. But the carved side chairs? The heavy tables? Something feels so wrong here."

Was Cameron finally realizing that the furnishings weren't right for their home? Harper held her breath. Her phone jangled. It was Julep. "Can you get Bella some lunch?" she whispered to Cameron.

"Sure thing." Just then the dog romped into the dining room, pawing at the shimmery lime ribbon draped around his nose.

"Pipsqueak," Bella scolded.

"Be with you in a sec, Julep," she told her friend, trying to get away from all the noise.

Excited to be a part of everything, Pipsqueak started barking. Harper was relieved to see the three of them disappear down the hall, Bella working at untangling the dog from a string of lights. Harper walked down to the parlor and plopped down on one of the Victorian sofas covered in velvet. It was like sitting on a brick ledge. "Phew, at last we can talk."

"Did I get you at a bad time?" Julep asked.

"No, I was just going to call you."

"Oh goody. I hope I was doing something outrageous in your mind."

"Kind of. I was just talking to my sister, who had some terrible news." She filled Julep in about the dress.

"Hallelujah. From the comments you made about that dress, I'd say this is a welcome disaster."

"Exactly, but time is short. Do you know any consignment shops that would carry dresses?"

"Oh my dear," Julep said in her thickest Vidalia accent. "There's only one place for a Savannah girl's wedding dress. Bleubelle's."

"The name practically drips with southern charm."

"You mind if I tag along?"

"You are leading the way, Julep. And thank you." They agreed on the time for Tuesday.

When she joined Cameron and Bella in the kitchen, she told them about the planned trip with Julep. "Can I come?" Bella asked.

"Oh sweetie," Harper said, giving her a hug. "You will be in school. But I do want to order a very special dress for you. Maybe we can go online tonight and work on that, okay?"

Looking up she caught Cameron's glance. His eyes held the look of grateful love. Just what any girl would want to see in a husband's eyes.

Husband. Soon she could call him that, and her heart brimmed with that one word.

That night she had a terrible time falling asleep. Next to the bed, her notebook had pages folded over or ripped out. It was a total mess, but this wedding could not be set aside.

When she finally did fall asleep, she had a terrible nightmare. In the dream, she was trying to reach Cameron but ribbons of red and green woven into a wall blocked the way. She could not break through. Finally, she was able to swim up and out of sleep. Damp with sweat and sick from the threads of the dream that still clung, she pushed up on her elbows.

The third floor room felt too big and too lonely. Making her way carefully downstairs in the floppy dancing reindeer PJs that she saved for Christmas, she slipped in behind Cameron on the sleeper sofa. He usually slept commando, and she wound her arms around him, laying her head on his warm back. One hand flat on his heart, she felt the steady beat. Her fears fell away. He turned with a sleepy grin. "What is it, sweet thing? What's wrong?"

"A bad dream," she mumbled and snuggled closer. Man, he was a furnace. Careful not to bump his right foot, she fit her body to his. "I couldn't find you. Couldn't get to you."

"I'm always here for you." His arms tightened and he kissed her forehead. "Always."

One of his hands slid over the flannel. "But what the hell are you wearing?"

"My reindeer PJs." She giggled. "I only wear these over the holidays, remember?"

"Hmm. Right." His hands stroked the soft flannel. "Probably bad for your health. Way too warm."

Harper kissed his chest. Gave it the slow tip of her tongue and he shivered. "You're the best nightmare medicine ever."

"Glad to hear it. But darlin' these pajamas are just like wrapping paper." Oh, so gently he slipped the top over her head while she inched off the bottom. "The gift is hidden inside."

Chapter 16

When Julep picked her up the following Tuesday, Harper was so excited she could hardly speak. And that never happened. "All I've thought about since we talked is this dress," she admitted, climbing into Julep's low-slung Mercedes. "Whoa. Pretty awesome, Julep." She ran a hand over the burled trim on the dash.

"Tuck is all about cars."

"Isn't every man?" Harper said, thinking of their own garage.

"He insisted on this, not me." The V8 engine rumbled under them as Julep pulled away.

Settling back into the black leather, Harper said, "So tell me about Bleubelle's."

The ride down Abercorn felt short because Julep described her own wedding and the role Bleubelle's had played. Sounded like something from *Gone with the Wind*.

When they reached the unassuming shop in a strip mall near Bonefish Grille on Abercorn, Harper felt her heart pumping. Busy with a million other things, she hadn't realized until now just how much this dress meant to her. How much she'd been missing by not shopping for it.

"I've already called," Julep told her. "Courtney's waiting for us."

Getting out of the Mercedes, they walked up to the window

where three mannequins were dressed in gowns that exceeded any childhood wedding expectations. In fact, Harper felt like a little girl pressing her nose to a candy store window. "Oh, Julep, the dresses are beautiful. Beautiful and expensive, I bet. And you probably have to order them, right?" The designs were high fashion. Fitted gowns with restrained trains. Capped sleeves tailored to fitted bodices, all beautifully detailed with pearls. Not a lot of fuss or frills here. Just stunning elegance.

"Usually, yes. But Courtney does have some samples." Opening the door, Julep ushered her inside.

"But why would she sell one to me?" Harper whispered. "I don't see any sale signs."

"Because my wedding was the biggest order they've ever had. I think it had to do with my eight bridesmaids." And Julep chuckled. How Harper loved this girl.

"Eight? I have two."

"You're smart. Why, I hardly ever talk to most of those girls anymore. Although, I will be in their weddings."

"Come right in, ladies." An attractive young woman came into the outer display area with an air of quiet competence. "So good to see you again, Julep." The two women air-kissed. "And you're expecting! Mercy, doesn't time fly?"

While the two of them chattered in the breezy, southern manner that could take forever, Harper was drawn to the racks that edged the rectangular showroom. Dealing with the heavy gowns wasn't easy, but she began to search.

"Come on, Harper." Julep waved her over. With one long,

lingering glance at the rack, Harper joined her. The two of them followed Courtney into the inner sanctum where they settled onto a puffy banquette. Right then, Harper decided this was a once in a lifetime experience. She was going to enjoy it. While another younger girl materialized to ply them with sweet tea and macaroons, Courtney showed them gown after gown, narrowing her choices from Harper's comments. She didn't want a train. Didn't want a lot of lace or beading. And she certainly didn't want long sleeves. Later, she realized that she'd nixed any gown that looked like her mother's wedding dress.

Unfortunately, she was drawn to high-end numbers, the kind of gown sold on Michigan Avenue in Chicago. "This must be so expensive," she murmured to Julep when Courtney left the room for a moment.

"Don't even think about it. Sample prices."

So Harper decided to take her time. "Just one thing," she finally interjected, hating to bring it up. "I'm getting married on Christmas Eve. You won't be able to get another sample in by then, right?"

Courtney and Julep exchanged a look. "Now don't you worry about that. I'll handle it," Courtney assured her.

When the number narrowed to six, they reached the try-on stage. Harper felt like Cinderella. Julep helped her in and out of the gowns that rustled with silky wonder. Walking out into the show room in the heels she'd brought, she pirouetted in front of the three-way mirror.

Since she'd never liked fussy clothing, her final choice was a simple strapless gown with a heart-shaped bodice that accented her figure. The three-tiered silk organza skirt flared into asymmetrical layers. At the waist was a small bouquet of flowers in a demure pink—which of course she intended to change.

As Harper twirled in front of the mirror, Julep narrowed her eyes. "Sweet and simple, but oh, so sexy. I love it."

Although the gown was a sample size, it was a little large on Harper and Courtney assured her the changes would be made. A woman came in with a pincushion and measuring tape, and then told her when the dress would be ready. And the price was actually something Harper could afford.

"And now lunch is on me," Julep told her when she came out dressed again. Why argue? By this time, Harper had learned that you didn't argue with Julep Tucker.

As they headed down Abercorn, they took in the Christmas decorations. All of the windows were decked out in green and red. "We went to the Bedfords' party last Saturday," Julep told Harper as she drove. "You just wouldn't believe how many compliments were flying through the air about your decor. And Brittany gave you the credit. You are going to be very busy."

"That's good news. We had to cancel. Cameron didn't want to go in his cast."

In the Gryphon Tea Room, they ordered the high tea. Harper preferred the African Autumn blend while Julep chose Smokey Cinnamon and Apple. The shopping expedition with her new friend had given Harper a thrill she'd always remember. "Oh Julep, this has been a wonderful morning. Thank you."

Selecting a thin cucumber sandwich, Julep smiled. "A woman

should be excited about her wedding."

"I know," Harper said, nibbling on a tasty tuna tea sandwich. "I guess the wedding has become a list of chores for me. It's been so stressful since Thanksgiving."

"You're in the home stretch. How is your mother-in-law coming along?"

"Oh, she and Lily sent me a tentative list for the buffet. I have to sit down with Connie and go over it. We're hoping that the weather will be mild enough that we can eat outside. Cameron's ordered a tent." Digging through her purse, she came up with the list that Cameron had printed off for her. "This is just a rough menu."

Scanning the typed page, Julep reached for a miniature éclair. "Mind if I make some suggestions?"

"Not at all. Gee, that lemon tart looks good."

"It's yours. I'm swearing off lemon this month." Julep took out a pen. "Let's see. Just a few more things, like hush puppies."

"Oh my God? They're not there? It's a good thing I've shown you that list."

All too soon, the lunch ended. When the waiter brought them the check, Julep insisted on paying, even though Harper protested.

"Have you set up a wedding registry?"

Harper just looked at her. Sure, she always went to a bride's registry for her gift when she was invited to a wedding. But they didn't need anything. As if she could read her mind, Julep smiled. "What am I ever going to get you for your wedding? Let's make this day my wedding gift to you."

Who could argue with that? "Sounds fabulous."

"Why don't we do some window shopping?" Julep asked once they walked out into Madison Square. "I don't get down to Bull Street that often."

"Sounds wonderful. Makes me feel like a student again to come down here." How Harper's life had changed.

"How is the decorating going?" Julep asked.

"Exhausting, to be honest. Cameron's frustrated because he really can't help with his ankle. In fact, he's doing far too much now. And his guys are all busy with jobs they need to finish before Christmas."

"Maybe I could come over with Patricia and a couple of her girls."

"Who's Patricia?"

"My cleaning lady. She has a lot of young girls who might enjoy decorating, as long as you direct them."

Finally, Harper could see a light shining at the end of the tunnel. "Oh, that would be such a help, Julep, if she has some hours. I don't care what she charges."

Wearing a sassy smile, Julep wagged a finger. "Remember everything today is on me. And that includes anything we mention."

Well, Harper wasn't quite comfortable with that. But she'd deal with that later. "I can see the wheels moving in Cameron's head as we decorate. And I think he realizes that the decor doesn't match the vintage furniture, and I use that word kindly."

"That's a good thing right?"

"It sure is. I'm hoping someday we can look at some new pieces together."

Julep tugged her into one of the shops, and before Harper knew it, her friend was snapping up ornaments and table decorations that fit her new theme. She especially liked the silver jingle bell doorknob wreaths and a welcome mat sporting a reindeer. When they turned onto Broughton Street, Julep took Harper to a gift shop with coastal holiday decorations. Harper picked out a three-foot tree made of white shells. "I should've moved the car closer," Julep grumbled.

"Here, let me take the heavier bags." Arms full, they giggled all the way up the cobblestone sidewalk to the car. For the first time, Harper felt not just the stress but also the giddy excitement of her Christmas wedding.

Their Christmas wedding. And that was the best part.

Chapter 17

When Harper got home, Cameron asked if she'd had any success. "Not telling...but yes. And you can't see my dress when I bring it home. That's not allowed."

Although the wedding was unfolding in close quarters, she desperately wanted her gown to be a surprise. "Not for us girls," she later whispered to Bella. "You can have a sneak peek after they make the alterations." A beaming smile and tight hug from Bella's spindly arms were her reward.

Ornaments and garlands in hand, they continued to put up Christmas decorations, while Cameron tapped in hooks, arranged stuffed elves on the highest shelves and held up sparkling ribbons so she could gauge the effect. They were a great team. The house began to take on a festive air, despite the museum-like furnishings. Grabbing Jack's trimming shears one day, Harper led Bella outside to cut short branches from one of their pine trees. The fragrant boughs filled the house with a piney smell that had always meant Christmas for her. They were all relieved when neither she nor Bella had any breathing problems.

Yes, it was beginning to look and feel like Christmas. She'd become Cameron's wife. No other gift could ever top this. The realization still brought her to a sudden halt. She might be grocery shopping or filling up at a gas station. *Mrs. Cameron Bennett.* She practiced writing it on her notepad, just to make it more real. Gazing at the name, her head spun.

When her mother called full of apologies about the wedding dress, Harper had to work at sounding disappointed. She'd be picking the dress up at Bleubelle's soon.

"All these years I've been thinking one of my girls would be married in that dress, feeling as happy as when I married your father," her mother lamented during their phone call.

"Oh, I am, Mom. No problem with that. I am happy. You know that." But the happiness would have nothing to do with a dress. Not really. Her joy had everything to do with the man.

"Of course, dear. Of course you'd say that."

Travel plans were shaping up. Most of the Kirkpatricks had a family tradition of alternating holidays with their in-laws, which had always seemed fair and right. When Malcolm and Mark sent their regrets, it wasn't a total surprise. They both had children and busy lives. "But we'll see you soon, won't we?" Malcolm asked.

"There's talk of a party in Chicago. You know, when the ice floes melt."

"Don't laugh, Harper. We had another snow emergency last night."

"Good lord." With each day, she felt more relieved that the wedding would be in Savannah.

The Saturday of Christie's birthday party came. Harper took Bella to her friend's, looking so pretty in a new red dress, a plaid headband holding back her dark hair. The gold-wrapped gift on her lap held a container of giant pop pearls. "Have a great time," she said, walking her to the door. "And don't forget to thank Christie's mother."

A wave of relief washed over her as she drove home. Her role as a nanny had given her a taste of what it felt like to be a parent. Is this how her mother had felt when they were growing up in Oak Park? Was her heart in her mouth every time she sent them out into the world? If kids were mean or they didn't get picked to play on the volleyball team, did her mother's heart sink? Being a parent had its downside. Harper could see that now. But Bella and Cameron were definitely worth it.

"You'll make a great mom," Cameron said when she raced up the back stairs and burst into the kitchen, eager to return to her decorating.

"Really?" But they'd never talked about any family plans. Maybe they should. "How would you, ah, feel about that part of it?"

"You make it sound like homework, Harper," he teased.

"The idea is just new, I guess."

"Hold that thought." He kissed her on the nose. "No need to rush anything."

When she went to pick Bella up, she was so relieved to see her happy smile. "Christie's mom wants to make a playdate with us," Bella announced as she snapped her own seatbelt. Bella was growing up. "She's gonna call you. I gave her our phone number. And she has a new baby brother."

"Oh?" This was news, but then the school was new for them. Pulling away from the curb, she slowly started home.

"Yeah, they just picked him up."

Laughter bubbled in Harper's throat but she swallowed it fast. This was too good to miss.

"He was crying," Bella continued. "Real loud. But Christie's daddy took care of him. I guess just like Daddy took care of me when I was a baby. Right?"

Smiling at her charge in the rearview mirror, Harper said, "Right." Imagining Cameron coping with a crying baby touched a tender part of her heart.

"A playdate," Harper told Cameron later. "We're coming up in the world."

"Glad to hear it." He gave her a rueful smile. "And thanks for being the chauffeur. I hate to unload all this on you, darlin'."

"Aren't we a team?" Harper didn't mention the baby brother to Cameron. They'd decided to table that, which was probably smart thinking. She had enough on her plate, building her new business, and so did he.

When Cameron came through the door the following Monday, he seemed to bring a wave of fresh pine with him. Bella came barreling from the foyer where she'd been playing with Pipsqueak, who followed, chasing a pinecone down the hall with her nose. "I've got a surprise for you, Bella," Cameron announced with a sparkle in his eyes.

"What is it?" Her daddy always had good surprises.

Stepping aside, he held the door wide. Rick and one of the other guys from Cameron's crews were lugging a huge pine tree up the steps. The sheer size of it left Harper in awe. It took some maneuvering to fit the monster tree through the french doors, leading from the verandah into the family room.

"And here I thought I'd be going up to the attic soon to bring down the artificial tree," she murmured.

"Hey, girl." Cameron's brows drew together. "Have faith in your man, please."

Running her fingers over the soft, full needles, she was taken back to the magical days when her brothers and McKenna would help her dad set the tree in the stand. It took forever to decide how to angle it to hide bare spots, which were always few. And then they wired it to the wall, just to be sure, before arguing about which ornament went where.

"The parlor's down the hall, guys, on the right." Cameron directed them. After they'd moved past, Harper pulled him into a pantry for a private moment. "You know you're wonderful, right?"

"Yeah. Sure," he said with a cocky grin. "But I like hearing it."

She gave him a quick kiss before pushing him back toward the action. "Don't let it go to your head, Boss Man."

The look he shot over his shoulder gave her shivers.

Watching him disappear down the hall, Harper sent a quick SOS text to Julep. *Do Patricia and her crew have any time to help with massive tree decorating?*

No problem. I'm on it. And sure enough, the following day Julep pulled up with Patricia and two young women who looked as if they could get this job done. Although Myra came once every other week to do the serious cleaning with Connie, they needed a bigger team for the tree.

"Connie, I think our decorating reinforcements have arrived," Harper said peeking from the kitchen window.

"Thank goodness. That is the biggest tree I've ever seen." Connie shook her head. "Jack said it looks like it's growing right through the ceiling."

Of course, Julep had brought even more decorations for the doorways, the powder rooms and a million other places that Harper hadn't had time to consider yet.

"Hey, you're good at this, Julep." She looked at her friend with new respect when she stopped in the first floor powder room under the main staircase. The small narrow room had been transformed into a winter wonderland, its shelves and counter filled with musical snow globes.

"You think so, sugga?" With glittery silver garland twirled around each arm, Julep looked like a pregnant Mother Christmas as she showed one of the girls how to loop the wiry strings over the powder room lights.

"Absolutely. Maybe one day I'll need a partner in my business. What do you think?"

Tilting her head, Julep chuckled. "That all depends on the benefits."

"Maybe some sangria once you have that baby. You know, so you wouldn't be so introverted."

"Right, that's me." And she gave Harper one of her saucy winks.

The activity in the house felt good, but there was one task Harper had been putting off. Grabbing her folder from the hall table, she looked for Connie, who was arranging a crèche set with Bella in the library. Harper crooked a finger. "Connie, can I have a word with you?"

"Sure." Handing a wiseman figurine to Bella, Connie wiped her hands on her apron and followed her to the kitchen. Harper took a deep breath. From the first moment she stepped into this mansion for that bachelor party, she'd had a special relationship with Connie. She sure didn't want to screw it up now.

Since she hadn't heard from Esther, she felt a lot might depend on settling the menu. Maybe Esther was waiting for some word from them. All this tiptoeing around was getting on Harper's nerves. "We've asked Cameron's mother to, ah, be a part of the wedding."

"Wonderful. What a good idea. So they're coming?"

Harper licked her dry lips. "Yes, I hope so. I thought if Mrs. Blodgett was involved in the menu..."

Connie looked at her as if she were speaking a different language. "You don't trust me?"

"Of course we trust you. It's just that, well, I'm in a pickle." Connie's frown wasn't something she saw very often. "I'm afraid Cameron's relatives won't come unless his mother feels she has to be here to help. My back is against a wall."

Happy chatter drifted down the hall while Harper started to sweat. The look on her housekeeper's face told Harper she was walking on eggshells.

Harper handed her the list as if it might be radioactive.

Face flushing, Connie bit her lower lip. She must be holding back words with that bite.

Fumbling around, Harper flipped through her copy of Esther's suggested menu, where she'd jotted down notes. "And Julep suggested we add hush puppies."

"Another deep-fried dish at a wedding?" She threw Harper a cautious look as if asking her to see some sense.

The list of southern dishes might not be the usual wedding fare, but it sure looked better than tarragon chicken. Harper had to acknowledge it was different. Could she take some things off without hurting Esther's feelings?

"Do you know how much those big fryers smell up the house when you do a deep-fried turkey? It's not like roasting it in the oven where it smells so good." Obviously Connie had strong feelings about this. Cameron had been right.

Inhaling the scent of pine from that wonderful Christmas tree, Harper wondered. "Is it that terrible?"

Connie's nose twitched. "Cream of roasted garlic soup, barbecued ribs, deep-fried chicken, spicy hot black-eyed peas. Hoppin' Johnny cakes?" Her voice slowed.

Taking a pen, Harper scratched that one off. "Oh, Connie, she could never make hoppin' Johnny cakes as good as yours. Let's forget about that one."

"Cheesy cornbread. Coconut cake. Banana pudding?" Connie's voice rose.

Harper gave a silent groan. Seemed like trying to please everyone, she wasn't making anyone happy. "We wanted to have a lowcountry meal, Connie. I thought it would be nice if my family tasted southern cooking."

Lordy, she was digging herself into a hole. If that was all her family wanted—a lowcountry menu—they could just come and visit. Connie would cook a fabulous meal. Seconds ticked by, although the hands of the clock on the wall didn't seem to move.

Taking a deep breath, Connie finally said, "Everyone has a different recipe for Mississippi mud cake or red velvet cake." Now wasn't the time to tell Connie that most of these entrées did not have written recipes.

Searching desperately for a diversion, Harper said, "Do you think we can put that deep fryer out on the veranda or in the garden?"

Eyes sliding to the window, Connie muttered, "I'll have to ask Jack where it will be safe." She said it as if Harper had suggested putting a cannon in the yard.

"I'd appreciate your help," Harper managed to squeak out.

Connie's attention fell back to the list. "Some good selections here, I guess. I do like okra and shrimp gumbo."

"Well, good. I'm glad you agree." Usually Connie was her biggest ally. Facing off with her felt uncomfortable.

"Anybody can make biscuits," she huffed, sliding the list onto the counter.

"Now I understand the problems Lincoln had in the 1800s," Harper told Cameron that night when she was cleaning up the kitchen.

"Food is a regional thing. Every pocket in the South cooks differently," Cameron said. "I'm amazed that Mama sent you a list.

That's saying something. Maybe she is thinking of stopping by."

"It came from Lily." No way was she portraying his mother as cooperative when she still hadn't even RSVP'd for the wedding. Her stomach was tumbling. "Just looking at the menu makes my stomach feel a bit tippy. Barbecued cashews? Never heard of them. Boiled peanuts. Tried 'em once. Not at the top of my list."

Coming up behind her, Cameron laced his arms around her waist. Her fingers traced the tendons in his biceps. Connie had gone home, and they'd finished a quick dinner of ham leftovers. Harper never realized a ham could stretch this far. She had to learn how to bake one. Suddenly they heard a strange sound out in the hallway. "What the heck?" She turned toward Cameron.

They both rushed from the kitchen—well as fast as Cameron could rush— to find Bella speeding toward them on the knee walker. "Look what I found in the hall closet!"

Just what Harper needed. Glancing over, she sent Cameron the look. "You never did tell me where you put that thing."

Looking oh so innocent, Cameron shifted his shoulders. "Connie must've stowed it there. Glad someone found use for it." Mischief glinted in his eyes. He must be feeling better.

Cameron turned back to Bella, her eyes glowing with her discovery. "Best two out of three. I'll race you." Disappearing into the library, he reappeared with some kind of stopwatch and handed it to Harper.

"Sometimes I think you're never going to grow up," she murmured, taking her place at the end of the hall.

"Sometimes I think you like that."

He knew her way too well. "Ready?" She clicked the stopwatch.

Chapter 18

A few days later, Harper cornered Cameron after Rick dropped him off. Usually he loved to find her waiting for him. But usually she was smiling. This time her face was stormy. "I have to ask you. Is your mother coming or not?" Sliding a finger into a rip in her jeans, she looked upset. Watching Harper twist that finger through one of the shabby tears now fashionable, he couldn't help thinking about the soft skin under those jeans.

"Cameron? Are you listening?"

Slinging his briefcase onto the nearest chair, he cleared his mind. With her hair in pigtails and that sweatshirt slipping off one shoulder, she looked terminally cute, as if she were eighteen again. He wished he'd known her then. Maybe someday, they'd have little girls who looked just like her.

Whoa. Head spinning, he gripped the nearest chair.

"Hey, you okay?"

Brushing her soft cheek with his knuckles, he said, "Yeah, I'm fine."

Thinking about little Harpers had felt scary but exciting. "I heard you and Connie talking about the meal and thought it was a done deal."

Standing there wringing her hands, Harper said, "I don't want to say anything negative about your family, Cameron. But when it comes to your mother and siblings, I can't take anything for granted." And she turned those pretty greenish-brown eyes to him in appeal.

She was right. They were running out of time. Plans were being made. Why, Connie had sent Jack over to the hardware store for one of those mammoth deep fryers. Right now, it was taking up way too much room in his garage. Time to settle things.

Rocking back on his good heel, he took out his phone and gave Harper a confident smile that only felt skin deep. She still looked skeptical. Darn thing rang and rang and he started to count, relieved when Mama picked up at fourteen.

"Hello?" Her voice sounded tentative, as if she wondered if the darn thing really worked.

"Mama, it's me. Cameron. Why does it take fourteen rings for you to pick up?"

"Oh, did it now?"

"Yes, it did."

"The sales people usually stop calling at five," she said begrudgingly. "I want to know there's a live person."

"Well, they could be dead by the time you say hello."

Harper put a hand over her mouth.

"I just want those darn people selling stuff to forget I live here. How dare they call me when I don't even know them."

That sounded so much like his mother that he burst out laughing. "Mama, I've got Harper here so I'm going to put you on speakerphone." His darlin' bride looked like she just might faint.

Hands pulling at her neckline like Bella, she said, "Hello, Mrs. Blodgett."

Cameron rolled his eyes. That whole name thing annoyed him. "Hello, Harper. I trust you're well?"

This was definitely going to be a sit-down conversation, and he took a chair. "Mama, we were just wondering if everything is set now. You and the family are coming to the wedding, right?"

"Well it is Christmas Eve, you know."

He pressed his fingertips into his closed eyelids. "Yes, it is Christmas Eve. December twenty-fourth and that's when the wedding will be. I think you received a revised invitation?"

"Yes, yes, I did."

"Are you saying you might have other plans?" Now that would be a first. As far back as he could remember, Christmas Eve was just like every other day in their house, except that his mother insisted his father go to church. They'd have a standoff. His father would come up with some lame excuse, like helping a friend out with a broken truck. But from the shape he was in when they got home from church, he'd been back in the woods at the still. That was just Homer Blodgett through and through. He'd ruined every damn Christmas in Cameron's memory.

"But where would we stay?" his mother asked.

Harper nudged the phone closer to herself. "We have two guestrooms on the second floor," she said. "Those would be nice for you, Lily and her husband."

Anticipating this issue, Cameron had asked Rick to work on it. "And as for Henry and Fred, one of my men has lined up some rental homes…"

"Sounds expensive."

"Let me finish. Some of my clients who have rentals not being used are lending me their homes." That was pretty close to the truth.

His mother sucked in a breath. "Well then, I'll have to check with them."

Harper had grabbed a list from the counter and waved it as if his mother could see it. "And I want you to know that Connie said the menu was fine."

"Oh she did, did she?" The sharp edge was back in his mother's voice, and he hated to see Harper squirm.

"I mean, she thought it was just fine." Trooper that she was, Harper kept in the game. Cameron gave her a thumbs up. "I did add just a couple of things. Items that you may have forgotten…"

"I'm not known for forgetting things."

Good God. Cameron slid lower in his chair. Reaching over, Harper patted his hand. "No, I'm sure you're not. I always remember that wonderful spread you had when, well, your husband passed away…" Okay, Harper looked like she wanted to choke those words back. But he loved the way his honey spoke her mind, even when it got her into trouble. Reaching out, he explored one of those torn places in her jeans.

Turning back the corners of the list, Harper said, "I wonder if you and Lily could send us a list of the ingredients? You know, anything unusual. I want to make sure our pantry has what we need on that day." She swatted at his hand.

"Why, there's nothing on that list that's unusual. Not for an experienced cook."

Cameron had to cover his eyes with the hand that was free. Thank God Connie had gone home for the day. "Mama, you can send that list to my email."

Silence. Harper glanced down and he nodded to tell her everything was all right. He was just glad that she hadn't met his family at very beginning, before she worked her miracle with Bella, before he'd fallen in love with her. She might have turned tail and run.

"Thank you for doing that, Mama."

But Harper needed more. He could see it on her pale face. Forgetting his boyish fantasies for a moment, he smoothed her jeans with both hands. "Then you will be coming, Mrs. Blodgett?" She leaned over the phone, her body like a question mark.

"Why, yes. Of course. Just one more thing. How fancy will this be?" Had that been the problem all along? His mother was worried about what to wear?

"Just wear that red sweater you wear every Christmas."

"That old thing?" Mama didn't sound convinced.

"You look beautiful in it." Lily had given her a beaded sweater one holiday season. She wore it proudly every year. Had some kind of bird on it. "After all, this is a Christmas wedding."

"Well, all right, son. Then I guess it's all settled."

Harper pumped a fist, the color flooding back into her face. When they all said good-bye, Cameron felt as if they'd just wrapped up a summit conference in Geneva.

Soaked through, his shirt felt clammy. "Look at me," he said, standing up and pulling the damp material away from his body. "You'd think I'd been laying bricks."

"Well it's your family," Harper said with a laugh. Then a strange look came over her face. "But it's going to be mine."

"Does it scare you?" Encircling her with his arms, he wanted to protect her.

"Sometimes." Knotting her fingers on his chest, she looked lost.

"Do I scare you, sugga?"

Her face relaxed. "Are you kidding?"

She looked so darn cute. He bent to kiss the lips that had sealed a deal with his mother. He was getting cozy, thinking about those jeans again, when she pushed away. "Eeew. You're all sweaty."

"So that's how it is, darlin'?" Rocking her in his arms, he whispered, "Oh, I remember when you told me you liked sweaty."

There was that lip nipping going on again. The pinch zinged right from her lips to certain parts of his body. "I think working on the wedding thing with you is making me hot."

"Oh, is that why you're sweaty?" Her eyes opened in mock innocence, and he tightened his hold.

"Maybe. Maybe not. Where's Bella?"

That coy smile came as she played with his top button before sliding it open. "She has a playdate with Christie."

"Oh, how will we spend the time?" he whispered, lips traveling over her soft cheeks.

"I've got some ideas."

Chapter 19

Julep asked to go with Harper to pick up the dress. "I think we should make a party of this," she told Harper. "A cause for celebration." Sounded good to Harper. While she waited for Julep to pick her up, she studied the list of ingredients that Cameron's mother had sent.

"But there's nothing that special here," Connie had said adjusting her glasses. "Brown sugar, mustard, red beans. There must be more to this."

"Cameron's family will be here a couple days before the wedding. If there's something that we don't have, I can just run out and get it."

Why had Harper ever started this? But at least the Blodgetts were coming to the wedding. Glancing through the kitchen window, Harper saw Julep pull into the driveway in her black Mercedes. "I wish I could help you out, Connie. Really I do. But you know me. Toasting bread is a big deal for some of us. Gotta run." She grabbed her handbag. "Final fitting today. Will you be able to pick up Bella at three if I don't make it home in time? Julep said something about a late lunch."

"Of course. You have fun now. You only get to have one wedding dress in your lifetime." Connie shook her head. "I mean for most of us."

Straightening her red headband, Harper dashed out the door. The December day felt crisp, and she tipped her face into the sunlight. With any luck, their wedding day would be just this golden.

Hurrying through the garden, Harper noticed that Jack had done a great job of trimming bushes and pulling weeds. She almost missed the wreath of magnolia leaves around the mermaid's neck as she hurried past. Rick's crew had wound garland over the wrought iron railings on all the verandahs. A crew was coming tomorrow to wash the windows inside and out. After that, an artificial candle would be put in each window of the house. She couldn't wait to see that.

If this weather held, they might be able to have the wedding party outside. Extraordinary Celebrations would be setting up a tent out here that could seat seventy guests. But she didn't know about the actual ceremony. After all, the tree was in the parlor, and the wide doorway offered a view from the other rooms.

"Don't you look pretty today," Julep said, giving her a once-over when Harper slid into the car. "I'm loving your red leather jacket. The ruffles on the black skirt might look innocent if it weren't for those high black boots."

"Me? Innocent?" Harper smoothed a hand over the ruffles scattered with embroidered holly leaves. "Julep I can't wait to see my dress again."

"I don't blame you. We should have snapped a picture of you in it that day with our phones. You looked so gorgeous." The tires squealed and took a tight turn onto Victory Parkway. "How are all the plans coming?"

Feeling a little dizzy, Harper expelled a sigh. "Our lists have lists. Sticky notes everywhere. Connie is all flustered about Mrs. Blodgett's list for the menu."

"How did she take it?" Julep asked.

"Not well but we smoothed things over, I think. At least the family is definitely coming now."

"So it's really going to be a lowcountry wedding? How yummy."

"You bet. A lowcountry Christmas wedding. Pinch me. Three years ago, I never would have believed this. Billy Colton—my old boyfriend—can just kiss my grits."

"I've got something exciting to tell you," Julep said, her eyes sparkling.

Harper loved being with this woman who found joy everywhere she went. "Tell me."

"Now that you're having the wedding right here, I told Tuck we absolutely had to come."

Harbor squealed with delight. "That makes me so happy. If you weren't driving, I'd reach over and hug you." It just seemed like the wedding got better and better every day. All their troubles and uncertainties had been put behind them. She could exhale and enjoy everything.

"I told him we can just drive up to Vidalia on Christmas morning. One day with the clan will be plenty."

Then it hit her. "But Julep. I stole your Christmas."

"You did not. Whatever are you talking about, girl?"

They were driving down Victory, and on either side were homes and businesses decked out for the holidays.

"No, really," Harper continued, the holiday glitz making her feel downright guilty. "You let me have all those tubs of decorations, the ones I'd planned for your house."

But Julep gave her head a playful shake. "Oh, darlin'. You got that all wrong. Let's think of it this way. You stole those decorations from Georgina Darlington, not me." Harper had never heard Julep cackle before but she joined right in.

"Besides, I can just share your decorations while I'm there. You've saved me the trouble of taking everything down. I always hate that part." One manicured hand fluttered in the air, and Harper didn't miss the green nails with the holly berries on the tips.

"Now, where are you two going on your honeymoon?" Julep asked. "I never did ask you? The Bahamas? The Caymans?"

"We decided we'd wait a little while. You know, until Cameron has rehab for his ankle. Seems like we'd be asking for trouble having him heave luggage around or doing a lot of touristy walking."

Julep shot her a wicked look. "Well, honey, if your husband's like mine you won't be enjoying the sites during your honeymoon. If you do, there is definitely something wrong." They both burst out laughing.

"Hey, I have a great idea." Julep got another one of her conniving looks. "Why don't you just give Connie the week off, and Bella can stay with us. I mean, if she's willing. Just think about it."

Harper didn't know how Bella would feel about that, but the idea of having Cameron alone for one week made her weak in the knees. "Thanks, Julep. Let me run it past Cameron. You are so sweet."

They were still chuckling when they entered Bleubelle's ten minutes later.

A younger woman and her mother were looking at dresses. For a second, Harper wished her own family could have been here for that—at least her mother and McKenna. But she had made a choice. And when she chose Cameron, she chose Savannah. That much was clear to her now.

Courtney came hurrying out from the back, dressed smartly in a well-cut navy dress that sure didn't come off the rack. "Your gown is waiting for you, Harper. Let me show you to the dressing room. I think you're going to love it."

And as she looked at herself in the three-way mirror a few minutes later, Harper felt transported.

"How are you going to wear your hair that day?" Julep asked from where she sat in a velveteen club chair.

Twisting a shank of her long hair up, Harper turned her head this way and that. "What do you think?"

"Very much the sophisticated bride," Julep said with approval. "Besides, that neck of yours goes on forever. Show it off."

The overhead lights made her skin glow. "Cameron does like my neck." Did she say that out loud? The surprised look on Julep's face told her that she had. And she flushed. "That is, I'll talk it over with Adam. He's doing our hair that morning."

She'd chosen a simple veil that fell just to her shoulders, and Courtney perched it on her head now for the full effect. The white satin heels she'd picked up at Belk's completed the picture. When she played dress-up with her friends years ago, they all talked about what they'd wear when they were a bride. But the reality brought a lump to her throat.

Smoothing her hands over the bodice, she cinched them at her waist and took stock of herself in the mirror. "One good thing about this dress is that it makes me look buxom," she said with approval. "I just feel different."

Julep only nodded and smiled. "It's a good cut on you."

After they stowed the wrapped gown carefully in Julep's car, they decided to have lunch at Bonefish Grill, only a couple doors down.

"My appetite's off," Harper told her friend, patting her tummy as she surveyed the menu. It all looked like so much food. "Maybe just a salad."

She glanced up to find Julep studying her over the menu. "Have you been nauseated lately?"

"Yeah, I think I still have a touch of that flu or sinus infection. You know, whatever Bella had at Thanksgiving. Maybe it's all the excitement." Setting the menu aside, she decided to order a salmon salad, even though she really didn't feel like eating it.

The waitress brought their iced tea and took their orders. But Julep had fallen quiet— really unusual for her. "Something wrong?" Harper asked. "You okay?"

"This is absolutely none of my business," Julep said with some hesitation. "But I'm always poking my nose in other people's business. You don't think you could be pregnant, do you?"

Setting her glass down with a thump, Harper choked. After the coughing spell was over, she fixed her friend with an indignant stare. "Absolutely not. What would make you say that?"

Julep fiddled with the back of her hair. "As I said, this is none of my business. But yes, you are very buxom, and I don't recall having that impression before. For me, the minute I got pregnant, the estrogen started pumping. For a while, Tuck was quite pleased. You know, before my tummy outgrew my boobs. And the nausea also started like that." And she snapped her fingers.

Harper was so glad that they were in a booth because this conversation had turned very personal. "I do feel different," she said slowly, thinking back and counting days. "And I don't have any appetite. I just figured it was the wedding and all."

The waitress brought the salads, and Julep began to eat. But Harper played with her fork, breaking up the salmon that she just couldn't eat. She didn't even know where the bathroom was here. That had become critical these last few days. Lots of trips to the bathroom.

Looking over at her, Julep said, "I hope I didn't upset you. Me and my big mouth. The only reason I even mentioned it is that I was pregnant about two days before I started to see my figure start to change. And I had absolutely no appetite for the next three months. But that all went away, and I've been starving since then. That's the benefit of being pregnant. Fat is okay."

This just could not be. "But I'm on the pill."

Julep gave her a crooked grin. "A lot of women are on the pill, Harper. But a lot of women still get pregnant, unfortunately. You know, not a ton but just enough to make things interesting. Didn't you tell me you were on antibiotics for a while?"

"Sure but only for ten days or so."

Julep held up a finger. "Only takes once. Think I read antibiotics can contribute to the failure rate of the pill."

The fork Harper had been playing with clattered to her plate.

"Everything all right here?" Their waitress appeared at her elbow, but Harper was numb.

"I think we're fine," Julep told the waitress. "Just fine."

"I hope I didn't upset you, Harper." Julep said finally, while Harper's mind was working through a hundred what-ifs. How would Cameron feel about this? What had he said? They'd "table this." Boy, she'd made some mistakes in her life, but this? This could be epic. Excitement prickled underneath her shock.

A baby. Their baby.

"You're so quiet," Julep said when the waitress brought their checks. "I never should've brought this up. Really bad timing on my part." She gave a pointed look at the salmon salad that Harper hadn't even touched.

"No, I'm not sorry, Julep. Just stunned. I need to find out." Taking a deep breath, Harper tried to steady her beating heart.

"How about a little Christmas shopping then?"

Although she was tired, she loved being with Julep. And she sure didn't want her to think she was going home to sulk. For the next half-hour, they trailed through shops, where of course Harper could not resist buying more Christmas baubles. That house was so huge. Everywhere she looked, there was another shelf, small table or alcove that seemed to need a bit of holiday joy. "Whatever is this?" Harper plucked a sparkly green pickle from a tree in one of the gift shops.

Dangling the glazed pickle from a finger, Julep chuckled. "You didn't have this tradition in Chicago? Whoever finds the hidden pickle on your Christmas tree gets a special gift."

"Amazing. I'll take it," Harper told the sales girl. For a lot of reasons, Christmas would always be her favorite time of year. And this year, they were making so many memories. After all, their anniversary would be on Christmas Eve.

Good thing the delicate ornament was already on the counter or she might have dropped it. Julep snapped up a few ornaments, and they were on their way back to the car. Still feeling dazed, Harper didn't say much on the way home. Her mind was too busy, and she couldn't carry on two conversations at once. When they pulled up to the house, Julep helped Harper lift her dress carefully from the back. "What a fun day," Harper told Julep. "A day to remember."

But her friend could hardly look at her. "You'll probably remember this as the day I made you worry needlessly. Harper, I feel just terrible about that."

"Don't, Julep. This is the season when everybody should feel happy and grateful, right?"

"Oh, sugga, I'd hug you but I don't want to crush that beautiful dress. I am so glad you're my friend."

"But I have to run." Being careful with the dress so she didn't snag it on a thorny bush or drag it through the mud, which would've been so like her, Harper headed for the house. It was no small feat to get her keys out and get through the door. The house felt quiet. Connie must have left for the day. A note on the table said that Cameron had walked Bella over to Daffin Park. Terrific. She was panting by the time she got the dress up to the third floor. She would let Bella see the dress when the right time came. And then she was back downstairs dashing for her car. She had one more errand before Cameron and Bella came home.

Chapter 20

When Cameron got home from work that night, he was bushed. Sure, his ankle was feeling better, but he was so over this walking cast. He hated having to depend on Rick and the other guys for rides to sites. But Dr. Welch was pretty sure it could be removed next week before the ceremony.

After he dragged himself up the stairs and opened the kitchen door, he stopped dead in his tracks. Bless her heart, Connie was making his favorite pork roast. He sniffed the tantalizing smell mixed with pine. This Christmas the house smelled so damn good, so homey. All because of Harper.

With the kitchen this quiet, no one seemed to be around. Tossing his briefcase onto a kitchen chair, he lifted the cover of the slow cooker. Yep, and Connie would probably make gravy to go with it. Potatoes, onions and cauliflower were cut up and ready to be roasted. Harper had tried cooking. He smiled, remembering her efforts and how he'd choked them down. She'd never be a "Martha," as she put it. Fine with him.

He smoothed a hand over the list Lily had sent. The menu had become like a war map. Why had Harper asked his mother to help plan the food for the wedding? Flipping through the pages, he noticed Harper's handwriting and smiled. She'd scrawled Mrs.

Cameron Bennett about fifteen times in different angles, playing with the C and the B. That sweet thing. She must have been doodling while she was on the phone. Seeing his name with the Mrs. in her handwriting brought a lump to his throat. He pushed the list back where he'd found it.

The house might be quiet now, but it sure wouldn't be quiet next week. Not after his family arrived, and from what he understood, they would be first on the scene. Grabbing his briefcase, he headed for the hallway where the smell of pine grew stronger. All the decorations and doodads that Harper and her crew had scattered around sure dressed up the place. You couldn't move without running into an angel or an elf. And then there was the tree. Towering to the ceiling, with ribbons cascading down from a Christmas angel over a mess of ornaments, icicles and silver baubles, it could have graced a department store. It was just that grand.

He glanced around the parlor. Problem was, all the glitter and glitz made the furniture look dated. The mansion was a show piece, not a family home. Bella's Christmas coloring book and her box of crayons looked like they didn't belong. How had he missed that? To see Pipsqueak stretched out on a Victorian sofa was hilarious. Even the dog looked uncomfortable. Of course, she wasn't allowed on the furniture, but like Bella and Harper, the dog made her own rules. He was seriously outnumbered.

"Anybody home?"

Somewhere a vacuum was buzzing. Usually Myra took care of the heavy cleaning, but Connie often ran the vacuum. The mail was set out on the side table, and he leafed through bills, more bills and some magazines that he set aside. Some pieces that looked like advertising had Harper's name on them, and he stared at the envelopes. Not too long, and her name would be Harper Bennett. Maybe his curious sense of pride was silly.

Vacuum in hand, Connie appeared in the parlor doorway. Frizzy curls escaping from a topknot, she looked done in.

"You fixed my favorite dinner."

"Right." Her glance flicked toward the stairway. "But I don't think it's Harper's favorite. She came in the door with her wedding dress, took one sniff and headed for the stairway." Connie looked hurt.

"Maybe she was just in a hurry. Wanted to hang up her dress." What the hell did he know? He sure hoped she wasn't getting the flu again. "Where's Bella?"

"Up in her room, comforting Pipsqueak." Looking defensive, Connie drew herself up. "Okay, I yelled at her. She gets all excited and that tail of hers knocks ornaments off the tree. They're expensive. Harper's friend Julep bought a lot of these."

"Can't we put the inexpensive ornaments on the lower branches?"

His housekeeper turned a stern gaze on him. "I'll put that on my list."

With the wedding switched to Savannah, she had a lot on her plate. Connie liked a reliable schedule and that had been blown to bits. Having people stay in the house hadn't helped but Harper had insisted. "They're family," she'd said with that glint in her eye.

Some days he thought this was a terrific idea, and other days he wondered what they'd gotten themselves into. Tonight he'd sit Harper down, and they'd go through everything that still had to be done.

Connie headed back to the kitchen, and he continued into the library taking the mail with him. Throwing it onto his desk, he set his briefcase on the chair, anxious to talk to Harper.

Able to handle the steps now, he carefully made his way upstairs, slowing when he heard Bella's voice. She was learning how to read, and the tale she was spinning sounded kind of like Snow White. Must be her own version of the fairytale. "And they lived happily ever after," he heard her say in that decisive manner she'd picked up from Harper. "Pipsqueak, you be good and I'll read Cinderella now." Yep, she was making all this up. A tiny yip and Bella began, the dog her captive audience.

Harper always kept the door to the third floor open. That had endeared her to him right off the bat. Seemed like so long ago, but the other nannies had closed that door every night. Not Harper, she wanted to hear any peep Bella might make. Taking the stairs, he detected her scent. One whiff and his whole body kicked in. The way she smelled, how her hair felt, the way her body moved—there was nothing he didn't love about the girl.

Maybe she was getting the three upstairs guest rooms ready for her family. They were going to stay up here, along with Harper in her room. How they would all use that one bathroom was beyond him, but she had assured him it was possible. "When I was growing up, we had one bathroom, Cameron, until my dad added on the family room." And she was kind enough not to remind him that he hadn't grown up with a lot of bathrooms either.

Peeking into her room, he found it empty. "Harper?"

"I'll be right out." Her muffled voice came from the bathroom.

Going to the window and pushing the filmy drape aside, he looked down at the garden that would be transformed in a week. Extraordinary Celebrations would set up their tents and work their magic. Thank goodness, the yard was large enough that the turkey fryer his mother had insisted on could be set off in a corner, roped off as a safety precaution. After all, there would be children there.

The soft footsteps on the pink carpet made him turn. "Hey," he said and stopped. Her eyes were red and her lips trembled. "What is it? Did my mother call again?"

With a shake of her head, she grabbed a tissue. "No. It's not your mother." And she looked at him in a strange way, like she had bad news and didn't want to deliver it.

"Out with it. It couldn't be that bad, could it?" Coming closer, he took her in his arms but felt the tension in her body.

Tipping her head to one side, she gave a shuddering sigh. "That all depends."

"On what?" This wasn't like her.

"Cameron, I think I'm pregnant."

The words echoed in his brain as if they were in a sound chamber. "What? What did you just say?" Heart pumping, he held her away, wanting to see her face while she said the words.

She opened her hands palm up. "I know, I know. You said you wanted to table it. Hold off for a while. I don't know what happened. Julep told me I looked different. I got the test at the drugstore."

Cameron felt as if he'd been zapped in an electrical storm. Emotions charged through him before settling in his stomach in a warm ball that rolled up to his smile. "Darlin'. Love of my life. Why are you crying?"

"Because the timing is so bad…and I can't keep anything down. And…" When her eyes flicked up to him, her long lashes formed wet peaks. "Because I thought you'd be mad."

"Mad?" He felt like climbing onto the roof, beating his chest and telling the world. "I am the most excited man on the planet right now. Aren't you excited?"

A smile finally finding her lips, she nodded. "Yes, I am. But bad timing, right?"

"I don't give a damn about timing. Is that why you don't feel well?"

"From what Julep tells me, this goes on for three months. Can you imagine?" Her amazement made him chuckle. Bad move.

"But how?" His mind spun back.

"The antibiotics." She looked crestfallen. "Another one of my mess-ups. That first week, you know, after Thanksgiving."

He thought back and smiled. "Good times. Totally worth it."

"But it's such bad timing…" To stop the complaining, he sealed his lips over hers. She tasted sweet, like toothpaste and mouthwash and something else he couldn't identify. She was going to become his wife, but suddenly he didn't know how to hold her.

Pulling away, she frowned. "Hey, what's up with you?"

"What do you mean?" He'd seen this expression before. Pure exasperation.

She cuffed his shoulder. "I'm not a piece of china. I'm not going to break."

Good to know. The first time he became a father was so long ago. He'd been so young. This time would be different. Better. "Oh, darlin'. I've got so much to learn."

"And I am just the girl to teach you. I think." For a second, uncertainty clouded her eyes.

"Yes, you definitely are." Cameron gave her a kiss that let her know she'd been kissed. Warm and wet. Slow and thorough. "Nothing's changed, babe," he whispered against her lips. "It all got better."

"You really mean that?"

Caught in a happy haze, they studied each other. "I really do."

Her smile widened. "Me too. Oh, Cameron, I am *so* excited."

Chapter 21

When Harper heard Mrs. Blodgett in the kitchen, there was no mistaking that flat, crushing monotone. Straightening her shoulders, she hoped she'd be able to control the nausea. Thinking back to playing dress-up in grade school, she didn't know one girl at St. Edmund Grade School who dreamed of being a pregnant bride. That hadn't been in the plan. But here she was, thrilled beyond belief despite the upset tummy. They'd decided not to share this latest development. "The wedding ceremony is the main event," Cameron told her. "That and Christmas. Let's keep our other news for another special announcement."

"Is it, Cameron, really?'

He gave her that sweet, endearing grin. "It sure is, darlin'. Hiring the Goodyear blimp to trail a sign across the sky wouldn't come close to being enough."

Coming down from the second floor, she smiled remembering that conversation. She'd done a final check of the guest rooms. Apparently, Cameron was giving his mother a tour. She could hear Lily exclaiming about the Christmas decorations. When they reached the parlor, just as Harper reached the bottom of the stairs, there was a general gasp. "Just like a department store," Mrs. Blodgett exclaimed. "Isn't it, Lily?"

Harper grabbed the newel post. Tugging at the hem of her bright red skirt, she smoothed her black top and adjusted the holly headband. As she crossed the hall, one of Cameron's brothers said, "Now, Cameron, don't tell me you cut down that tree yourself."

The boisterous laughter quieted when she entered the room. Bella was pointing out her favorite ornaments. But all eyes turned to Harper, including Cameron's. His smile was pure encouragement and lit her up like a Christmas candle. Looking from her mother to Harper, Lily opened her arms. "And don't you look wonderful. We are so excited for both of you." Then she laughed. "Well, all three of you."

Her mind on the whole pregnancy thing, Harper thought Lily meant the baby. Had he told them after all? Her hand went to her stomach, but she caught Cameron's raised eyebrows. They were so in sync. Letting her hand fall, she turned to Mrs. Blodgett. "So nice to see you."

A brief nod and a quick hug. "Why you've had your hair done, Mrs. Blodgett. How nice it looks." It was hard to keep the amazement from her voice. The thought of Esther Blodgett entering a beauty salon was a leap for Harper.

"I convinced Mama to come with me," Lily explained, while Cameron's mother ran a hand over her bouffant hair-do.

"You look beautiful." Enjoying Esther's shy flush, Harper meant it as she turned to the rest of the family.

Sometimes Harper thought Henry and Fred looked like Cameron and other times she didn't. Hands down, when they were on the farm at Hazel Hurst dressed in their overalls, the family similarity was a stretch. But cleaned up in V-neck sweaters, khaki slacks and loafers, these two were completely different men. And she didn't miss the ruddy blush in their cheeks, as if they knew what she was thinking.

"You remember my husband Walt," Lily said, turning to her husband.

"Of course, how nice to see you again." When he went to shake her hand, Harper hugged him. The group seemed to shine and she was touched. For them, this trip to Savannah had been a big deal. For a second, she was ashamed that she hadn't realized that earlier. Chicago might have seemed as far away as the moon. No wonder Esther had hesitated.

After that awkward exchange, Cameron continued the tour of the house. Of course, Esther and Lily had seen it on earlier visits, but not Walt or the two brothers. Harper couldn't wait to relay their comments about the decorations to Julep.

And oh yes, Bella made sure that they saw everything. Every little figurine in each crèche set, each gilded star on the mantles. Harper never would have believed the powder room could fit six people. By the time Lily had wound up the third snow globe, perspiration was breaking out on the men's foreheads.

"Maybe your grandmother and Aunt Lily would like to see their rooms, Bella," Harper said. Bella gave her a frown until Harper added, "Want to show them *your* room first?"

With an excited giggle, Bella led the group up the stairs, chattering all the way. While Bella showed the Blodgetts her bedroom, Harper dashed back to the powder room. Surrounded by cinnamon potpourri and snow globes, she wondered if she should create another bout with the flu as an excuse for her tummy trouble. But she didn't want people fussing over her. Accessing the mouthwash and the toothpaste that she now kept in every bathroom drawer, she steadied herself and stepped out. Cameron was waiting. "Everything okay?"

"Perfect." The last thing she wanted was him hovering, although it was kind of sweet.

Since Cameron had planned to take his family on one of the trolley tours of Savannah, she didn't have to be too concerned about the Blodgetts today. The day before, Cameron had his cast taken off, so he was able to drive them around. The only tension came when Connie and Cameron's mother faced off in the kitchen. The rest of the family was upstairs when Harper came across the two women, both with copies of the list in their hands. Bless Connie's heart. Although very territorial about her kitchen, she was showing Esther what she had in the freezer. Together the two women planned what they would cook the next day. And neither one mentioned or brought out a recipe. How amazing.

"She's got a good start on it," Harper overheard Esther tell Lily when she joined them.

"Mama, I never doubted that she would."

"I'm taking Bella with us," Cameron told Harper, taking her chin in one hand while the others got their coats on. "You look like you need a nap."

"Very perceptive," she said as he kissed her.

After a tour of downtown Savannah, Cameron was going to

take his brothers to a house on Jones Street that would be their home for the next four days.

When he returned, Cameron had the strangest expression on his face. "You know, I think Henry and Fred are thinking of going out tonight."

The two of them were in the library alone. Cameron had picked up a dinner from Fresh Market, and his mother and Lily insisted on helping Connie serve it, with Bella's assistance. They seemed to think that the bride shouldn't lift a finger. Harper wasn't going to argue with that.

"Why shouldn't Henry and Fred go out? Wouldn't you be curious to see a new city?"

Cameron gave her this blank stare. "I just can't imagine my brothers out on the town."

Harper laughed at his expression. "You are still thinking of the farm boys you grew up with. Maybe they think of you that way too."

They both had plenty to consider as they walked into the dining room for dinner. Bella had brought out the Christmas placemats. And when Harper saw the green mats with holly appliqued in the corners, it took her back to a disastrous dinner when she first came. Cameron had asked Kimmy, his girlfriend, to join them. Connie was off that night. Eager to prove herself, Harper had mistakenly set the table with these Christmas placements. Of course, Kimmy called it to their attention. She was just like that.

Tonight everyone seemed tired, and the atmosphere may have been a little stilted. Still, it was a family meal. One where Cameron and his siblings shared stories that made their mother smile. Eventually, Harper trudged up to bed, exhausted but excited about the next day when her family would arrive. When she heard the knock on her bedroom door, she thought it was Cameron.

Turning, she was ready to read him the riot act. She made it plain that they would definitely be in their own bedrooms before the wedding. But opening the door she found, not Cameron but Bella. Eyes wide, she stood there in her blue Frozen nightgown. "Harper, I bet you forgot that you told me…"

The wedding gown. Of course. "I did forget, but you have to keep it a secret. You can't tell your dad what it looks like." When she opened the door to the closet, Bella's eyes got even wider. Still encased in protective plastic, the dress belonged in a fairy tale. Instead of the pink bouquet at the waist, Harper had replaced it with shiny magnolia leaves with sprigs of bright holly beads in the center.

"Just like mine," Bella said. "Right?"

"Kind of, yes." Bella's dress, which had been ordered online, was very similar. The skirt was layers of long silk organza, wired at the hem. At the waist was a small clutch of magnolia leaves with the bright berries. As flower girl, she'd carry a white basket of holly with the instructions not to toss any in the air because it could be prickly. That had been the only disappointment for Bella. Because they'd decided to have the ceremony inside, there would be no aisle, only the staircase.

"I can hardly wait," Bella told her, shivering with excitement. "I don't think I'll be able to sleep tonight."

"You better get to bed. I'll take you down. Tomorrow is a very big day."

"Oh I know," said Bella, her hand gripping the handrail. These steps were a little steeper than the grand staircase that swept from the first to the second floor. "Daddy said I could go to the airport with him to pick up Grandpa Mike and Grandma Reenie. And McKenna is coming too." She hopped from step to step with excitement. McKenna was a favorite with Bella since she came for the St. Patrick's Day parade.

Poor Cameron. He was making two trips to the airport that day, since Seth and Selena were coming on a later flight. In a surprise development, the rest of the Kirkpatrick clan had decided to come. Apparently, Mark and Malcolm's wives did not want to miss a Christmas in Savannah. McKenna and Logan, Seth and Selena, along with their parents were staying up on the third floor. Cameron had made arrangements for the others. "I'm beginning to feel like a travel agent," he grumbled. But he looked as pleased as she felt.

Realization that her entire family had come made her downright teary-eyed. To Harper's disgust, everything made her either nauseous or teary-eyed. And she had no time for it.

After she tucked Bella in, she was tiptoeing past the rooms occupied by the Blodgetts when Cameron stuck his hand out of the master suite and beckoned. Harper approached with mixed feelings. "We're not fooling around tonight. I know your foot is better but..."

"This has nothing to do with my foot." Sliding his arms around her, he took her chin between his finger and thumb. "Are you laying down the law with me, Mrs. Bennett?"

She wagged a finger. "Not yet but just wait." Right. As if she could ever deny this man anything.

"I just want to kiss you good night." With a cheeky grin, he added, "I don't know how I was so lucky to get a woman so beautiful and so sassy."

"You like that, do you?" She knew he did.

When he launched a full onslaught of kisses, she was glad she was wearing her reindeer pajamas. Anything less and she'd be slipping out of them. Although for all the stroking that was going on, he seemed to find the flannel appealing. Feeling her earlier resolve melting, she backed away. "Everybody's asleep and we should be too."

"I'm all for it but in the same bed. It's lonely down here." And he tried that pathetic little boy look that usually worked. But not tonight.

"Watch it. Your mother might hear you." She eased away.

The love in his eyes followed her all the way to bed.

When she awoke the next morning, her body went on alert almost immediately. Today her family arrived. Getting dressed quickly, she bounded down the stairs. When she passed Bella's open door, Harper could only see the tip of her nose above the Ninja quilts. Good. Let her sleep. This was going to be a long day. Pipsqueak, however, didn't want to miss out on anything and trotted next to her down the steps.

Headed toward the back of the house, she enjoyed hearing

voices in the kitchen. Usually it was quiet in the morning. The smell of coffee, once warm and comforting, turned her stomach. Now she always carried soda crackers in her pocket. And her mother had gone through this seven times? Harper couldn't imagine it.

"Everybody sleep well?" She circled the room with her eyes and everyone nodded. Well, everyone but Cameron, who was slowly shaking his head. But he stopped when his mother turned his way.

"Now today," Connie began, "Esther and I have agreed that you will not be allowed in the kitchen."

Whoa, really? "So you've heard I'm not a great cook?" Everyone broke up at that. But she was serious. That list of yummy food? She never made any of it. Never even tried. She could do a lot of damage here.

"How would you like to drive with me to the airport? Seth called and he's been able to switch their flight to the one your parents and McKenna are on. It'll save us one trip. Jack will drive the SUV."

"No problem."

Lily was at the coffee maker, pouring mugs for everyone. "Coffee, Harper?"

"No, I don't think so. Usually I have my orange juice first." Right, that was so not the truth.

The rest of the day Harper felt like a transportation service. Fine with her. The busyness kept her mind occupied. When she heard Esther and Connie raising their voices in the kitchen about what went into a pecan pie, she had to intervene. "Cameron must have some bourbon in the house." Esther's voice held a fretful note.

"I wouldn't know." Now, that would be the day when Connie didn't know everything that was in this house. Connie was a little conservative about things like that. Since she and her husband were teetotalers, she never cooked anything with alcohol. That issue had never come up.

Just when the argument was getting heated, Lily sauntered out of the pantry holding a bag of chocolate chips. "Have you ever had chocolate pecan pie?" she asked the room in general. Harper wanted to hug her. Cameron's sister had probably always played the peacemaker in their family. "Best thing ever."

Since no one protested, Lily slit open the bag, pouring at least half of it into the syrupy mix. A serious chocoholic, Harper couldn't wait to sample it, until she remembered that chocolate was off-limits too. Too much caffeine. She'd been spending time on the Internet. That's when she went back into the powder room to study the snow globes.

On the trip to the airport, Harper felt both excited and nervous. Would the two families get along or would it be stiff and awkward? And would her family notice something different about her? Since the Blodgetts didn't know her that well, they weren't picking up on anything. But her family? She just didn't know. Luckily, Bella was riding in the Bentley with Cameron.

When they reached the airport, the flight from Chicago was delayed. So she took one of the giant rockers at the head of the exit ramp while Bella sat in the other. They both rocked while Cameron paced the perimeter of the small courtyard and Jack visited the golf shop. Keeping an eye on the people streaming down the concourse, she saw McKenna's flaming red hair the moment she came into view.

"You see her, Bella?" And she pointed.

Jumping from the rocker, Bella ran to the head of the ramp. Big Mike and Reenie came first with many hugs and carry-ons that were probably stuffed with gifts. And then it was McKenna and Logan. She hadn't seen McKenna since Selena's and Seth's wedding. Now McKenna was about seven months pregnant and due in February. "I don't know if I can get my arms around you," she teased.

"Just you wait, little sister," McKenna shot right back, giving her a quick hug.

Harper froze. Did McKenna see something?

"Hey, you okay?" Her sister pulled back. "Got the wedding jitters?"

Their mother gently nudged McKenna aside. "What wedding jitters? Nonsense. You're not nervous, are you, sweetheart? Why, it's high time." Now, what did that mean?

Smelling like Old Spice shaving lotion, her father kissed her cheek. "How's my little girl?"

"Nervous," she admitted.

"You?" He pulled away, his eyes laughing. "Never."

"So good to see you, Dad."

"My turn." There Bella stood, arms outstretched. Of course, Harper's father picked her up and swirled her around, just as he used to do with her. "How's my princess? Have you been good? Is Santa going to come to you this year?"

When he set her down, she put her hands on her hips. "I certainly hope so, Grandpa." So little and yet so old. That was the expression Harper caught on Cameron's face. How would things change once Bella was a big sister? Seth loped up the ramp holding Selena's hand, and they went through the whole welcome routine again. Bella loved Harper's huge family. They seemed to fill a hole that had been empty way too long. Harper's hand went to her stomach until she realized what she was doing and dropped it. They headed for the baggage claim area. The laughter and teasing continued all the way to the parking garage.

What a good visit they had that day. Once again, Cameron played tour guide. Harper had a chance to stay home and visit with McKenna and Selena, since they'd both been here before. That night they all went to bed early. The next day was Christmas Eve, their wedding day.

But Harper could hardly sleep. She kept going to the window, wondering if Cameron was awake too. Sure enough, the light fell from his window onto the verandah below. But this was the last night they'd spend apart. The thought comforted her.

After a quick breakfast, Harper drove to Adam's salon, along with McKenna, Selena and Bella. At the end of the appointment, Harper slipped him a copy of their vows. "I've been waiting for this, you know," he said, whisking the sheet from her fingers.

"Sorry. So much to do."

"Sure you're feeling all right?" Adam gave her a scrutinizing glance, no doubt wondering why she'd dashed to the bathroom once or twice.

"Nervous," she supplied.

"This is so right for you," he whispered with a tight hug. "And you will make a beautiful bride."

Overhearing them, McKenna joined in. "You got that right."

A bride. The words switched a light on inside her. The glow lasted all day. Their families were here. All was right with the world. When they reached the house all kinds of wonderful smells filled the air.

"It stinks in here," Bella said.

"And don't you look beautiful," Harper's mother exclaimed, scooping Bella up and saving her from a certain beheading from Esther. "And now I think we could use some help, right, Esther? Isn't there a job Bella could help us with?" As Harper swirled to the powder room, she heard Esther teaching Bella how to devein a shrimp.

"Everything okay?" Cameron asked when she reappeared.

"Perfect. Don't hover, okay?"

"Don't all grooms hover on their wedding day?" He gave her a saucy smile. Sliding his arms around her, he tried to touch her tummy. She tapped his hand.

"None of that either," she said between set teeth. "It's so obvious."

"That I love you?" he whispered.

"Oh, Cameron." He was hopeless. Love didn't seem like enough for what she felt for this man. Just then Pipsqueak raced from the parlor, an ornament swishing from her tail.

"Come here, you!" While Cameron was diverted, Harper dashed upstairs.

Chapter 22

Piano music drifted up the staircase from where a pianist had set up a keyboard in the wide hallway. While her mother was arranging her veil, Harper felt a wave of panic. What if she couldn't get through this day without making a fool of herself? She flattened one hand against her stomach. What if she didn't make it to the bathroom in time? Downstairs the place was packed, and she was wearing a gown that felt wide as a hot air balloon. "What is it, sweetheart?" Her mother stopped fussing.

Harper sucked in a deep breath. *Buck up, girl.* "Nothing, Mom. It's just that I hope everything is ready downstairs." No way was she admitting to her situation. Not today. Besides, she'd tucked a few saltines into her tiny, white satin bridal bag. If she just kept her stomach reasonably full, she should be fine.

Cameron would see to it. Like always, he'd take care of her. Her nervousness eased.

Kissing her on the cheek, her mother whispered, "It's fine, Harper."

"Thanks, Mom." The last month had been such a rush. With Christmas, the wedding, Cameron's accident and now a pregnancy, it felt as if life had rushed at her from all sides. But he'd always been there.

She could almost feel his comforting arms around her now. Not only was she his wife, she was having his baby. Contentment eased her jittery stomach.

Looking up, she found her mother staring at her, eyes sweeping the gown. The butterflies returned. Harper checked her dress and patted the hair that Adam had swept up into an elegant wave. "What, Mom?"

"I think this dress is way prettier than the one I wore years ago." And she winked.

"You really think so?" And she checked the magnolia leaves at her waist to make sure the red berries were still in place.

Appearing in the doorway, McKenna glowed in a red gown that flowed with liquid grace over her baby bump to the floor. Holly was pinned in her hair to match her bouquet. Selena came in right behind her, her long dark waves a stunning contrast to the red dress. The three of them had decided on Candy Apple lipstick. "I don't know where you got those dresses," Harper told them. "But they are gorgeous. Love the one shoulder strap. Very Grecian."

Putting her hands on her hips, Selena said, "Talk about gorgeous. Your dress is pretty hot. Strapless?"

Suddenly self-conscious, Harper ran a hand across her bare chest. "Do you think it's too much?"

Casting a pointed glance at Harper's cleavage, Selena chuckled. "Too much of that? Not possible and I'm sure Cameron will agree." McKenna joined the laughter.

When she heard Pipsqueak yapping, she knew Bella was on her way up. There had been no restraining her once she was dressed in her flower girl dress. No waiting. She had dashed down to show everyone.

Bustling into the room, Bella shoved a blue Tiffany's box at Harper. "Daddy said to give you this."

"Oh, my." What was this? He'd been acting so weird since she gave him the news.

Bella eyed the gift. "Can I open it?"

"Not this one," Harper said, taking it over to the dressing table. Her hands trembled as she opened the box. McKenna, Selena and her mother all leaned in. A wave of sighs swept the room when Harper took out a necklace with a beautiful heart made of tiny diamonds. Her eyes filled.

"Cameron has such wonderful taste," her mother said. "Let me help you put it on."

"Of course he does, Mom." McKenna exchanged a look with Selena. "After all, he chose Harper, didn't he?"

"Do I get one of those too?" Bella asked, patting the bodice of her dress. "I don't have a necklace."

"Believe it or not, your daddy did give me a box for you." Opening the upper drawer of her bureau, Harper took out an identical box. Of course, Bella was ecstatic when she opened the gift. Her heart was smaller, white gold with one diamond, but equally beautiful. McKenna helped her put it on.

"Just like yours...Mommy." Bella smiled up at her.

If it hadn't been for this little girl, Harper never would have been here. Bella's need had called to her, or so Harper supposed.

"Mommy." Bella repeated the word slower, softer. Harper

loved hearing it. Behind her, she heard sniffles and tissues being swiped from the box on her dresser.

"Okay, let's not ruin our makeup." Harper blotted her own eyes. Just then the sound of the wedding march wound up the staircase. The pianist had been given a schedule and looking at the clock, Harper realized they were already ten minutes late. They all grabbed their bouquets.

"Your father will be looking for me." With a quick kiss, her mother disappeared, Selena and McKenna right behind her.

"Do I look all right? Do I?" Bella asked.

"You look perfect," Harper said, taking her hand. "Let's get going. Be careful. Use the handrail." Although Julep had repeated her offer to have Bella stay with them after the wedding, Harper wanted her here. After all, the house was decorated for the holidays, and they hadn't had time to really enjoy it. She pictured cozy evenings, just the three of them. Well, four. They'd reached the landing. The wedding march continued and Bella squeezed her hand.

Standing at the top of the steps, she watched McKenna walk down to where Adam was stationed, looking very official in his navy jacket and red tie. Who knew what her old friend was going to say? She hoped it wasn't too outrageous. The only thing that mattered as far as their families were concerned was that Adam had the authority to legally marry them.

On either side of Adam, chairs arced back into the library and the parlor, plenty of room for their seventy guests. At the very front, her parents sat next to Esther, with Lily and the family on her other side. Both women were already dabbing their eyes. Her own mother didn't surprise her, but Esther's obvious emotion did. Scattered throughout the two rooms were her siblings. Catching her eye, Julep gave a small wave from where she sat with Tuck.

When McKenna reached the first floor, Logan was there to offer his arm. Selena went next, with Harper's brother Seth watching her with pure adoration in his eyes.

"Your turn, honey."

Dropping Harper's hand, Bella began her descent and Harper held her breath. Just as they'd rehearsed the night before, Bella kept her right hand on the banister while her left hand held the basket of holly. From the expressions on the faces of the guests, she made quite a picture.

But there was only one face Harper needed to see. One pair of blue eyes filled with such love for her. Love that rocked her so deeply that she had to reach for the railing herself. "My wife," Cameron whispered as they turned to face Adam. "Love of my life."

"Oh, Cameron." She clung to his arm.

The service passed in a blur. Oh, she was aware of Adam speaking. Knew that he'd injected some humor into the comments, which was no surprise. Somehow she overcame her dry mouth when it came time to recite their wedding vows. The truth was, "I do" was enough for her. But the guests chuckled at the words that were open and honest and very much them. At the end, Cameron kissed her and the house filled with applause and laughter. Harper even thought she saw ornaments on the tree shiver from the noise.

In the side garden, the tent stood ready. Connie and Esther had been supervising the menu all day, along with the staff members Candace and Miles had supplied from Extraordinary Celebrations. Because they wanted to enter the garden without passing through the kitchen, they exited through the front door, which they seldom used. Leading the way, the family stood on either side, showering them with artificial magnolia petals that Jack would have to sweep up the next day.

When they reached Victory Parkway, they turned, now in full view of the holiday traffic on the busy street. Horns honked and people shouted "Congratulations" through open windows.

"Are we making a spectacle of ourselves?" she asked Cameron, feeling giddy.

"Darlin', I could not care less." Cameron laughed, patting her hand. He still had a slight limp, and she was glad that this would probably be the longest walk they'd take today. Once inside the tent, there was a short reception line. The decision had been made to just have candid shots taken and that seemed to be fine, with the photographer darting here and there.

A table for the bridal party had been set up at the end of the long, narrow tent. Without further ceremony, they passed through the sumptuous buffet. "Your mother did us proud," she said to Cameron as they slowly moved past the steam tables.

"Down home cooking." Heaping his plate with deep-fried turkey and jambalaya, he left plenty of room for black-eyed peas and mustard baked beans. Harper tried to keep her plate simple. The turkey would be fine and then a small serving of sweet potatoes. This wasn't the time to try the okra, and she took a pass on the boiled peanuts. But she was pleased to see that Bella ate something. Their little girl had come a long way.

As the group ate and champagne was served, Harper dipped into her bag for the soda crackers. Then came the toasts and the incessant clinking on the glasses, not that she minded all the kissing one bit. Harper was glad when the music started. Of course, the first dance was for Harper and her dad. "You have a good husband," he told her. "And well, he's damn lucky."

"Thanks, Dad." He was being so cute.

Esther looked so flustered when it came time for Cameron to step onto the floor with her. The cardinals on her pretty Christmas sweater sparkled in the glittery light suspended from the ceiling of the tent.

The last couple days had been a revelation. Harper had been so wrong about Esther. What she'd first seen as detachment now seemed to be shy uncertainty. Her son's grand house might be difficult for Esther Blodgett to comprehend. Harper had once felt that way herself.

When the song ended, the band began to play another dreamy tune. Her dad whisked her mother onto the dance floor. Cameron turned to her but she held up one finger. "Be right back," she told him, scooping up her dress. "Gotta visit the snow globes."

"Don't be long, darlin'." His eyes warmed.

She nearly stumbled. Tearing her attention away from that man wasn't easy, but she made it out of the tent. Getting up the steps was a real challenge with the long skirt. Suddenly she felt someone else lifting the weight. Harper turned, expecting to find Cameron or Julep.

"We don't want this beautiful dress to get ruined." Mrs. Blodgett's cheeks flushed just the way Cameron's did when he was uncomfortable.

They'd reached the back door and with her mother-in-law's help, Harper smoothed her hands over the skirt. "Mrs. Blodgett, thank you."

"Well, now." Esther clasped her hands in front of her. "I think it's high time you call me Mama, instead of Mrs. Blodgett. That is, if that sets all right with you."

"Oh, well. Yes." Harper almost felt light-headed but she nodded. *Mama.* She'd have to practice saying the word until it felt right.

"Then that's that." Esther looked like she needed a hug, and Harper had one ready. Her new mother-in-law felt so small and vulnerable, the delicate backbone ridged along the sweater. "I really do love your son, you know," Harper said, pulling back.

Esther Blodgett's eyes filled, shocking Harper with the blatant emotion. "You're the best thing that ever happened to my son," the older woman said with a sniff. "Don't take any guff from that boy. None of his highfalutin' nonsense."

With a chuckle, Harper gave Esther another careful squeeze before releasing her. The bathroom really was a priority. "Oh, I won't, Mama. I most certainly will not."

"And you'll come to visit with Bella and Pipsqueak? You're always welcome, you know."

"Why, of course we will."

Her slim shoulders straightened. "Then that's settled. Because we miss, well, that hound and everything." A puppy at the time, Pipsqueak had been given to Bella as they were leaving the funeral for Cameron's father.

Nodding slowly, Harper said. "Right. I know."

Ten minutes later, she was in Cameron's arms dancing to an old tune about love being wonderful, wonderful. "I've had orders from your mama who is now *my* mama."

His chuckle tickled her chest. "What's that?"

When she tried to shake a finger at him, he grabbed it. "None of those highfalutin' ways, mister. I'm having none of it."

Harper loved the shocked look on his face. "Good God, you even sound like her. Is that what she said?"

Harper nodded, knowing it would always be fun to shake him up like this.

"So you're ganging up on me. That gives me the chills."

"Yes, it should. And you're giving me chills right now. A different kind." She melted against him. Felt the firm chest, his thudding heart and the muscled arms around her.

Holding her so close that her skirt would be wrinkled, he whispered, "I can warm you up. Later."

"Can't wait." She giggled. "Cameron?"

"What darlin'?"

"The music stopped."

He looked around, his cheeks reddening. "Well, damn."

Their laugh was shared by the people around them. Her

brothers loved it, and she recognized her brothers' guffaws. Since so many folks had plans for Christmas Eve, the guests said their farewells early. Julep gave her a tight hug.

"Any news?" she asked, fluttering her lashes outrageously.

"Later," Harper whispered. She wanted to hold this secret to her heart for a little while.

They kept dancing. Settling against him, she felt so grateful. Finally, all the pieces of their lives had fallen into place. Harper made a special request for Christmas songs and when "Have Yourself a Merry Little Christmas" came on, a sigh swept through the remaining group.

"So, what do you think, Mr. Bennett?" she teased, tightening her arms around his neck. "Are our troubles out of sight?"

With a mischievous smile, he twirled her around. "Oh, darlin', I don't know. Sounds way too boring for us."

"And that is one of the many reasons why I love you," she whispered.

Epilogue

Three days later, the guests had gone and the house felt empty. They'd given Connie and Jack the week off, partly so they could have total privacy. The weeks leading up to Christmas had been so rushed that they'd had little opportunity to enjoy the season. This would be a wonderful break in routine, days of unwinding and nibbling on leftovers, if Harper could stomach them. The three of them were sprawled out in the TV room watching the latest Star Wars movie, when Harper realized she'd forgotten one thing.

"Bella, have you found the green pickle on the Christmas tree yet?"

Harper glanced at Cameron and he nodded. They'd talked about this earlier and agreed.

Bella brought her head up with a jerk. "Oh, my gosh. I completely forgot about the pickle. Do you believe it?" She sounded so adult that Cameron and Harper both laughed. Dashing out the door, they had trouble keeping up with her.

The three of them paraded down the hall until they stood in front of the beautiful tree, still splendid with white lights and the dizzying color scheme of lime green and aqua that everyone claimed to want for next year.

"I want to keep our tree up forever," Bella said so seriously they broke into laughter again. "Can we, Daddy? Mommy? Wouldn't that be great?"

"That would be a fire hazard." Cameron checked the freshness of the needles but they still bent easily. "After New Year's, we'll have to take the tree down."

"Maybe you'd like to wait until then to find the pickle?" Harper dangled the possibility before Bella, knowing what her reaction would be.

"No, no I don't want to wait."

"And why is that not a surprise?" Cameron teased from the side of his mouth.

"Okay, then." Harper waved a hand toward the tree. "Have at it but don't knock anything off, please." The next few moments were filled with Bella's frantic hunt. Of course, Harper had buried the green ornament deep among the boughs, low enough so Bella could reach it.

"Look, I see it!" Bella plucked it out, dangling it from her fingers. "Do I get an extra present?"

"The last thing you need," Cameron said in a voice so stern, he almost sounded believable.

But Bella knew better. "Pretty please with whipped cream on top?" she pleaded.

Walking over to the mantle, Harper took a gift from among the magnolia leaves, where she'd hidden it two days ago. The little box fit perfectly in Bella's outstretched hands. The box may have been small and wrapped in silver foil, but the red bow was huge. Excited, Bella could hardly undo the bow. In the end, she slipped the ribbon off and opened the box. "What the heck?" Puzzled, she lifted out the ornament of a baby in a cradle. "What is this? Just another ornament? But it's so late."

"Would you like to have a little brother or sister?" Cameron asked.

Her eyes grew larger. "You mean, a baby like Christie has?"

"Could be." Harper knew it was early in the game, but what better gift could they give Bella?

"When?"

"Next summer," Cameron told her. "You'll have to be very good. Help your mom with some things."

So that's how it was? Sounded good to her. "We'll have to make some calls tomorrow," Harper said, watching Bella hang the ornament at the very front of the tree. "Before she tells the world."

Whipping around, Bella trotted off down the hall. "Pipsqueak! We're going to have a baby!"

"What a Christmas." Settling onto the Victorian sofa, Harper was so glad Cameron had agreed to switch out the furniture for something more comfortable. "Now we can relax."

But he started laughing. "What?" She poked him in the arm.

"With you? That will never happen." The finger he ran down her cheek sent shivers through her body. "Yeah, I was hoping you'd break out that Catwoman costume. Remember the dance you did that first night?"

Oh, he really was something. "Private show?"

He nodded slowly.

"There's always New Year's Eve."

"I'll wait. Come 'ere, darlin'." The grin was naughty. And the kiss? Oh, so nice.

THE END

262

Finding Southern Comfort

If you have not read *Finding Southern Comfort,* here is a quick look at how Cameron and Harper met.

Harper circled the block for the third time. Why go through an interview bound to be humiliating? *Overdue rent.* And she'd be giving up. Despite what her former boyfriend Billy said, she was not a quitter. She pulled over and parked. At least this time she wasn't wearing a black Catwoman suit.

"Just come back with the job," Adam had told her when he handed her the keys to his red Ford Focus. "Hey, girl, you can do this."

Sure. Right. In the morning sunlight, the pale brickwork of Cameron Bennett's mansion glowed. But the black trim and shutters gave a no-nonsense touch. The house had an edge, just like its owner. Her stomach knotted. What if he recognized her and laughed when she walked in?

But he wouldn't. Cameron seemed like the perfect southern gentleman.

Hadn't he taken her home when her car wouldn't start? He'd paid her something even though she hadn't delivered. Cripes. She drummed her fingers on the steering wheel. How could she face him again? Chest tight, she dug in her pink peony purse, found her inhaler and breathed in. After her lungs expanded, her stomach settled. She could do this.

Once out of the car, she marched toward the steps leading up to the house. The wrought iron railing felt warm under her hand. Harper hesitated on the bottom step, heart galloping.

Still time to turn back but she'd run out of options. She wouldn't be surprised to find everything she owned piled at the curb when she returned, her Frida Kahlo posters sandwiched between the drafting board and a box of dishes.

On the way over in the car, she'd practiced a different voice so Baby Blues wouldn't recognize her. Mary Ann Lacey, a classmate in college, had been from Charleston. How she teased Harper about the broad, Chicago vowels and her constant use of "yah."

Yah, today Harper would become Mary Ann Lacey.

She pushed off from the bottom step.

The eye-popping salary in the online ad for a nanny made her former jobs look like volunteer work. Harper had set her mug down so hard, the coffee slopped over the lip. Was she qualified? Her list of employers over the past two years was pretty pathetic. The Kirkpatrick clan had all chipped in for her education at the elite Savannah design school and she was working at Maisy's Resale Shop? She owed her family more than a series of part time jobs, but she'd hated her New York internship. Her career plans needed a serious readjustment.

Maybe this job could give her some breathing room—a chance to figure out her future. Only one child to take care of, or so the ad said. How hard could this be? She was blown away when a request for an interview came back two hours after she'd pushed the send button. Stretched out on her futon, she was watching *The Notebook* for like the fiftieth time. Even soaking wet, Ryan Gosling still sizzled. Her sobs were interrupted by the ping. She had mail.

One casual glance and she sat bolt upright. Gulping and pausing dear Ryan, she started typing. Sure, ten o'clock Wednesday would be fine. But when she did an Internet search for the address, hot and cold flashes danced across her skin.

The mansion on Victory Drive. Cameron Bennett. Holy cripes. She closed the laptop, only to reopen it fifteen minutes later. The pay was too good to pass up. Time to put on her big girl pants.

Now she squinted up at the building. "Here goes nothing."

Harper took the brick steps slowly so she wouldn't get all sweaty. Her stockings felt like sausage casings. Her older sister's words kept her climbing the dang stairs. "You only have one chance to make a good impression, Harper. Make it count."

She might not even have one chance if Cameron recognized her as the stripper who couldn't strip a few nights ago.

Her flounced skirt swung around her thighs and her hair was coiled into a demure bun at the nape of her neck. Just a touch of lip gloss and some mascara this morning. One more deep breath from her inhaler before she tucked it in her bag. The tortoise shell bracelets she'd scored at Maisy's shop jangled on her wrists when she punched the doorbell.

A couple beats and Connie opened one of the heavy black doors.

"I have an appointment at ten o'clock. Harper Kirkpatrick," she said, as if she'd never seen Connie before in her life. With some effort, she lifted the end of each sentence, just like Mary Ann had told her. "Just a tad, Harper, darlin'. Like you're lifting the edge of a flapjack?"

No hint of recognition when Connie stepped back. "Please come in."

"What a lovely foyer." Diving into a southern accent that clung like syrup to every word, Harper babbled about the marble floor, Oriental rugs and priceless antiques like she'd never seen them before. The same pink tulips flopped from the crystal vase.

Hah, so they were artificial.

Well, so was she. Thinking maybe she'd overdone her Scarlett O'Hara imitation, she zipped her lips.

"Won't you sit down, Harper?" Connie motioned to an ornately carved bench that sat under a watercolor of the marshes. The library pocket door slid open while Harper tried to get comfortable on the hard surface.

"Thank you so much for coming, Miss Daniels. Connie will get back to you. We expect to make a decision soon." Immaculate in gray pinstripe slacks and an alabaster shirt, Baby Blues stood in the doorway, his mauve tie a jaunty splash of color. The man had style.

"Then I'll wait to hear from you." The gorgeous Miss Daniels smiled with the confidence of a candidate who knew she'd aced her interview. The classic lines of her suit screamed designer and the sand color accented her blonde bob. Mile-long legs ended in nude peep-toe heels.

Harper smoothed one hand over the ruffles of her tiered skirt patterned with purple flowers. Suddenly, her pink jacket seemed too bright, the skirt too girly. She'd drawn the line at wearing the navy "interview suit" her mother had given her as a graduation gift.

Navy wasn't in Harper's color palette. Now she wondered.

Cameron gave Harper a brief nod before sliding the door closed. Thank God for the mask she'd worn that night.

"I'll just tell him you're here," Connie murmured after she'd shown the girl out.

Right. Like he hadn't seen her sitting there. Harper expelled a tight breath as the library door slid closed behind Connie. Reaching into her bag, she fingered her inhaler. Touching the plastic ridges eased her anxiety.

Finding Southern Comfort is available on Amazon, iBooks, Nook and Kobo.

Other Books by Barbara Lohr

Windy City Romance series
Finding Southern Comfort
Her Favorite Mistake
Her Favorite Honeymoon
Her Favorite Hot Doc
The Christmas Baby Bundle
Rescuing the Reluctant Groom

Man from Yesterday series
Coming Home to You
Always on His Mind
In His Eyes

About the Author

Barbara Lohr writes heartwarming romance with a flair for fun and subtly sexy love scenes. In her *Windy City Romance series*, feisty women take on hunky heroes and life's issues. Her *Man from Yesterday* series provides a provocative glance back at "what if." When she's not writing, she loves to bike, kayak, golf or cook. She makes a mean popover. Barbara lives in the South of the USA with her husband and a cat that claims he was Heathcliff in a former life.

For more information on the author and her work, or to sign up for her newsletter, please see:
www.BarbaraLohrAuthor.com
www.facebook.com/Barbaralohrauthor
www.twitter.com/BarbaraJLohr

Acknowledgements

Many thanks to Romance Writers of America and Central Ohio Fiction Writers. The loops and forums of writers who address writing and publishing issues are also invaluable to me. An extra loud shout out to my Street Team, the readers who support me in so many way!

For my daughters, Kelly and Shannon, when we shared Judy Blume and Madeleine L'Engle together, we never saw what lay ahead. Keep those reading lamps on over your beds. My grandchildren, Bo and Gianna, bring me such joy and will probably appear in quite a few of Mama B's novels. To my husband Ted, words aren't adequate to thank you for your love and support, especially when my computer crashes and you have to provide tech support. May we have many more wonderful years together that include trips to Leopold's for ice cream.